Advance Praise

"An urgent and beautiful story, told in braided timelines, of a mother and daughter, each fiercely loving and clear-eyed yet trapped by circumstances inside a cult controlled by a charismatic and dangerous leader. The genius of debut novelist Alexandria Faulkenbury is her ability to create a world that is both alluring and terrifying, and characters who are deeply dimensional and human. *Somewhere Past the End* is sure to hold you from the dark magic and mystery of its beginning passage to its spacious yet gratifying end. As for Teresa and Alice, they're yours now. They'll imbed themselves in your heart."

— Ona Gritz, award-winning author of *Everywhere I Look*

"Written with sureness and visceral emotion, Faulkenbury gives us a tense, close up view of the formation of a cult and one woman's courageous escape, all wrapped around a gripping mystery that will have you questioning what is real. Both a vivid page-turner, and a nuanced examination of human nature, *Somewhere Past the End* is a nourishing read. I highly recommend it."

— Sara Read, author of *Johanna Porter* is *Not Sorry and Principles of (E)motion*

"Faulkenbury's novel weaves together the stories of two women as they fall in and out of enthrallment with The Collective. Two questions drive the story: What is the Truth? and How did we end up like this? This novel explores the different ways that men control, how they prey on the vulnerable and keep them faithful. If you, like me, find yourself drawn to the stories cult members have to share, pull up a seat at Faulkenbury's Somewhere Past the End and get your fill."

— Shay Galloway, author, *The Valley of Sage and Juniper*

"With meticulously and compassionately crafted characters, *Somewhere Past the End* is a haunting exploration of human vulnerability and the ongoing yearning for unconditional love. Through alternating narratives, Faulkenbury masterfully intertwines past and present, suspense and psychological depth. Her novel depicts a dangerous, all-too-believable world where mothers struggle to protect their young daughters, and subversion must lie quietly in the baking of pies, in the steadfast questioning of authority over laundry.

In a world of fake news and false prophesies, misinformation and misplaced trust, this book is a timely testament to the dangers of blind faith and the power of the individual in the midst of mass hysteria.

There are no easy answers in *Somewhere Past the End*, but there is a kind of peace. A true homecoming: the coming back to self. Faulkenbury's women thoughtfully navigate the complexities of belief, inviting readers on a journey that is as unsettling as it is compelling. A must-read for fans of psychological thrillers, cult documentaries, and anyone fascinated by the complications and complexities of faith."

— Brittany Micka-Foos, author of *It's No Fun Anymore*

Somewhere Past the End

Somewhere Past the End

a novel

Alexandria Faulkenbury

Apprentice
House Press
Loyola University Maryland

First Edition

Casbound ISBN: 978-1-62720-560-3
Paperback ISBN: 978-1-62720-561-0
Ebook ISBN: 978-1-62720-562-7

Design by Molly Gerard
Editorial Development by Rylee Miller
Promotional Development by Olivia Cresser

Quote by Ursula K. Le Guin (copyright © 1985 by Ursula K. Le Guin) first appeared in ALWAYS COMING HOME, published by Harper & Row. Reprinted by permission of Ginger Clark Literary, LLC

Cover Photo: Reba Spike, Unsplash+

Published by Apprentice House Press

Apprentice
House Press
Loyola University Maryland

Loyola University Maryland
4501 N. Charles Street, Baltimore, MD 21210
410.617.5265
www.ApprenticeHouse.com
info@ApprenticeHouse.com

For Evan, Clara, and Miles

-1-

ALICE

I decide to watch the end of the world from the storeroom window. Outside, members of the Collective stream into the meadow. The late summer light makes it look like a fairy garden, and I remember Jennifer once saying summers in rural New York were as close as we could get to heaven. Angelica had swatted her hand at that comment, affronted that anyone would equate our temporary stop on earth with the riches awaiting us in the beyond.

Jennifer's long gone now, of course. Far away from the meadow and far away from New York for all I know. I'm sure Angelica is out there somewhere, but I don't see her. The window frame obscures some of the meadow, but Brother Richmond is front and center, so I keep my focus there. He's surrounded by a ring of wildflowers and a growing assortment of his followers. His family. My family. I see Joanne walking with Eric. They're all wrapped up in one another, like they need the support of the other to move forward. Last year, when they finally realized they were in love, I rolled my eyes. Now my chest squeezes tight at the thought of losing these people who have made up so much of my life.

I've never known any home but here. We lived in a few other places before Brother Richmond bought the Farm, but I have trouble recalling them. Everyone who does remember says Brother

Richmond was different then. They say he sought out the down-trodden with offers of help instead of threats veiled as promises. They say he gave out love like he gave out money, freely and without strategy or manipulation. They say he walked on water, raised the dead, and performed all those miracles that belong to someone else in the worldly stories. They talk like those days were made from sunlight and hope. Maybe they were, but the few bright memories I have are too fleeting to stamp out all that's happened since.

I cling to them all the same. I weave them together like squares of a quilt that will keep me warm when I'm gone from this place. The soft brush of my mom's hair against my cheek as we pressed together singing hymns after Evening Table. The steady rhythm of the rocking chair on our front porch. The tiny fish glinting silver in the creek where Edwin and I played as kids.

Edwin. I peer into the growing gaggle of people. I don't see him.

I forget about Edwin when my dad marches into the center of the meadow. He looks stoic, as always. He's holding my mom's hand. Her eyes dart back and forth, anxiety etched across her face. A thread of uncertainty weaves through my middle, and I feel her absence already. Her strawberry blonde hair, streaked with gray, falls across her shoulders as she turns her head. She's looking for me.

The lines in her face look softer in the waning sun, and her hair catches the light in a way I haven't seen since I was a child. But it's not just the sun giving her a glow. There's some other kind of light rising around the group, but I can't tell where it's coming from. I squint and people blur together across my vision, but my mom stands apart from all the rest. She looks my way, so I raise myself up on the wooden bench below the window. I place my hand on the bump I've been so diligent in hiding over the last seven months. I will her to hear my thoughts. She doesn't move. Her face doesn't change, but I know my mom. I can see the almost imperceptible flick of her eyes down to my hand. And then, in her eyes, something like hope. I step back down off the shelf before anyone else looks out of the cloying light at me. My dad is now further up on the hill, and I can't see his face in the glare, but his shoulders sag like they do when he's worried. My mom reaches her hand toward the window where I watch. By now Brother Richmond is there, and my mom's hand falls back to her side. He wraps his arm around her and mouths something. I can't hear it through the window, but I can guess what he's saying. Something like, "It's time."

Brother Richmond lets go of my mom's shoulders and moves to the center of the meadow. I know I should go now. Slip away before Brother Richmond's big speech. Before everyone's anxiety bubbles over. It's a hard thing to be led to the end of days without the end ever arriving. We've been here before, and I was out there with everyone else then. We waited to be called up to heaven while the rest of the world perished. We waited to be proved right. In the end, I fell asleep lying in the grass at my mom's feet and woke to Brother Richmond's shaky voice telling us it had all been a test.

Now, Brother Richmond raises his face and arms toward the sky, like he's conducting whatever's happening out there. The windowpane shakes and I feel a shift in the air, like it's vibrating at a higher frequency. It smells of burnt sugar. The glass reflects the fear flickering across my face. Some in the meadow join Brother Richmond with their eyes closed and arms raised. Their faces are ablaze with a hunger I haven't felt in years. Others fall to the ground, their hands buried in the tangled weeds around them, as if they can somehow root themselves to the earth. I scan the group for my parents, but I no longer find them in the crowd. I let the grief of their loss wash over me. Even if nothing happens, I've drawn a line in the sand. I'm lost to them now.

A flash of movement catches my eye, and I look up. I spot Jason, but it can't be him. He's at home waiting for me. And yet, there he is, standing in the middle of the crowd, waiting for a shiny ride into the hereafter. My brain scrambles to work out why Jason and I are now on opposite sides of this glass. I can no longer see my reflection in the glass because I am pressing my face against it, anxious to prove to myself that it's a trick of the light and not Jason after all.

We've been planning our escape for months. Ever since Brother Richmond made the announcement. The Homegoing was the perfect cover. Everyone would be out in the meadow for hours, and when they straggled back to their homes, exhausted and emotionally drained, we'd be gone. It was a good plan. Still, Jason worried.

"What if it's real this time?" he whispered to me in the dark of our bedroom. His voice had the same quaver that had been there when we asked Brother Richmond permission to marry at eighteen.

I squeezed his hand. "I'll risk fire from heaven before I let someone take our child." Speaking out loud about the baby made my palms go clammy.

"You'd rather suffer unspeakable torture? The baby would feel that too," he said, anger edging its way into his voice.

I scrunched the bed sheet between the fingers of my free hand in exasperation. "It's not real, Jason. There's no Homegoing. No cosmic plan. There's only Brother Richmond."

I sounded more confident than I felt. I couldn't tell Jason I'd wanted to leave so many times before but failed every time I thought about it. Fear and love and something else I couldn't name rooted me to these fields and, even though I hated to admit it, to Brother Richmond. I couldn't tell Jason I sometimes woke in the deep recesses of the night, terrified Brother Richmond really was the prophet he claimed to be. In those moments, my pajamas sticky with sweat, I prayed and cried and bargained with God about the irrevocable damage I would be doing to my soul if I left. But then one day I had something more important than myself to think about. Something I hoped would unearth me from this soil.

I'm still staring, slack-jawed, when Jason looks in my direction. I don't know if he sees me, but the pained expression on his face makes me abandon all reason. I push against the window, trying in vain to open it. Streamers of light billow around the group and encircle the meadow. Tears blur my view as I press my forehead against the glass. The heat on the other side of the window forces me to take a step back. A hazy fog ribbons itself through the beams of light. It's beautiful, really. A sudden pounding rings out from somewhere near the center of the meadow. The pounding grows louder and louder until my field of vision vibrates with the sound. I drop my head and cup my hands over my ears to block it out. Then, as suddenly as it began, it's gone. All is silent. I look up. The window is laced with cracks, but I can still see the meadow beyond. There's nothing. My parents, Jason, Brother Richmond. They're all gone.

-2-

TERESA

The night Tom and I told my parents I was pregnant, I felt sick. And it wasn't just the baby.

Tom's grandma, Vivian, sat on our maroon sofa. I'm sure she never pictured herself working out the details of her teenage grandson's girlfriend's unplanned pregnancy, but Tom's parents had died in a car accident when he was two. So, there she sat. Her ever-wringing hands were the only thing that betrayed her nerves. They made the little flower on her outdated hat bob back and forth.

My father's presence filled the room without leaving space for my mother, Vivian, or us. There wasn't enough air left for anyone to breathe easy. Still, I wasn't worried. I knew and loved the Bible stories we learned in Sunday School. I knew sins could be forgiven. Fallen women could be reborn. Babies who didn't quite start out in wedlock could still be loved and cherished if they ended up that way. I figured all would be forgiven once the shock wore off.

"Teresa, we'll take care of this. Bill Turner knows someone in Binghamton who handles these things. You'll only need to miss a day or two of school. We'll say it's the flu."

I blanched at my father's words. Some kind of strangled sound escaped Vivian's throat before she turned it into a cough. My mother's face had gone white, but she didn't say anything. She just continued rolling and unrolling her handkerchief in her hands. Years later, I would see someone with a handkerchief and feel bile rise at the back of my throat.

"Sir, that won't be necessary. I love your daughter. I want to marry her."

Tom stood when he spoke. It felt like a lifetime ago that I'd first asked him for an extra scoop at the ice cream shop where he worked after school, but it had somehow only been six months. Still, I loved him more in that moment when he stood up to my father than in all the moments we'd spent together before. I took his hand. I started to speak, but my father cut me off.

"Like hell you'll marry my daughter. No. This is going away. You, this problem, all of it. You have no idea what it takes to raise a child. You're still children yourselves."

On the sofa in the corner, Vivian cleared her throat.

"Steven, I can see you mean well here, but once the test came back positive, these two stopped being children. They've got to make their own choices now, and it sure seems like they want to keep this baby and start a life together. I'd say it doesn't much matter what we think anymore." I stared, open-mouthed, at this tiny woman with her baggy pantyhose and rumpled hat.

My father looked as though he couldn't decide whether to shout at the old lady who ran the church bake sale or punch a hole in our living room wall. I decided I wouldn't stay silent like my mother. This was my life, and I needed to have a say in it. I spoke, cognizant of my father's scarcely constrained rage.

"We know what we're doing, Daddy. I love Tom, and–" I didn't get a chance to finish. My father walked out of the room without another glance at me. The front door rattled the windows as it slammed shut.

My parents never threw us out. I knew my mother wouldn't let it go that far. But after that night it was clear we had little choice. We couldn't live with my father. Vivian offered to let us stay with her, but my father wouldn't let me leave his house and move in with my boyfriend and his grandma. We needed a fresh start. At sixteen, that sounded so easy.

The night I left, I snuck into my parents' room and took my mother's pewter compact. I wanted to have some part of her, some part of the only home I'd known. The top of the compact was engraved with ribbons worked in a circle. My mother's initials were carved in the center. She liked to have her initials on everything she owned. With my father looming so large in her life, those three letters spoke her into existence in a way she couldn't. I opened the compact and the light scent of powder took me back to playing dress up in her closet. After I'd tried on her shoes and pearls, I'd beg for some of her powder. She'd laugh and dab my nose with the little puff inside the compact.

"A puff for a pretty," she'd say.

I snapped the compact closed and waved away the memory with the powder in the air. As I switched off the lamp to leave, I noticed the green notebook I'd given her for Christmas sitting on her nightstand. I'd had it embossed with her initials. I picked it up, curious about what my mother had kept note of in the months since Christmas. I opened the front cover. There was nothing. No words, no date, not even her name penciled in the top corner. The spine was smooth and unbroken, the pages unbent. Sadness welled up inside me for reasons I couldn't explain. I put the notebook in my bag and slipped out of my parents' room.

Michael was sitting at his desk when I walked into his room. He knew what Tom and I were planning, and he'd promised to cover for me until it was no longer possible, but I knew he was still angry at me for leaving.

"You can probably have my old room now. You've always said it was bigger, right?" I smiled, but he didn't look up. "Michael, come on. You know once we're settled, I'll have you over. This baby is definitely going to need its cool uncle."

"If you don't go soon, you're going to get caught," he said as he flipped the pages in his math textbook, clearly not reading a word.

I crossed the room in three steps and put my hand on his shoulder, careful in case he jerked away from me. He didn't. Instead, he slumped over the desk, and I could hear the catch in his throat when he spoke again. "What am I supposed to do without you?" He closed his math book. "You're going to be late," he said.

I squeezed his shoulder. "I love you, Michael."

He didn't reply but reached his hand up and put it on mine for a moment before standing and walking out the door. His voice faded down the stairs, something to our father about watching the baseball game.

*****

Two hours away from Dover Springs, Cyrene felt just far enough to be a buffer between our old lives and the new one we hoped to create together. Vivian had given us what little money she could for a promise to call weekly. We combined that gift with the babysitting money I had in a tin under my bed and Tom's last check from the Dairy Freeze. It was barely enough to cover a couple of gold-plated wedding bands and first and last month's rent.

Apartment was a strong word for the space where we lived. One room with a curtain around the bed, heat that hardly worked, water stains and cracks that crisscrossed the ceiling like abstract art, drafty windows, and a bathroom door that slammed into your knees when you sat on the toilet.

I tried to cheer the place up. Empty jam jars of wildflowers that

I'd picked at the park, a floral scarf my parents had given me for my last birthday draped over the single lamp in the living area. I told myself it was romantic. That we were doing it. We were making it on our own.

Tom got a job at a garage a short walk from our apartment. He was a natural with cars, like his dad had been. I did my best to contribute. So many job interviews in those first few months. I wore my wedding band proudly and tried to conceal my growing stomach, but I couldn't wipe the youth off my face. I almost had a shot at Newberry's. I chatted with the girl at the register about the weather, told her I liked her charm bracelet, then mentioned I was looking for a job. She said their morning girl had just left. The store manager appeared from behind a curtained wall like the wizard of Oz. He smiled and complimented my eyeshadow. My spirits lifted. Then he walked around the rest of the counter and saw my stomach.

"Actually, we're not refilling the position. I'm sure you understand." He walked back through the curtained wall before I had a chance to speak.

They were all the same after that. I kept getting bigger, and no one wanted to hire a pregnant teen. One restaurant manager asked me if my parents knew I was out so late. I was useless. Tom's job barely supported us. He told me not to worry, but I could see enough worry for the both of us blooming in the dark circles under his eyes. We called Vivian every Sunday afternoon from a payphone. Yes, we were eating, and yes, I was going to the doctor. We left out the parts about the water stains and our empty wallets.

Taking long walks seemed to lull the baby to sleep, so I spent a lot of time on the sidewalks of Cyrene. Every time I saw change lying on the ground, I would gather it up for the old pickle jar on our kitchen counter. With each plink against the glass, we'd imagine what our new lives would look like.

One day, somewhere in my third trimester, I turned down Melody Lane. It sounds prettier than it was. I sidestepped several spots where dog owners had neglected to pick up after their pets and quickened my pace when passing the corner where the drunk vets gathered in the afternoon. I was about to turn toward the park when I saw the bright gleam of silver along the bottom steps of the office supply store. A treasure trove of coins. I looked up and down the street, anxious that the owner of this bounty would soon be back. Surely, they would realize their coin purse had spilled a small fortune across the dirty sidewalk. There was no one. Just a man in an orange baseball cap who toasted me with a bottle wrapped in brown paper. Lowering myself to the ground was taking longer and longer, but I managed to make it to the coins and counted them before stuffing the lot in the pocket of my jacket. $3.25. I used the stair rail to pull myself back up and hurried past the vet as I moved toward home.

"Hope you got it all," he called after me as I passed. My face burned, but for $3.25 I would have done it again.

At home, Tom was already in the kitchenette, boiling water for pasta. Flashing my biggest smile, I reached into my pocket and my face fell.

"Ooof. Is it that bad? Do I still smell like the garage? I showered. Scout's honor." He held his wooden spoon up like a boy scout and grinned. I sat in the chair next to the tiny table pushed against the wall. My jacket pocket had a hole. All the change was gone. I imagined a glittering trail following me home like breadcrumbs and then imagined someone luckier than me collecting the coins. I sobbed. Tom kneeled in front of me, so we were face to face.

"Hey, what's wrong?"

I told him the whole pathetic story. "That's two loads of

laundry, washed and dried!" I wailed.

Tom slumped into the chair opposite me. His shoulders sagged and he set his wooden spoon between us on the table. "I'm sorry, Teresa."

I sniffed. "Why are you sorry? You didn't lose a week's worth of laundry money."

"This isn't the life I wanted to give you. I wanted something better for us, for this baby," he said.

"You mean you didn't imagine your pregnant wife coming home with holes in her pockets like a character out of a Dickens' novel?" I looked up at him, but he was still looking at the table. I picked up the spoon and poked his arm with it. He gave a weak laugh.

"No, can't say I saw that one. I was never much of a Dickens fan anyway."

I feigned shock and he laughed, a real laugh this time. Some of the tension in my shoulders settled. A fizzing sound made us both jump. The pasta was boiling over. White rivulets of starchy water streamed down the sides of the pot. Tom jumped up and turned down the burner. I pushed myself up and out of the chair and went to find a needle and thread to sew my jacket pocket.

-3-

ALICE

I close my eyes against the meadow's emptiness outside the window and curl up on the bench seat. If I lay here long enough, maybe I will absorb into the earth, and then I won't have to face the fire and destruction waiting for me. I weep for my disbelief and my loss and the fear of what will come next. I wonder how long I have and bury my face in my hands. Then there's a warmth spreading across the back of my neck, and I raise my head. This must be how the end begins. I peek out into the field, almost against my will. The certainty that a lake of fire is already brewing there makes me dizzy. Rays of sun bounce off the cracked window, bending and refracting into prisms of color that dazzle, but no sea of destruction greets me. There's only a meadow of wildflowers, a few overturned crates, and a blanket of grass stretching to the hills. There's some movement at the edge of the meadow, but the glare from the sun keeps me from seeing what it is. Maybe they are all still here. Maybe this was all some kind of misunderstanding. Maybe Jason is still at home, waiting for me.

I tear into the home Jason and I have shared for the last ten years. I comb through each room like I'll find him perched on the sofa, writing a report for Brother Richmond. But of course, he's not there. He's gone. They're all gone. And here I am. Alone. I put my hands on the laminate kitchen counter and take a deep breath. I don't know how I can leave without Jason. What do I know of the world outside the Farm? My last bit of strength crumples with this thought. I don't understand why he would abandon me when we'd worked so hard to get away. And why was this Homegoing different? Where did everyone go? How could I have been so wrong? My brain sprints through questions without stopping to consider the answers. I sink to the floor and lay my head on the cool tile. I study the patterns of the wood in the kitchen cabinets and try to quiet my mind. Outside, the light fades to gray in the thickening night.

*****

I wake with a start. I'm disoriented, and for a fraction of a moment, I forget everything that's happened. When it all comes rushing back, I close my eyes. I will myself to go back to sleep and forget again, but there's a sharp jab in my stomach and I remember something else.

"What are we going to do?" I whisper down at the bump barely concealed by my loose top.

"How about we start with some food? Got anything good?"

I jerk my head up so fast a jet of pain shoots down the side of my neck. Tabitha Morales stands framed in the doorway of my kitchen.

"Tabitha! What are you doing? How are you here?" I look frantically beyond her, wondering if I'll see Jason or my mother behind her.

"What? Thought you were the only one who got left behind?"

"I was scared. I saw the light and I ran." I improvise. I can't tell her I wasn't supposed to be there in the first place.

"You weren't the only one. Jordan ran off as soon as it happened too. Saw him loading stuff into a car when I was walking over here. I don't think he even went to the meadow."

"How many others are there?" I ask, to keep Tabitha from asking why I wasn't in the meadow.

"Almost twenty of us. Some were on the edges of the meadow and hadn't quite made it into the circle when it happened. Some hadn't even left their houses yet. Jacob said he fell asleep. Justine says she was putting out some extra food for the pigs since she wouldn't be back to feed them. Everyone's got some kind of story as to why they weren't right in the center of things."

"Where were you?" I ask. Her gaze travels past me and out the window.

"It doesn't much matter now. We're the ones still here, so we've got to muddle forward as best we can."

I sink back against the cabinet. I've never understood Tabitha. She's around my mother's age, but she's only been in the Collective a few years. When she joined, she was, by all accounts, very together and not the lost sort of soul Brother Richmond usually preyed on. Watching her rummage around my kitchen, so self-assured, I still can't figure out what drew her here. Being born here, you can't help feeling like this is all your life will ever be. But I can't imagine what would bring Tabitha to choose this mess of a family. Brother Richmond is charismatic; I'll give him that. And some of his messaging still retains its earlier aura of love and acceptance, but he's had that angry gleam in his eyes for years. His little spies report everything you eat at Evening Table on Sunday, who you talk to on Wednesday, and what you wear on Saturday. You can't sneeze without his permission. Then there are his more sinister habits. Those unspoken sins that permeate life on the Farm.

"If you're going to lay on the floor like a lump, then I guess I'm cooking." Tabitha turns on the stove and places a large frying pan on the front burner. Then she opens the fridge and pulls out a carton of eggs.

I should ask her more questions. I should be furious. She's looking for a spatula when our world has turned upside down. But I find a strange emptiness where I should be panicking, like I'm watching from very far away.

"What are you even doing here, Tabitha? Why come looking for me?"

Tabitha pauses, a freshly cracked egg poised between her rough fingers. Tendrils of egg white sizzle and steam as they hit the hot skillet. She doesn't speak as she releases the rest of the egg into the pan, discards the shell, and washes her hands. The only sound between us is the crackle and pop of the egg on the stove. She looks as though she's about to speak, but instead she turns back and sprinkles salt and pepper over the skillet. I watch in silence, mesmerized by this ballet of domesticity when everything feels upside down and under water. I trace the grooves in the cabinet door I'm leaning against, noting the places where flecks of food and drink have made their way down from the countertops over the years.

"It wasn't my time." Tabitha's voice breaks the sizzle of eggs, and I jump.

"But it was everyone's time. Anyone left is supposed to be burning up in a lake of fire. Or did you miss that lesson on your first day?"

"Here. Come eat. The others are gathering at the meeting house to figure out what to do next." She sets a plate on the table and pulls out the rickety chair parked in front of it.

"I'm not hungry," I say even as I feel my legs propelling me up and into the chair. Some people don't eat when they are depressed or traumatized, but I've never been that way. Edith Baker lost 25 pounds when Brother Richmond put her on Separation for sneaking around with Giles Hayden. Everyone talked about how great she looked, if only she'd stop crying. I couldn't understand it. Depression, shock, fear, worry, they all churn together in my stomach and make me ravenous. It's like I eat so I don't have to think about whatever horrible thing is happening. The baby seems to feel the same way. I couldn't stop eating in the weeks leading up to the Homegoing. I'd get sick if I went more than two hours without snacking on something.

I look at Tabitha between bites of egg. She doesn't seem the least bit upset. Her eyes show no tell-tale red rings or puffiness. She's acting as if the end of the world is just another day at the Farm and cooking eggs for me is one of her daily chores. My head feels tethered to my body only through sheer will. I can't make sense of anything.

"Why do you think we're still here?" I say, my mouth full of eggs.

"I think that's a question above my pay grade. Finish up and we'll walk over to the meeting house together. Edwin says there's a message from Brother Richmond."

*****

I follow Tabitha in a daze. I'm not sure what I'm planning to do now. For months, years, if I'm being honest, I've thought of nothing besides leaving this place. Getting away from Brother Richmond. Telling my parents goodbye without saying a word. Making a life with Jason and our baby somewhere far away. And now? Brother Richmond is gone. I'm free to do as I like. But I feel as tethered to this place as I've ever been. This isn't what I pictured. I can still leave, but my feet don't seem to know that. They plod along, one in front of the other, behind Tabitha.

When we first moved out here, the paths were cut to Brother Richmond's exacting vision. All vegetation was cleared to form a neat grid that reached every part of the Farm. Precise. Planned.

Perfect. But the land had other plans. It grew up and over the paths in the summer, creating lush green tunnels that turned eerie when the branches lost their leaves and stretched up to scratch the sky. In other places, the ground resisted even the idea of a path and plants sprang up to disrupt the walkway in such patterns that you might find yourself walking into a cornfield when you swore you started out toward the meeting house.

Brother Richmond handpicked a garden team to prune the errant branches, force the path into a clean and weedless Eden, and plant only those flowers he said were pleasing to the Lord. But the soil refused all such notions. We all wondered why creation would rebel so intently against something sent from the Creator. No one wondered out loud, of course. But the wondering was there. It sprouted like a weed in the smirks of the garden team, as they yet again chainsawed through the brambles so those walking could have a clear view of the sky and of God. It shone in the delighted eyes of a child, as they squealed at a patch of dandelions newly appeared in the middle of the path. It rustled through the whispers of the women who tended Brother Richmond's yard, as they pulled more of the long grass that threatened to overtake his beloved daisies. It was as inescapable as the berry brambles that grew along the meeting house path, snagging girls' dresses with their thorns. And now that Brother Richmond is gone, the land seems to know it's been left to its own devices. Already the paths curve out of their grid, and the weeds eat at their edges. Brambles drop their late summer offerings wherever they please. Purple smears of juice blot the smooth white gravel.

We approach the meeting house from the Village path, so we come to it at an angle. It looms over us. It was built to look welcoming, or so my mom said, but there are too many windows, and they are too large against the stark white wood of the building. It looks as if it's in a perpetual state of surprise, the casements creating a gaping mouth and widened eyes. I crane my neck to see who I can spot through the glass. I'm surprised to see Angelica pacing back and forth in the front of the room. She's been here forever and never put one toe out of line that I remember. I wonder why she hasn't been taken with the rest. Jacob Parsons stands to her left. He makes more sense. He was in Separation just a couple of months ago for sneaking beer onto the Farm. As we pull open the heavy double doors at the front of the building, Justine Harding runs up to me, her teary face now blocking my view of anyone else inside.

"Oh, Alice. I'm so sorry. I mean, I'm sorry for all of us, but Jason and your parents and you're still here. We've all lost someone, I guess. But it just doesn't make sense. Why didn't Brother Richmond tell us some would be left behind? Do you think this is some sort of punishment? It's got to be a punishment, right?"

Her harried words overwhelm me, and I try to sidestep her without answering. She misinterprets this as a move toward her, wraps her spindly arms around me, and holds tight, my face smothered in her long blonde hair. But then Tabitha is there, gently patting Justine on the back and easing me out of her death grip. Everywhere I look people are distraught, hugging one another, pacing the room, staring at the ceiling. I feel like an imposter. Why did I even agree to come with Tabitha? To see who else didn't make the cut? To find out if the world really is about to end? I'm about to turn and slip out the side door of the building when I hear my name. I turn and see Edwin jogging over to me.

"Edwin!" I rush toward him, and he pulls me into a hug. "I'm so glad to see you. Well not glad exactly, I'm sorry you're not...I'm sorry we're not...do you know what's going on?" I realize I sound just like Justine, and I take a deep breath and try again. "I'm sorry. I just haven't been able to get my bearings since, you know. It's comforting to see a friendly face." I say, hoping I've chosen the right words.

Edwin smiles at me that same way he used to when we were kids and I'd just convinced him to sneak an extra dessert at Evening Table. He seems calm, considering. "It's ok, Alice. It's all going to be ok. Brother Richmond left a message for us."

"A message?" My voice raises in a squeaky, worried tone. Edwin doesn't answer. He walks to the front of the room. I follow him and then stand to the side as he jumps up onto the stage. His voice isn't very loud, but this room's been built with acoustics in mind, so the sound carries well.

"Um, hello, everyone. I know we're all scared and worried and we're trying to figure it all out, but," he pauses and I'm not sure if it's for dramatic effect or so he can figure out what to say next, "we're all going to be ok."

"Get off the stage, boy. We're lost. We're all lost. The world is ending, and we're lost with it." Angelica speaks from her spot near the window. Her voice is barely audible over those still crying or blowing their nose, but the calm way she pronounces judgment makes my skin crawl. Several others in the group shout their agreement.

"If you believed that, Angelica, you'd still be sitting in that meadow waiting for your fate, but you came here."

Edwin. Ever the optimist. When we got called into Brother Richmond's office for putting salt in the sugar bowls, he squeezed my hand and told me it wasn't going to be so bad. We got off with only extra cleaning duties.

"Brother Richmond knew we would still be here after the Homegoing, and I think that means we've been left behind for a reason. Look at Alice here." He puts his hand out toward me, and I shrink away from it. He flicks just the ends of his fingers and his eyes plead with me.

Oh hell, I think, and take his hand as he pulls me onto the podium.

"Alice has been in the Collective since birth. She's always worked to advance the mission of the group."

I hear a few whispers in the crowd, and I can imagine the things they are saying. I edge toward the stairs so I can get off this cursed stage, but Edwin's hand grips my shoulder. He raises a hand to hush the whispers.

"I didn't say she was perfect. We've all made our mistakes, but we keep showing up. We keep believing. And so does Alice. She's here. We're here. Figuring it out. Now, if you're willing to trust me and we're willing to work together, I think we can get through this."

"We're all ears." says Jacob Parsons from the back of the room.

He should be telling them about the message, I think. He must have a reason for not mentioning it.

"We need to head over to Brother Richmond's house," he says.

People seem dubious about this suggestion from the various whispers and gasps that slink through the small group. Going into Brother Richmond's house has long been forbidden by all but his most trusted advisors, but, as Tabitha points out, he's no longer here to fuss about it.

As we file out of the meeting house to make the trek back to the Village, a hand grabs my shoulder. I whirl around, expecting Tabitha, but it's Bekah. Her eyes are puffy red, and her hair is a tangled mess. Sarah is standing next to her, looking just as disheveled. I look past Bekah toward the meeting house, my eyes raised in a question I don't want to ask. Bekah shakes her head.

"My family isn't there. They've gone with all the rest," she says.

I look past her to Sarah. "And your mom, Sarah?" I ask, even though I already know the answer.

"She's gone too." Sarah says.

I pull them close to me, trying to offer some measure of comfort. They're just teenagers. It doesn't seem right to have left them without anyone to look after them. Bekah's the latest in a generational lineage in the Collective. I can see their loss weighing heavy in her eyes. Sarah only had her mom. She joined when Sarah was ten or eleven. It feels somehow worse to lose your family when that family is one person. Sarah pulls out of my hug and speaks without looking at me.

"We were wondering..." She kicks at the gravel in the path. "We were wondering," she begins again, but can't seem to finish the thought.

"We were wondering," Bekah cuts in, "if we could stay with you, until we figure out what's going on. It's just that our houses are both empty, and we're not sure what to do, and we heard from Tabitha that you were still here, and she suggested..." She must see the shock and hesitation on my face because she trails off. "Never mind. We'll be fine. It's fine."

I sigh, my arm still wrapped around Bekah's shoulder. I'm supposed to be leaving. I can't babysit two teenagers if I'm leaving. I can't. It won't work. But their faces are so worn. They've been alone for less than twenty-four hours and already they've aged well beyond their youth. I pull on the low hanging branch of a tree next to me and say in a rush, before I can think about it too much, "Of course you can stay with me. I wouldn't have it any other way."

The girls seem buoyed by this news. We spread out, a three-knot strand across the path, and continue walking toward the Village in silence. I'm so lost in thought that it's a shock when Brother Richmond's house appears before me. It sits in the middle of the Village, the lone brick structure towering over a sea of white clapboard. It's the only two-story building on the Farm. Brother Richmond claimed he needed to live in the old farmhouse when the land was purchased because certain demonic forces were at work even in the very foundations of the house and he was the only one who could keep them at bay. It always seemed curious to me that expelling those demons required the installation of central air and granite counter tops.

The front door of the house is original, and we enter, one by one, through the narrow opening. Once we cross the threshold, everyone falls silent. I wonder if this is some kind of test. Brother Richmond was fond of those, and I think maybe he'll pop up from behind the sofa and tell us our families are all out hiding in the corn fields.

Edwin leads us to the living room. It's dark at first. Velvet drapes are pulled tight against the two front windows, and the gloom feels like a film on my skin. I walk a few steps into the room before someone pulls the curtains, and then we're all wincing as our eyes adjust to the scene before us. It's not a very large room, but it's stuffed with plush sofas, reclining armchairs, and ottomans. There are several side tables stacked with books. Mostly copies of *The Collective Code*, one of them opened and heavily underlined. But there's also a book on astrology, a faded *New York Times* from 1999, and a couple of old hymnals, their bindings frayed with colored threads that stick up in wild angles. A round table in the middle of the room holds several burned down incense sticks, their perfume an afterthought in the musty air. Ashes tumble to the floor as someone knocks into the table.

At the front of the room, pushed against the wall, there's an old rolling cart, the metal chipping off in places to reveal rust underneath. On top of it is a television. Of course Brother Richmond has a TV. No one else has ever been allowed one, but since when did that matter. I hear a few people echo what I'm thinking, but I keep my mouth closed. I don't need any extra attention on me right now.

There's an envelope sitting on the shelf under the television. It reads "The Remainder" and it's propped against what looks like a VCR. Edwin goes over and picks up the envelope. Underneath it, atop the VCR, rests a video tape. Only Brother Richmond would commit his last will and testament to a piece of technology that peaked in 1995. He opens the envelope and takes out a thin sheet of pale blue paper. He reads aloud,

"To my beloveds. These are trying times. I know you must be scared and worried and unsure of what is next right now. I understand. I prepared for this day with everything that is in me, but I could not reveal all the Lord's plans to you. His plans have their own timing, and the Lord works all things together for good, as you know. Never fear, beloveds. You have not been forsaken. While it is true that the weary world is nearing the end of her time, it is not just yet. The rest of us go ahead to prepare a place for you, but you, the chosen few, will prepare for the final Homegoing. The Lord has revealed to me that it will take place two months from the time you view this message. Time is short, so you must get ready. Please see my video for further instructions."

Murmurs break out as Edwin finishes the letter. Never has there been discussion of a second Homegoing, only the one where the faithful would be ushered into paradise and everyone left would perish as the world imploded. Tabitha shifts uncomfortably on the edge of the sofa. Jacob gets up off the floor and walks out of the house without a word. No one follows him, but he and I lock our eyes as he brushes past on the way to the door. He looks afraid.

I close my eyes and try to think. Even from wherever he's gone Brother Richmond is trying to control us. I was already planning to leave, so I'll just leave now. Walk out like Jacob and leave this place as Jason and I planned. Jason is gone, but I still have this life growing inside me and I owe it to whoever this person is going to be to get far, far away from here. Someone else can look after Bekah and Sarah. There's got to be someone else. They'll understand. I have the money Jason and I saved. How much does a hotel room cost? What about a doctor's visit? I envision myself out in the world. I feel like an infant trying to walk for the first time. How could I have gotten this far knowing so little about surviving on my own? Maybe Jason and I wouldn't have made it even if he were still here. Brother Richmond always said it was a gift to be free from the world's worries, but it was really just another way to keep us here. I'm still wrestling through all the obstacles piled in my way when Edwin turns on the TV.

The static is bright as daylight. Everyone moves to sit down, like it's a family movie night. A few people find space on the couches while the rest perch on the sides of armchairs, plop down on the floor, or hover in the doorways. Everyone looks to Edwin. It seems he's been unofficially elected our leader in this end of world journey. I stand near the doorway that leads back to the front door, unsure if I want to know what comes next.

He puts the tape in the VCR, and we wait. Memories of being in Brother Richmond's office flood my brain. I look down at the blue carpet, but before long I find my eyes trailing back up to the screen. My stomach lurches and I wonder if the baby is protesting. Maybe it already understands that whatever this is will lead to no good thing. At first, the screen is black, and then it fills with technicolor tracking bars before a high-pitched whining noise and a loud pop come from the VCR, then the screen goes black again. Edwin crouches in front of the VCR and brings the tape out, the mangled ribbon spilling down over his hands like black ink. He cradles it like an infant and gasps go up around the room. He stands.

"Friends, I have a confession to make. After the Homegoing, I felt led to come back here and pray over what happened. When I came into this room, I was drawn to the television, and I found the letter and the tape from Brother Richmond. Self-control failed me and I viewed the tape before I gathered everyone together. I offer my confession and my apology for betraying you in this way."

"That doesn't matter, just tell us what was on the video," Angelica screeches from her perch on one of the ottomans.

"Brother Richmond shared his love for us, and he left instructions to gather for the second Homegoing just as we did with the first. The only difference is that Alice and I are to lead the group into the meadow this time."

Ice floods my veins and I gape at Edwin. Everyone else turns to stare at me. They know I haven't exactly walked the straight and narrow since, well, ever. And if anyone knew about the baby, then I'm sure the murmurs would be more like the shouts of an angry mob.

"Alice," Edwin looks at me. "I know this is a shock, but I'll be here to help you. Brother Richmond was clear that we are in this together. You and I and the rest of the faithful gathered here. Afterward, we'll be reunited with the departed and the world will finally be sanctified through fire, just as Brother Richmond always told us."

He closes his eyes as if in prayer. There's one hushed moment and then everyone talks at once. People are clapping me on the back, smiling, happy to have been told what to do once again. My head is a swirl of emotion, but one thought rings out above the rest: *No.*

-4-

TERESA

"I told you I put the quarters in that little zipper bag in the laundry basket." I leaned over the table meant for folding clothes to push the laundry basket toward Tom. My huge stomach bumped against the cracked table of the Sunshine Laundromat and snagged one of my only maternity shirts. All those quarters from our pickle jar. And now we couldn't find them.

"I told you I don't see it here," Tom said as he pushed the basket back toward me.

An exasperated older woman heaved a cracked laundry hamper onto the table next to us. It landed with a brittle whack. Broken plastic on broken plastic. I pulled at the snag in my shirt and tried not to look at her, but she lowered her entire body to catch my eyes.

"I don't care where your quarters are. It's my turn with this machine. It's the only one big enough for my comforters. I'll be lucky if I finish half before this place closes, so get your stuff out. Now."

"Sorry, ma'am." I piled our wet clothes onto the table. The prospect of carrying home our heavy wet clothes to drape over the backs of chairs where they would mildew before they dried in the damp apartment made me want to sob.

"It's got to be around here somewhere." Tom was on the floor feeling underneath the washing machine, trying to stem the flood of my tears.

"Tom, stop. It's gone." I began stuffing wet t-shirts and jeans into our laundry bag, my hands already pained from the cold, wet material.

"Excuse me? Would these help?"

At first, all I noticed was the roll of quarters. The brown paper, ridged in orange, and the gleam of the stacked silver coins just peeking out through the crimped edges. My eyes followed the rolled coins to an outstretched hand. Nails edged with dirt and fingers rough with calluses. The hand was attached to an arm draped in a maroon sweatshirt, which led to the smiling face of a man I'd never seen before. His hair stretched down well past his shoulders, deep brown but edged with red where the afternoon light shone on it through the laundromat windows. As I studied him, he tucked his hair behind his ears in a gesture I would soon come to know. A trim beard grazed his chin. He looked vaguely like the Jesus in my childhood story Bible, if that Jesus also wore Converse tennis shoes and a digital watch.

Only after staring at the man for what felt like a beat too long did I notice the woman. She had the same placid smile, the same light in her eyes. She didn't wear any makeup, and her long pink dress was tattered on the bottom where it dragged the linoleum floor. Her hair was a vivid red, styled in loose curls that fell over one shoulder in a way that looked haphazard, though I guessed it wasn't. She held a zippered pouch, much larger than the one Tom and I lost, with neon yellow smile-y faces all over it. Other wrapped coins stuck out of the top. They didn't have any laundry. Still, I stared. Somewhere, deep inside me, an instinct to leave our wet clothes and run far, far away from these people and their quarters welled up like a gushing spring.

"We couldn't take your money. Really. Thank you, though. That's awfully kind." Tom was still on the floor but rocked back on his heels as he studied the couple. I reached out my hand to help pull him up, and the rushing feeling inside me passed.

"Please, we insist. We've got plenty," the man said. He gestured at the woman, and she hoisted the bag full of quarters in the air. She must have sensed my hesitancy because she smiled as she said, "Don't worry. We're not going to give you quarters and then make you listen to a sermon."

The man laughed like it was the funniest thing he'd ever heard and swatted his hand in the direction of the woman. I looked at Tom. He cleaned his glasses with the edge of his t-shirt and tried to keep himself from laughing. It wasn't that funny, but their joy was contagious, and I found myself smiling back at them as Tom replaced his glasses and put his arm around me. He turned toward the strangers.

"Ok, then. Thanks. We appreciate it." He shook the man's hand and took the coins.

"You're so welcome." The man's body was turned toward Tom, but his eyes remained on me. "No one likes to feel called out when they're doing their best to get through the day."

A little shiver went up my spine and into the back of my head, where it buzzed around like a bee caught in a tin box. I wasn't sure if I liked it or not. I looked at the table piled high with the rest of our wet clothes. I began loading them into the nearest dryer.

"Thank you, sir," I mumbled more to the clothes than to the man. I wanted to get home where I could sit down and put my aching feet in a tub of hot water.

"Whoa, I bet I'm not more than five years older than you. Way too young for that 'sir' business." He tucked his hair behind his ears again. "I'm Richmond. Rich, actually. And this is Jennifer." He stepped back so he was standing even with the woman in the pink dress.

I continued throwing the clothes in the dryer. Tom handed me the roll of quarters and leaned against the table. His usual awkward cadence relaxed into a conversational tone I hadn't heard with anyone but me.

"Thanks again. You guys are lifesavers. Do you go around to all the laundromats playing dryer fairy?"

Rich laughed, and I was surprised to find that I liked it, despite my earlier feelings of unease. It was big and deep and sounded like warm honey. I finished loading the laundry and pulled at the top of the rolled quarters. I ripped a little too far down and the coins spilled out of their paper wrapper. They clanged against the dryer and rolled across the gray linoleum like shooting stars in a storm. I began the lengthy process of lowering myself to the floor to pick up the dropped coins. Jennifer was by my side in a second.

"Let me! It's so hard to get down on the floor when you're this far along. My son's almost one. I remember the feeling."

I let her retrieve the coins, feeling stupid as tears once again sprang to my eyes. "Thanks. It's hard to do almost anything at this stage." It felt easy to admit this to Jennifer, who loaded the quarters into the dryer's coin slot. She tossed the rest of the loose coins into her zippered bag and pulled out a new stack.

"How far along are you?"

"Eight months." I rubbed my stomach.

"You look amazing. I looked like a watermelon stuffed into some pantyhose when I was at that stage. It will get easier, I promise. Until they start walking, and then all hell breaks loose." Jennifer's laugh was the total opposite of Rich's. It was light and quiet. But you could feel it in the way her face changed, in the way her eyes crinkled shut, the way she put her hand on your arm right at the end. I laughed too. I could see Tom smile at me out of the corner of my eye.

"How long do these dryers run anyway?" Rich said. He and Tom had moved to stand next to Jennifer and me.

"Usually around an hour," Tom said, and held up the book he'd brought to show how we planned to pass the time while we waited.

"It's so stuffy in here, and I'm starving," Rich said. "How about we head to the sandwich shop across the street while you wait on your clothes. My treat?"

"Oh no, we couldn't take any more of your generosity, really." I was glad Tom spoke up so I wouldn't have to reject their offer. They really did seem like nice people.

"Are you kidding me? Jennifer and I have been talking to nothing but boring people all day. You two are the first interesting ones we've met. You'd really be doing us a favor."

I didn't know what we had said in our two minutes of conversation to make us interesting, but I thrilled at the thought. We hadn't exactly been the life of the party since moving to Cyrene, and the possibility of friendship felt like a gift above and beyond the quarters.

"Well, Tom, we haven't had lunch yet. And this baby is getting hungry."

That was all it took. "The baby gets what the baby wants. Lead on, Rich." Tom did a mock bow.

"Hey!" Someone screeched behind me, and I turned to find the woman who had demanded our washing machine.

"Sorry. I thought I got everything out. Did I leave something?" She ignored me and stepped closer to Rich.

"You got any extra quarters in there for an old lady?"

"No," Rich said.

Surprised, I started to offer the woman the stack of quarters

Jennifer had just given me. But Jennifer put her hand over mine and shook her head.

"But I do have some quarters for the lovely lady with flowers in her hair." His fingers brushed the floral scarf tied over her head. She blushed and her face softened into something almost pretty. She took the coins from Jennifer, who had materialized next to her, and winked at me as she turned away. Rich jumped on top of the folding table next to us and stood. He was tall and his fingertips grazed the tiled ceiling as he raised his hands above his head.

"Who else needs quarters? We've got quarters for all! The God of love offers extravagant generosity!"

The other people in the laundry mat marched to our table as if they'd been waiting for the invitation. A man who looked to be in his forties with torn pants stained with white paint shuffled over. An exhausted-looking mother called her five children over from playing leapfrog in the corner. Several attractive girls a little older than me stared at Rich like they would wash his clothes in the river if he asked. I only had half a second to wonder if Jennifer ever got jealous of that kind of attention before she dumped several rolls of quarters in my hand. They were heavy, and I almost dropped them in surprise.

"Help me hand these out!" Her eyes were bright and charged with frenetic energy.

I pulled the rolls of coins against my stomach to keep them from dropping to the floor and handed some to the family with the five kids. What looked to be the oldest kid, a boy of maybe eleven or twelve, grabbed the first roll and hoisted it high above his head. The other children turned and followed him like a platoon over to the vending machines at the back of the laundromat. I heard the drop of a can and then their whoops of joy.

I kept handing out coins until I'd exhausted my supply, but

then there was Jennifer handing Tom and me more rolls of quarters. The people kept multiplying too. Just when I thought we'd given out quarters to everyone, there was someone new. Above me, Rich spoke about love and neighbors, but the babble of people was too loud to distinguish many details. I felt like I was doing something important, something meaningful, perhaps for the first time. My feet no longer hurt. My worries and fears seemed distant and inconsequential. I eagerly reached for the next set of quarters from Jennifer.

Tom had somehow migrated to the front door. I waved and he gave me a big thumbs up. It was good to be in the middle of this day that didn't quite feel possible. A day that, if only for a little while, removed us from our moldy apartment and our stress and our homesickness. I could tell by Tom's goofy grin that he felt the same way. I let myself be carried away by the feeling.

After the last person had been handed a roll of quarters, Rich jumped to the floor in one long and graceful stride. He pushed his hair back behind his ears and walked over to Tom and me. I was a sweaty mess, and Tom's glasses were crooked. Rich put his arms around us both and said, "How about we get that sandwich now?"

At the sandwich shop, we crowded into a booth and ordered the family style platter. The accordion of deli meat and cheese splayed across the tray reminded me of how hungry I'd been before the quarters, so I dove in and made myself a sandwich. Rich followed me with a grin and raised eyebrows but didn't say anything. When I couldn't eat another pickle or slice of Swiss cheese, I wiped my mouth with my napkin.

"Where did you get all those quarters? We must have handed out over a hundred rolls."

"The God of love provides." Rich leaned back far in his seat and tossed a chip in the air, catching it in his mouth just before it fell to the table.

"I thought you said you weren't a church," Tom said.

"You can believe in God without organized religion," Jennifer said. She curled her fingers into air quotes around the phrase, like it wasn't a real thing.

"So why give out the quarters? If you're not pushing a church or something, then why do it?" I couldn't fault Tom for asking the question. It was at the back of my mind too, but I was tired from the morning and full from the food, and I didn't want to get into a religious debate with our new friends. I turned to Jennifer.

"So, do you and Rich have other kids or just the one?" I asked, remembering her description of her almost one year old in the laundry mat. Jennifer sat up straight. The smile fell from her face, replaced by an almost fearful look. She dropped her voice low and spoke quickly.

"Rich and I aren't together. My husband, Anthony, is at home with our son Edwin today."

"Oh, I'm sorry. I shouldn't have assumed," I said.

"It's fine," she said, in a way that closed the subject. Her eyes trailed away from me and over toward Tom and Rich's conversation. Rich was speaking.

"Let me ask you something, Tom. How did it make you feel in there? Being in control of that kind of generosity?"

I wondered what Tom would say. He frowned a little before he spoke. "It felt really good. Better than I've felt in some time, if I'm being honest." He looked toward me for reassurance, and I nodded.

"You know, you look a little like my mother," Rich said abruptly and turned to face me. "She had hair the same color as yours. She got pregnant with me when she was fifteen." His eyes drifted down to my belly where it bumped against the table in front of us. I looked down, not wanting to discuss my pregnancy with him. "Her family threw her out. My father abandoned her. She slept on the street, begged for food, and delivered me all on her own in the parking lot of a gas station. A couple on a road trip found her and helped her get to a hospital. She spent the rest of her life trying to teach me the importance of helping others. She told me she never felt so good as when she was helping others. She always said that when you put something into someone's hands, something they didn't have before, it made them a new person. Right then and there. Like magic."

I felt tears welling up hot in the backs of my eyes as I thought about how much harder things would be without Tom by my side. Without his grandma. I thought of all the help that I'd been given even as it all felt so difficult. Rich handed me a paper napkin from the table and turned back to Tom.

"I think God wants everyone to feel like that. To feel that your life has been transformed and to feel like you've transformed someone else's life. This world is a hard and scary place, and so many people have a vision of this better kind of life they want to live without knowing how to get there. I believe in a God that wants to give people that better kind of life and who wants us to help others get it. That's what I've devoted my life to, anyway."

Rich's eyes lit up when he spoke. His voice was strong and sure and full of possibility. Listening to him talk made everything else seem dull in comparison. I could tell Tom felt it too, and we leaned in, eager to know more and hoping against hope that maybe we could be a part of that better life as well.

-5-

ALICE

I avoid everyone over the next week. I change the sheets in the bedroom I once shared with Jason and give the space to Sarah and Bekah. I can't sleep in there, so I take the spare room. The room that, in other houses, is meant for children. Not in our house though. I sleep and wake and sleep some more. I stare at the light changing through the window.

When it's almost completely dark, and everything outside the window is shadow, I listen to Bekah and Sarah talk in garbled voices outside my door. They leave food, and the smell of banana bread fills the room. I drag myself out of bed long enough to grab the plate and slink back, where I cocoon myself in blankets and try not to think about anything. After three days of this, I will myself into the bathroom. If the world isn't going to end, I might as well get a shower. In the mirror, my black hair points out in all directions like Medusa. I try to smooth it down, remembering how my mother's strawberry blonde hair fell down her back like silk. I always wished I had her hair instead of the unmanageable black mane I inherited from my dad. When I was thirteen, I convinced Edwin to sneak into town with me to buy a box of hair color to make my dreams a reality.

In the small pharmacy downtown, we ran our fingers along the shelves, marveling at all the options. An older woman with a faded blue vest and hair the color of dirty snow glanced up at us over the top of the magazine she was reading. I was trying to decide between Bountiful Blonde and Sunkissed Strawberry when the woman spoke, eyes still fixed on the magazine.

"You kids from the Farm?"

I froze. Everyone in town knew something about us. We had the free community dinners and Brother Richmond was always preaching outside the farm stand about love and generosity as people picked out corn and placed their orders for pies. We needed to be a light in the dark world, he said. People can't see the light if you don't show it to them. So we showed it to them. But some preferred the dark to the light if we were in it. Worldly people. They wanted to drag us back into the dark with them. We had to be on our guard against them.

My hand was still resting on the top of a glossy box, a blonde woman beaming up at me, when Edwin replied.

"No ma'am. Not from here. Just visiting."

I marveled at the ease in Edwin's voice. He was holding some shampoo and raised it toward the woman in greeting.

"Where from?" The woman looked skeptical, and I feared she could hear my heart beating all the way behind the register.

"We're from Tennessee. Visiting our aunt Trudy."

"Trudy Stapleton?"

"That's the one."

I closed my eyes. Now we'd be found out. There was no Trudy Stapleton or she didn't have any nieces or nephews. Something that would prove us to be the lying offspring of those crazies up at the Farm. And then what? She'd run us out or kidnap us for one of her worldly schemes, if the stories were to be believed. Nothing happened, though. The woman just shrugged.

"Didn't know Trudy had family that far south. Welcome to Cyrene."

Once we'd paid for the Sunkissed Strawberry, we ran down the street until we reached the outskirts of towns where buildings started to give way to fields. I fell into a clump of grass, gasping and holding the stitch in my side.

"Edwin!" I shrieked. "You were so calm! Where did you learn how to do that?"

Edwin shrugged and rolled over in the grass where I'd collapsed. "You just have to listen to people and then tell them what they want to hear."

"You've never met that woman before! How did you know what she wanted to hear?"

"I've listened to enough worldly folk to know what they want. They just want things to be easy. No fuss. No muss."

Back at my house, Edwin rubbed the dye into my hair. It tingled my scalp, and I swore I could feel myself changing. We wrapped an old towel around my head and waited the thirty minute application time with the bathroom window open to let out the smell. Edwin stood guard at the door in case my parents came home. I kept my eyes closed as I rinsed my hair in the bathtub, so I could get the full effect when I looked in the mirror. It felt like the start of something big. But when I flipped my head up and grinned in the mirror, it was the same old me looking back. My hair was as black as ever. In our haste to get out of the pharmacy, we'd failed to consider that I'd first need to bleach the black out of my hair before I could add the blonde. Edwin offered to go back for the bleach, but the failure felt too absolute to try again.

*****

I begin to feel myself coming back together and I venture out into the living room where Sarah and Bekah are sitting on the couch. They look startled to see me.

"Thought I'd join the land of the living, at least for today."

They stare, and I realize I haven't taken any care in dressing. The bump where my stomach used to be bulges beneath my shirt.

Bekah speaks first. "Are you—"

"Pregnant?" Sarah finishes the question with a tone of awe in her voice.

I guess there's no hiding it now. "Yes," I say, and leave it at that.

"Was it on purpose?" Bekah's voice is tentative. I can tell she doesn't want to risk me retreating to the bedroom again, but her curiosity is getting the better of her.

"It was. And before you ask, no, it was not approved. And yes. We did it anyway."

"Doesn't matter now, does it?" Sarah says. Her eyes are hard and there's a trace of bitterness in her voice.

"Are you scared?" Bekah asks.

I don't answer. Instead, I walk toward the front window and look out past our porch and toward the path that leads to the meeting house. The weeds have pushed their way into it at odd angles and from my view at the window, it looks like the opening to a maze.

"Do you think they are in heaven like Brother Richmond said? Do you really think they are coming back for us? Two months is not very long," Sarah asks. Her voice sounds far away now.

I continue looking out the window. "Do you think they are all in heaven, Sarah?" I answer, finally.

It's Bekah who responds.

"Brother Richmond said everyone would be taken to heaven and everyone is gone." She speaks like each word is a puzzle piece she's trying to fit in the right place. "He also said other things would happen that didn't, so—"

"Brother Richmond was bad." Sarah's voice is sudden and sharp. I don't question her, but I wonder what experiences led her to this conclusion. I wonder if they were similar to my own. I wonder why I never bothered to ask more questions.

"Sarah, you can't. Even though..." Bekah is grasping at words but can't seem to find the ones she wants. Sarah continues over Bekah's protests.

"Brother Richmond was bad, but he said this good thing would happen and it did. Only it wasn't that good. Not for us anyway." She looks up at me like she's asked a question, and I should supply the answer. I don't speak.

"So, we wait for the next good thing. God works all things together for good, so there's got to be a next good thing. The second Homegoing, like Brother Richmond's letter said," Bekah says.

They both look at me, and I am struck by the fact that I have been so focused on getting myself out of this place that I haven't really considered those I would be leaving behind. I assumed everyone who was still here wanted to be here. But I am still here. There are probably others like me, I realize. People who had all the same questions and doubts seething just below the surface but nowhere to go with those feelings. I'm still not sure what I believe, but I can't tell the girls that. Not when their eyes are begging me to help them put the pieces together.

"Maybe we should pray," Bekah says, and her face is full of such desperation that I agree, even though I'm not sure I remember how. We all kneel on the thin rug in my living room and ask for answers, answers I'm sure aren't coming.

After the girls go to bed, I walk down to the basement. I cross the dirt floor to the far wall, feeling my way in the dark. I don't want to turn on my flashlight until I need to. Who knows if someone is watching my house. I run my hand along the wall until I get to the sharp stone that juts out from the rest. Jason and I joked about it being the entrance to a secret room when we'd moved in. I pry the stone free to reveal the cavity we dug behind it. A jolt of shock and anger zings through me. All our money, everything we had to make it out in the world, is gone. All that's left is an envelope that says "Alice" in Jason's handwriting.

Dear Alice,

I'm sorry. I wanted to stay and make a new life with you. I wanted you to have all you've dreamed of and hoped for. But life isn't about getting what we want. It's about serving God, and our plan was only serving ourselves. I know the child you're carrying is a blessing, even if it was conceived in disobedience. You talk of not wanting to raise the baby in the Collective because of Brother Richmond's sins, but what about ours? How could we raise a child properly with such deception in our hearts? I look forward to one day being reunited with you when we can put this wearisome world behind us and embrace repentance.

Love,

Jason

I sink to the floor. Grief washes over me again, and I pound my hands into the dirt. Then, I feel another kick. A somersault inside me. I press my hand to my stomach and feel it again. A reminder. Something Brother Richmond tried to control and failed. I cradle my stomach and cry myself to sleep on the basement floor. I'm still asleep when the police come banging at the door.

-6-

TERESA

Tom and I weren't sure what to expect at that first meeting after the laundromat, but we agreed to approach it with an open mind. Fifteen or so people were crammed into Rich's tiny basement level apartment when we got there. It was bright for an underground space. Colorful scarves draped the lamps, and I tipped my hat, one broke interior decorator to another. Two blue futons were pushed end to end against the wall, both heavy with patchwork quilts and knit blankets. They looked more like they belonged in a grandma's sitting room than a basement bachelor pad.

Jennifer raced up to us. She seemed anxious to introduce us to her husband. He wasn't the man I would have pictured her with. Short and stocky, Anthony had close cropped blonde hair and wore a golf shirt and slacks. He had the handshake of a salesman.

"Did you guys find everyone here down on their luck in the laundromat?" Tom said, gesturing to the other people gathered in the room.

"Not the laundromat for me," Anthony said, a twinkle in his brown eyes. "I met Rich in my first job out of college. He was working as the janitor at the school where I was teaching, if you can believe it. At first it was just small talk. Hello, goodbye, nice weather, you get the idea." Anthony's voice was quiet, and I had to lean in to hear what he said.

"One night I stayed late in my classroom to finish setting up for our science fair. I teach science. Middle school. Anyway, Rich walked right in, sat on the corner of my desk and said, 'Mr. Belfry, I think you have a drinking problem, and I think I can help you fix it.' Of course, I got defensive and told him he didn't know what the hell he was talking about and to get out of my room. What he didn't know, what he couldn't know," he paused for dramatic effect, "was that I had a bottle of Jack Daniels in the bottom drawer of my desk underneath some old textbooks, and I'd been slipping a little into my morning coffee every morning of the school year. The principal came this close—" he pinched his thumb and finger together in front of his face, "—to catching me with the bottle out on my desk one morning, and I was sweating bullets thinking about what I would do if I lost my job. I'd been drinking since I was fifteen. I'd tried the twelve steps, cold turkey, even some hypnotherapy mumbo jumbo, but nothing worked."

"So, did you tell Rich he was right about the drinking?" I asked.

"Well, I went home that night and couldn't sleep. I felt this pressure on my chest, this buzzing, and I knew I wasn't going to be able to sleep until I dealt with it. Like it was nudging me back toward Rich. So, I said, ok, God, if I'm supposed to go talk to this janitor, you need to give me some kind of a sign. Right then, my lamp fell off my nightstand. Just tipped right over. I didn't need to be told twice. The next day after school, I found Rich mopping the cafeteria and I told him he was right. I said I was willing to try whatever he was selling. Two weeks later I had my last drink and haven't looked back since. Rich saved my life."

"Wow," I said. "What was the secret? How'd you finally give it up?"

"Prayer and hard truths. He got me involved with serving others rather than myself. He introduced me to my beautiful bride." His gaze panned toward Jennifer.

"Rich introduced you two?" Tom asked, his head now titled toward Jennifer.

Jennifer smiled and closed her eyes briefly like she was preparing for a performance. "I was teaching as well, not at Anthony's school, somewhere different. But there was a grief support group that met in the evenings at Anthony's school. My mother had just passed away from cancer. She'd been sick a long time, but I was still in a bad place when the end finally came. During one meeting, I just couldn't cope, so I left the group mid-discussion to cry in the girls' bathroom. There was no toilet paper to wipe my nose or eyes, which only made me cry harder. I looked like a racoon with all that mascara I used to wear." Jennifer rimmed her fingers around both her eyes. "Rich must have heard me because he came in and offered me extra toilet paper from his janitor's cart. I tore off a large swath and handed it back to him. 'Keep it,' he said. 'I don't think they'll miss it.' It was the first thing that had made me laugh since my mom died. Later, he introduced me to Anthony."

We heard similar stories all night. *I was on the verge of suicide and Rich brought me back from the brink. Rich cured me of my insomnia. Rich was my friend when no one else was there for me.* I wondered how this one man could be so many things to so many people. Edwin, Jennifer and Anthony's son, toddled around, babbling nonsense and asking for Rich.

I was just finishing up a third piece of pizza when Rich came in. Everyone went quiet. But it wasn't an ominous silence. Instead, it was like the conversation opened up to make room for him. He walked over to Tom and me when he spotted us across the room.

"Teresa! Tom! I'm so glad you both came. I knew I was right

about you two. Didn't I tell you, Jennifer? Didn't I have a good feeling about them?"

"You did," Jennifer agreed.

Rich gave the briefest nod in Anthony's direction and turned toward Tom and me again. Jennifer's smile faltered, but only for a moment.

"I think you're going to find a whole new family with this group." Rich handed me a Bible. "You may want one of these for when we get started. Hope you don't mind sharing, we only have a few right now. But we're planning to get more printed."

It was a plain, black leather Bible. Exactly like the heavy one my dad kept on our fireplace mantle and insisted we read from at Sunday dinners. Michael and I always joked that it made us feel like we were in *Little House on the Prairie.* My heart gave a little thud of sadness as I thought about laughing with Michael and wondered when I could get him up to Cyrene. It had been months. I'd sent him a few postcards, but he didn't write back. We didn't yet have a phone in the apartment, but when I'd tried to call Michael from a payphone outside the pharmacy, my mother picked up and I'd lost my nerve and hung up.

The book felt overly thick in my hands, lumpy, even for a Bible. I wondered why Rich needed to print Bibles when you could find a free copy in any hotel bedside table. I held the Bible out to Tom. His arched eyebrows drew a short laugh from Rich.

"Don't worry, Tom. We're not a church, remember?"

He winked at Tom and walked to the other side of the room. Even though the room was small and stuffed full, it parted around him. People tumbled into folding chairs, edged into the doorway of the bathroom, or pressed themselves flat against the wall to make a clear path for Rich. We continued eating pizza and drinking warm soda for close to another hour. It didn't feel like that much time had passed when I looked at my watch, though. I realized then how starved I'd been for conversation.

At some point, everyone seemed to know it was time to settle in because they all moved to sit down and the conversation quieted, as if on a dimmer switch. Tom and I sat pressed up against another woman on one of the futons. She had introduced herself as Angelica earlier in the night. She was old, but in that way everyone older than twenty-five seems old when you're young. Looking back, she probably wasn't any older than forty at the first meeting. Rich walked to the front of the room, and Angelica gazed at him like she was afraid he'd disappear at any minute. He stood directly in front of a floor lamp so there was a halo of light around his brown hair.

"Welcome to anyone new, anyone old, and anyone who's just here for the pizza."

Quiet laughter skittered around the room. I shifted, trying to scoot a little closer to Tom, but Angelica clapped her hand on my shoulder and whispered in my ear, "So glad you're here." Her other hand plopped, uninvited, onto my stomach.

"I think it's going to be a little girl. You're carrying high."

I shrugged my shoulders. I'd long tired of other people's comments on my unborn child, but they kept coming anyway. At the front of the room, Rich was reading a verse from the Bible in his hand.

"'The Lord has anointed me to proclaim good news to the poor. He has sent me to bind up the broken hearted to proclaim freedom for the captive. To proclaim the year of the Lord's favor and the day of vengeance of our God.' Can I get an amen after that powerful word?"

Amens peppered the room, but I was focused on the words he'd read. I knew it was from Isaiah, but I couldn't remember the verse or chapter. It sounded different when Rich read it. I felt like the captive in need of freedom. Tom pushed the Bible Rich had given us back onto my lap, uninterested in searching for the verse himself. I flipped it open to where I thought I would find Isaiah, and I realized why the book felt so thick.

The Bible was in tatters. There were some original pages, but other sections had been entirely torn out and new pages, thick and waxy, not the see-through pages with gilt edges I expected, had been sewn in their place. In other spots, long sections had been whited out or pictures had been drawn over the original text. On one page of Genesis was a flower with petals falling off it. The petals said 'poverty', 'sadness', 'anxiety', and 'loneliness'. There were new petals sprouting up where the old ones had fallen away. These read "Friendship," "Love," "Security," and a blank one that hadn't been filled in yet. I must have let out an audible gasp, because the room grew still, and Rich stopped speaking. I felt the blush creeping up my neck as several faces turned to look at me.

"Some of you may be surprised about our reading material tonight." Rich spoke out to the room, but I could feel his eyes on me, even as I looked down, embarrassed, at the piecemeal Bible in my hands.

"I realize our take on the holy Scripture is a little unorthodox, but you know who wrote these books? Stuffy old men who had no interest in actually getting out there and helping people, no interest in wanting to know what life looked like down among the people. They had little interest in a better world, but we know that's what our Lord wants for us. Oh sure, the message couldn't help but slip through from time to time. God's word will find a way, amen? And those are the parts we've left untouched, but the Lord has anointed me. No—" He stopped abruptly, and the lamp light wavered around his head. "No, the Lord has anointed us, my brothers and sisters, to bring good news to the captive. And that means shaking things up from time to time. Finding a way to let God's true message shine through the mess these insignificant men have tried to shove down our throats for two thousand years."

Angelica offered a loud "Amen!" and raised her copy of the mangled Bible in the air. I loved the Bible as a child, but I wasn't a stranger to difficult passages. The ones I skipped over. The ones I'd wished weren't there. But did that mean we could really just snip them out or color daisies over them? As would happen so many times, Richmond seemed to know what I was thinking.

"Now I know, that even though some of this gibberish in here is dead wrong, that many feel a little uneasy about tearing up a holy book. I get that. I don't really enjoy it myself. But it's important for us to get our message across. That's why we're currently raising money to print our own testament, with much of this holy scripture intact, but with our own wisdom as well. That way we don't have to go stealing Bibles from hotels and cutting them up anymore. Because we've got wisdom among us, don't we? Ladies, don't tell me these men got everything just exactly right as it concerns women, amen? We gotta fill in those blanks for future generations. Now everyone, stand up, on your feet!"

I could barely pull myself to standing in those last days before the baby arrived, but I was eager. That same energy that permeated the laundromat swirled around the overstuffed living room. I edged myself to the end of the couch cushion and held my arms out for Tom to pull me to standing. His eyes were shining, and I could tell that he was into this strange new way of looking at the world. We had learned some things in our lives, hadn't we? Men who lived a thousand years ago shouldn't get to hand out God's grace on their terms.

With everyone standing, I couldn't see Rich, but his voice

bounced around the room and into my ears like he was speaking right next to me.

"Put your hands up. Reach up to the heavens. And repeat after me: I have wisdom! I have knowledge! I have a voice!"

Everyone chanted the phrases in unison. I shouted until my lungs felt like they would give out and then I shouted more. It was a rush to shout out your place in the world, to lay claim to something you'd been told wasn't yours. That you were too young, too reckless, or too pregnant to have. The baby leaped and pushed against my skin. I pulled Tom's hand over and placed it on my stomach so he could feel the movement. His eyes got big, and we leaned into one another as Rich kept chanting at the front of the room.

-7-

ALICE

I've been in this interrogation room for at least an hour and have talked to two police officers. One asked me if I owned any weapons, and another asked me about my whereabouts during the disappearance.

"I ran home to get something just before. It was foolish, but I wanted to have my grandmother's Bible with me during the Homegoing," I wasn't sure she bought it, but I couldn't tell her I watched the whole thing from the storeroom window. She'd given me a grim smile and said someone else would be with me shortly.

Now there's a new officer seated in front of me, asking more questions I don't have the right answers for. I scratch at an unidentifiable brown spot on the metal table.

"Mrs..." The officer looks down at his paper. He's older, probably close to retirement. His hair is close-cropped and silvery. Salt and pepper hair, my mom always said. He's tall. Not as tall as my dad, but just about. His suit is old, a bit outdated, which says something coming from me. He looks like the type of man who would have a mustache, but he's clean shaven. "Mrs. Greene?"

"Yes, that's me. I'm sorry. What was your question again?" I ask, even though I remember.

"What can you tell us about Richmond Preston? What do you

remember about him in the days leading up to the disappearance?"

What do I remember about Brother Richmond? I remember the heat of his hands on my shoulders. I remember joy and awe as he spoke at Evening Table when I was a child. I remember confusion and what felt like doors slammed in my face at the slightest question. I remember fear and shame on Sunday nights in his office. I remember anger, so much anger.

"He was our leader."

"Was?"

"Is, I guess." I think, belatedly, that maybe it's not a good idea to start tossing around 'was' when someone has gone missing and I'm sitting in a police station.

"The leader of your group?" I can tell he's thinking cult even as he's so careful about what comes out his mouth. I've heard it before. I've defended us against the charge. He looks down at his manilla folder and shuffles through a few papers, though I know he knows what we're called.

"You called yourselves The Collective, is that right?"

"That's correct, officer."

"You can call me Detective Cameron." He smiles and pushes a paper cup of water toward me. I wonder if he's practiced this hospitality.

"So, Richmond Preston was the leader of the Collective. You've been in the Collective since birth. Your parents are Teresa and Tom Moffat, and you've been married to—" He looks at his papers again, and now I wonder if he's just trying to avoid making eye contact with me. "Jason Greene for the last ten years. Is all this correct?"

"Yes, my parents joined before I was born. But I was planning to leave, that's why I'm still here. I mean, here on the earth. Ok, I can hear how that doesn't make sense. There was this prophecy, but..." I don't want to sound crazy, but I feel like that ship has probably sailed. I catch Detective Cameron looking at me out of the corner of his eye. Is that sympathy I see? I rub my eyes, wishing I was anywhere but here. But here I am, answering for Brother Richmond.

"A prophecy about the end of the world?"

"Yes," I say and look past the table into the blankness of a gray wall. The room has two overhead lights that shine directly down on the table, but the corners of the rooms are all shadow. I strain my eyes against the gray nothingness, willing something to be there.

"But," he speaks gently, as if I will break at his coming observation. "The world's still here. And so are you?" He gestures around him, confident that the world still exists beyond the too bright lights and empty corners of this room.

"I guess he got that part wrong," I say. I am tired. So tired.

"But he got it right that 138 people would disappear into thin air? Listen, Mrs. Greene, I'm on your side, but you've got to give me a little more information. I know your parents and your husband were in that group. Can you tell us anything about where they may have gone? What they were planning? Don't you want to find them?"

That's a question I've been asking myself for days. The grief of loss, the shock of Jason's abandonment and that awful proclamation from Brother Richmond's tape, Bekah and Sarah, it's all such an utter mess in my head that I can't even parse out what I want. Besides, this detective is right. The world is still here. It's still spinning. This baby is still growing, and I could walk out of this police station and try to make it on my own. But if we found them all? If it was some kind of misunderstanding? Or worse, a test? What then?

"I would love to see my family again." I let each word linger in the air a moment before speaking the next. I rack my brain for the right thing to say to this man who doesn't know anything about me, my family, or our lives. I can't tell him about the letter and the tape. I can't tell him something that will only make us seem crazier. I look down at my hands.

"Mrs. Greene, I want to make sure you understand how serious this situation is. This is a federal case now."

I look up at him. "What does that mean?"

He folds his hands in front of him on the table. "It means that the FBI tends to get involved when close to 150 people go missing. We're not really equipped to handle a case of this magnitude. Nothing like this has ever happened here. Nothing like this has ever happened anywhere. We've had Preston on our radar for a while now, of course, but nothing this big. Nothing we could make stick."

"Tabitha," I say, looking up into Detective Cameron's green eyes. They remind me of my dad's eyes, and I look down again.

"Tabitha Morales?"

"Yes, she's still here as well. Maybe she knows something."

"Yes, we're aware. We've brought in Ms. Morales and a few of the others in for questioning. As I said, this is a major case."

"Oh." I look down again. "Look, I don't know what happened to them. I just don't know. I wish I had a way to make sure they are all right. To tell them I love them. To ask them. But I don't." My voice breaks and I have to take deep measured breaths and blink rapidly to hold back the tears starting to leak out of the corners of my eyes. I must look terrible.

"Ok, Mrs. Greene. I think that's enough questions for now. Please don't leave town. We may need to speak with you again." Detective Cameron stands and moves toward the door. "Is there someone here to take you home?"

I shake my head no. Sarah and Bekah weren't home when the cops arrived. I'm not sure where they are. Damn it. How am I going to be a mother if I can't even keep tabs on two teenage girls?

"How are you going to get home?" Detective Cameron asks.

"I'll walk."

"That's a long walk."

"I like walking."

Detective Cameron stares at the ceiling and shakes his head like he can't believe what he's about to say. "I'll give you a ride home."

"I'm fine to walk."

"I couldn't live with myself if I let you walk home in your condition. Or rather my wife couldn't live with me. My shift is ending, anyway. I'm happy to do it. Meet me out in the lobby in about fifteen minutes."

The lobby of the police station is dimly lit and cramped, like the designers hadn't considered that people would actually be sitting out here when they drew up the plans. There are two faded wooden benches against either wall. I sit on the bench closest to the main entrance. On the other side of the lobby is a large desk. It is encased, floor to ceiling, in glass, like the officer sitting at the desk is on display. Next to the wall of glass is a metal door with frosted window panes. Every time the metal door opens, it creaks like its hinges are about to fall off. Police officers and other ordinary looking people shuffle in and out. I don't know what's behind the frosted glass, but there's a woman sitting on the bench across from me who jerks her head up every time it opens. Her eyes are red, and she's bitten her nails down to the nub. She keeps rubbing her hands over and over one another like she's washing up for dinner. Further down the bench, a man in a suit sits looking at a phone. He seems bored and looks annoyed at the little gasps that catch in the woman's throat every time the frosted door opens. I wonder who they are waiting for.

The officer sitting at the desk is typing at a computer but periodically scans the small space as if a criminal may suddenly materialize on the benches with us. His gaze seems to rest on me longer than the other two, and it makes my head itch. Does he know who I am and why I was called here? This was a mistake. The now familiar creak of the metal door echoes through the lobby, and Detective Cameron walks through it. He looks different now, even though it's only been fifteen minutes since I saw him. He seems lighter, like he's left something burdensome on the other side of that glass.

On the drive back to the Farm, he is quiet. We cut through town, down neighborhood streets of houses with fenced yards and porch swings. Some are meticulously kept, and some are falling down. It's such a mixture here. So different from the Farm, where everything is the same.

"Can you...Were you allowed...Do you drive?" Detective Cameron finally says.

I smile to myself at how flummoxed our world seems to make him. "We are not of the world, but we must be ready when it comes knocking at our door," I say in response.

Detective Cameron looks sideways at me.

"Sorry. That was cryptic," I say. "Only folks who work off the Farm drive. Hey, how'd you find out about the Homegoing anyway? Did someone call you?" I wrack my brain for a face, a name, someone who would betray Brother Richmond in that way. My own face is the only one that comes up.

"People don't like it when their employees don't show up to work. And a lot of employees were missing Monday morning."

I nod, feeling dumb for having asked the question. I look out the window. The trees rustle in the wind and their leaves create a wall of impenetrable green. It's hard to believe they'll abandon their branches in a few weeks. The gates of the Farm appear between a gap in the trees up ahead. A mass of people mill about in front of them. Detective Cameron slows the car to a crawl. For a moment, I wonder if everyone's come back, and I think that maybe it'll be best to take whatever punishment is waiting for me. I see a shock of strawberry blonde hair in the crowd. My heart drops into my stomach.

But of course, it isn't her. It isn't any of them. As we draw closer to the gate, I notice the ring of news vans circling the crowd and realize, with sinking panic, that it's a group of reporters. At the center of the outstretched cellphones and microphones, I see Edwin. I must make some sort of noise because Detective Cameron looks over at me.

"Do you want me to turn back? Do you know another way in?"

I look back toward the way we came, and Detective Cameron begins backing down the long drive. I'm not ready to talk to Edwin about Brother Richmond's letter, and I'm certainly not ready to face reporters and answer any more questions. Let Edwin handle them. He likes that sort of thing. He looks completely at ease up there. Some of the people turn toward us as the car crunches backward over the gravel, but Detective Cameron's car is unmarked, and most seem to assume we've taken a wrong turn or come to gawk at the carnage like them.

"That's Edwin Belfry, correct?"

I must look surprised because Detective Cameron gives a short laugh. "Remember I said we'd brought in a few of the other members for questioning? Is that what you call yourselves? Members?"

I don't say anything. Is the Collective even still an entity now that most everyone is gone? I close my eyes and lay my head against the warm glass of the car window.

"Take a left down past that oak tree," I say, my eyes still closed. "Don't miss it. It doesn't look like much, but there's a path there through the fence." The car crunches over the gravel road, and I sway against the door frame. I grab the little handle above the passenger window to steady myself.

"You know," I say to Detective Cameron, "When I was little, I thought this was for swinging on when you got bored in the car."

"My daughters thought the same thing." His voice is all affection and I swallow hard to fend off another round of tears.

A memory plays, like a movie, in my head. I'm about fifteen, just before Brother Richmond started calling me into his office. I'm driving into town with my dad. The sun is shining, and it feels like a perfect day. I loop my fingers through the handle bar above my head in the front seat and tell my dad my childhood theory about it being a miniature monkey bar. My dad laughs and tells me I may just need a monkey bar in case I get scared of his driving and need to swing out the window. Then he does a few little swerves on the road. I squeal even though I'm too old to believe he's not in control.

"But Dad, Brother Richmond says we never need to be afraid," I say with mock devotion.

"Well, I guess the car manufacturers missed that lesson, so they put those handles there just in case." My dad is grinning.

"Just in case Brother Richmond is wrong?" I make a horrified face, expecting my father to laugh along with me or roll his eyes. Instead, he pulls to such an abrupt stop on the side of the road that my arm, still holding the handle above the door, feels wrenched out of socket.

"Alice, look at me." My dad's face is no longer playful. It is clouded over with concern and something like fear. "I don't want to ever hear you say that again. Do you understand me?"

"But Dad, I was just—"

"I don't care, Alice. I never want to hear that come out of your mouth again. Understand?"

"Ok, geez. I was just joking." He sighs and releases his tight grip on the steering wheel.

"Not everything is a joke, Alice."

The memory dissipates. My face is hot from the sun shining in through the passenger window. I roll it down to get some air and look for the gate as the car turns toward the oak tree.

"Are you and Edwin Belfry close?" Detective Cameron has shifted back into his cop voice, and I sit up a little straighter to better guard myself.

"I thought we were done with questions for today, Detective. Edwin and I were friends, but..."

"But?"

"But his faith grew and mine shriveled." I decide not to mention anything about the Separation.

"So why do you think he's not with the others?"

"I don't have a clue. I was shocked to see him afterward. The path's there." I gesture toward a dip in the tall grass where a rusted out green gate sits crooked but in-tact.

"Stop here, and I'll get out and open the gate. Or you could just drop me here. It's really no trouble to walk."

"This car offers door-to-door service, ma'am."

I wonder if that's Detective Cameron's attempt at making a joke. I get out of the car and walk toward the rusted gate. I haven't used this gate in years, but my hands still remember the just-so way to twist the bar to release the lock.

As we pull up to my house, I am relieved to see that the

reporters haven't made their way into the Village yet.

"Thanks for the ride, Detective Cameron."

"No problem. We may need you to come down and answer some more questions. In the meantime, if you think of anything, or if you need anything, give me a call." He hands me a small business card and I put it in my pocket.

Bekah and Sarah aren't home, and a pang of worry plucks at my chest. Where are they? I watch Detective Cameron pull back out toward the pasture gate. Once he's gone, I pull on a sweatshirt to ward off the evening chill and head out to look for the girls. The reporters are still there when I get close to the main gate, so I walk off the path and into a grove of trees. I crouch down around the roots and creep as close to the fence as I can without being seen. I hear Edwin before I see him. He is speaking in a loud stage voice, throwing his words across the small crowd gathered before him. His voice rises and falls as the wind blows.

It's a poor facsimile of Brother Richmond's booming tones, but I can tell, even from my crouched position, that several reporters in the crowd are transfixed. Edwin doesn't have Brother Richmond's height or broad shoulders. He's barely taller than me, which isn't saying much. His skinny arms are waving back and forth like a couple of windmills, but his dark hair falls almost to his shoulders now, and he studied well all those years I was breaking rules and getting into trouble. He actually read all the drivel that Brother Richmond put in the Village library, and it looks as though he learned something. I find myself falling into the old rhythms of listening with my whole body, ready to nod, clap or stand and shout where appropriate. One reporter waves her phone around in the air to signal she has a question. She looks down at her notes before addressing Edwin.

"Mr. Belfry, you haven't yet said where you believe the other members of the Collective have gone."

"Thank you, Ms. Sinclair. *The Cyrene Ledger,* correct?"

"Yes, that's correct." The tone of her voice doesn't change, but I can see from her face that she's surprised he knows her name and affiliation. *Listen to people. Tell them what they want to hear.*

"That's the answer everyone here really wants to know, right? You've all been yelling it at me since you pulled up here, so I guess I better give you a straight answer?"

I can't see Edwin's face, only his back, but I know he's smiling. I can hear it in his voice. There are a few polite chuckles in the crowd. He doesn't have them yet, but he's working on it.

"Now, I'd be lying if I said I knew exactly where my brothers and sisters have gone. Obviously, my itinerary must have gotten lost in the mail."

More laughter this time.

"However, I know they are in a far better place than this worn out and tired old world. And I hope, by God's good grace, to join them one day soon."

"Mr. Belfry, what do you mean by a better place? And when do you plan to join them? Is there another event planned?" Ms. Sinclair's crossed arms and pursed lips are a study in skepticism.

"Again, Ms. Sinclair, I don't know all the particulars, but I know it's a place without suffering, a place without worries, a place where we can find rest, and a place where there is peace. I know it sounds dopey. I know it sounds like pie in the sky crazy. But, ladies and gentlemen, you're here because 138 souls disappeared from this earth in an instant. So, even if you don't want to admit it to yourself, I think you know somewhere in your heart of hearts that this place exists."

I lean forward and try to catch a glimpse of Edwin's face. Behind me, I hear a branch snap.

"Why in God's name are you creeping around out here in the trees like a forest fairy?" Tabitha suddenly looms over me.

"Get down! They'll see you!"

"So? Let them try and step one foot inside that gate." She pats her pocket where a bulge pushes up underneath her red linen top. I roll my eyes and push myself up off the ground. It's getting harder by the day.

Tabitha holds out her hand and pulls me the rest of the way up from the tree roots. She lifts a brown leaf off my sweater.

"I'm looking for Bekah and Sarah. They weren't at my house when I got home from the police station."

She looks puzzled and tilts her head back toward Edwin. I follow her gaze and notice two girls off to the right. They're partially blocked by some branches, but there's no doubt it's Sarah and Bekah. Sarah is chewing on one of her fingernails and darting her head back and forth between the reporters and Edwin, but Bekah is as transfixed as Ms. Sinclair. I must have been so focused on Edwin's speech that I mistook them for reporters.

"What are they doing out there?" I hiss at Tabitha. "Where have they been?"

Tabitha walks a few paces out of the grove of the trees, and I follow her. I can still hear Edwin talking, but his voice is muffled now.

"When I heard the cops were starting to sniff around, I came to get you and the girls. Figured it was better for us to be together when outsiders started pushing in. The girls didn't know where you were."

I think about how I must have been asleep on the basement floor and curse under my breath. They'd just lost their whole family and then couldn't find me in a time of crisis. Some mother I'll make.

Tabitha continues, "I brought them to my house and then had them go back over to your place after I was sure the cops were gone. They were there when I got taken in. Where were you?"

I put my hand on my back and press hard to ease the pain, giving myself a moment to think before I have to answer Tabitha. As I do, I realize this baby is unmistakable now. There's no more secret about what I'm carrying.

"That one's not supposed to be here, huh?" Tabitha says as she eyes the tight stretch of my shirt across my stomach.

I wince. No one is supposed to know how many children each couple in the Collective has been allowed to have. But of course, everyone does anyway. So, I'm not surprised Tabitha knows Jason and I weren't supposed to get pregnant. But I can't relive that moment in Brother Richmond's office when he told us his decision. Or rather, his revelation, as he put it. It's too much.

"Jason said it was a blessing. Said it meant we could be surrogate parents to the kids whose parents weren't around or were busy with Collective business."

"That was probably true. For him. Not for you. You were always going to need more," she says.

"What did the police ask you when they called you in?" I say to change the subject. I am tired of her faux wisdom, her attempts to prove she knows me. She stops in the middle of the path and looks at me. I think she's going to do that thing again where she just stares at me without answering. Sometimes talking to Tabitha feels like looking into a kaleidoscope. You can't make out anything in all those shimmering colors, and in the end, it just makes you dizzy.

But she surprises me this time.

"Probably the same things they asked you. Did I know anything? Was it planned? Who else was left behind? That sort of thing."

"And what did you tell them?"

"Probably the same things you told them."

I roll my eyes and look back toward Edwin. "Why didn't Brother Richmond just pick him? He's a natural at all this."

Tabitha shrugs. "Guess you come as a set."

Edwin's mom used to say that about us. Can't have one without the other. Two peas in a pod. We'd even show up to each other's chore assignments. Everyone knew it was me and Edwin. Edwin and me. Until it wasn't. I push my hair out of my eyes and try not to think about the past. "What if I don't want to be chosen?"

Tabitha appears to consider this as she walks. Then she says, "When I was a kid, I would get in fights with my sister because she was constantly coming in my room and taking my clothes or messing up my dolls. When I complained to my mom, she would always say the same thing."

I'm not sure what this has to do with our current situation, but I decide to humor her. "What did she say?"

"She said, 'If you don't want her in your room, then don't leave your door open.'"

*****

When the girls get home from watching Edwin's speech at the front gate, I'm waiting in the living room. They both speak in a rush when they see me.

"Alice! You're back!"

"What did they ask you? Was it awful?"

I give them an abbreviated recap of my time at the police station. "And what were you girls doing up at the front gates? It seems like Tabitha went to a lot of trouble to keep you both off the cops' radar, and then I find you prancing around in front of all those reporters."

"We were just listening to Edwin. He said—"

"Bekah is the one who wanted to go," Sarah interrupts, and Bekah gives her a death stare.

"Look, you're both old enough to do what you want. I just want you to be careful, ok?"

They both nod, and then we go into the kitchen to figure out something for dinner.

-8-

TERESA

Alice was so small when they placed her in my arms. I thought something was wrong. I looked to Tom, but he just beamed at me. Alice cried her heart out. I felt helpless with her wailing. The nurse must have sensed my discomfort because she bustled over and showed me how to get Alice to nurse. I marveled at how such a tiny baby knew what to do right from the start and wondered why my baby seemed to come complete with so much knowledge while I knew nothing about being a mother.

Vivian showed up the next day with flowers and a package of diapers. The years melted from her face as Tom placed the baby in her arms.

"Meet your new great granddaughter, Granny."

"She's perfect. Just perfect."

I noticed then that Tom and Vivian had the same smile and wondered if Tom's mother had it too. I wished she was here to meet her granddaughter. I wished my mother was here as well, but I pushed that thought from my mind. Instead, I focused on my worry about how small Alice was. The newborn diaper swallowed her. But the doctor assured me that she was just right. Of course, we weren't calling her Alice yet. We weren't calling her anything, and Vivian pestered us about the name.

"I like Susanne, but Teresa likes Caroline," Tom said.

"We aren't going to decide for a few days," I said.

"You know," Vivian said as she placed the baby in the bassinet next to me, "they're not going to let you leave the hospital without giving this baby a name."

"But we want to wait until we can introduce her to our..." Church wasn't the right word. I wasn't quite sure what we were, but Rich had offered to do an informal blessing ceremony when we came home from the hospital and we wanted to wait until then to give her a name.

"We just want to wait until we get home," I finished.

But Vivian was right. The nurse on duty told us in no uncertain terms that she was not allowed to release us without completed paperwork for the baby's birth certificate.

"Change it later if you want," she said in a bored tone. It seemed we weren't the first new parents she'd had to set straight.

"I think you should go with Caroline. She looks like a Caroline," Vivian said.

We called Rich to get his advice. He was silent on the phone for so long I thought the line had disconnected.

"Alice," he said finally. "Her name should be Alice."

I hadn't expected a name from him, just some advice on how to get the hospital staff to let us leave without naming her, but once he said it, it felt right. We giddily wrote it down on all the forms. There weren't as many rules with Rich back in those early days, and there certainly wasn't a naming ceremony. We weren't worried over names for months and scared that our choice would be rejected. It wasn't like that then, but Rich still talked about our 'ceremony' years later, and the way the Lord gave him a vision of Alice across that telephone wire.

I cried sloppy wet tears all over the frilly green dress I'd sewn for the trip home from the hospital, even though I didn't know, you couldn't know then, whether it was going to be a boy or a girl. The dress swallowed her, but we oo-ed and aw-ed and Vivian snapped pictures as if it was the perfect fit. Tom said she looked like a cupcake.

"But a very, very cute cupcake!" Vivian said.

Once we got home, I left Alice with Tom and walked down to the payphone across from the pharmacy. I dialed my parents' number, prayed, hoped, and crossed my fingers that Michael would pick up.

"Hello?"

My heart soared at the sound of his voice, and I tossed up a silent thank you to God.

"Congratulations! You're an uncle!"

"Teresa? Is that you? You had the baby? When? Boy or girl?"

"Girl. Her name is Alice. She's perfect. And she's already wondering when her cool uncle Michael is going to come for a visit."

"Teresa, that's amazing. Uncle Michael?" He laughed. "That sounds so weird."

"So, when are you going to come meet her? You're out of school for break next week, right? Do you think you could get the bus up here? I can try to help with the fare."

"No, don't worry about it, Teresa. I'll be there."

"Great. And Michael? If mom wants to come with you, that would be ok."

*****

The day of Michael's visit, I fussed over everything. The way the pillows were arranged, the way the chairs were angled, if I should turn on the space heater. Tom was back at work and Vivian had left the day before. It was just me and Alice and I couldn't tell if I felt more nervous to be alone with my baby or to see my own mother for the first time since becoming one. A knock on the door startled me out of my indecision about the heater, and I rushed to open it. Michael wasn't standing on the other side of the door. It was Rich. Holding a casserole dish and smiling.

"I thought you might need something to eat since it's your first day on your own with the baby."

I didn't remember telling him that today was my first day with the baby, but he always seemed to know things like that. I pointed at the casserole dish. "Did you make that?"

"God, no. This is from Jennifer. I'm just the messenger. She didn't have time to drop it off, but wanted you to have it. Said she'll bring another one when she comes to see the baby tomorrow."

I opened the door wide for him to come in and gestured toward the counter so he could set the glass dish down. "I'm just getting ready for a visit from my brother and mother. I haven't seen them in a while."

"I won't keep you, then," Rich said, but he didn't walk back toward the door. Instead, he sat on the sofa. "How are things with Alice? Where is she? Sleeping?"

"Yes, thank goodness. I don't think she slept a wink last night." I shrugged and my shoulders felt a little lighter. I didn't necessarily want Rich there when my family arrived, but his presence was a calming distraction.

"I'm just so thrilled that Alice is the first official baby born into the Collective," he said.

"The Collective?"

"Just a little name I've been tossing around for our group. I figured we've got to call ourselves something and the Collective feels right. Like we've all been pulled together for something greater than ourselves, ya know?

"I like it. It fits." I sat down on the chair opposite Rich and felt myself relax for the first time that day. It was short-lived. There was another knock at the door almost before I'd settled into the cushions.

"That will be my family." I jumped off the chair and looked expectantly at Rich. He didn't move from the sofa.

I rushed over and threw the door open. Michael was holding a gift bag emblazoned with the word 'Baby!' across the front. It sounds trite, I know, but he looked older. I looked past him for my mother. My father stood in her place. His towering presence was a shock when I was expecting her diminutive frame. Michael pulled me into a hug before I had a chance to say anything.

"I'm sorry," he whispered into my ear. "He insisted on coming."

Before I could respond, Michael handed me the gift bag and walked into the room, leaving me to face my father.

"Hi, Daddy. Did Mom come with you?" I asked, even though I knew the answer.

He walked in and his presence filled up all the space in the tiny apartment. I breathed in one last breath of fresh air from the hallway before I closed the door.

"No, your mother has a meeting with the ladies auxiliary at church this afternoon. It's better that I'm here to assess the situation and then maybe we'll arrange for her to visit later."

"She didn't want to meet her granddaughter?"

"She'll come another time." My father spoke in that definitive tone of his, and I didn't say anything else.

"So, where's my niece?" Michael said, clearly trying to break the tension.

"She's sleeping, but I'm sure she'll wake up at any minute."

My father hadn't moved from the doorway. He was studying a water spot on the ceiling.

"Teresa, this place is..." It was clear from the disgust in his voice what he thought of our apartment.

"I think Tom and Teresa have made it quite homey here." Rich appeared at my side even though I hadn't heard him move from the couch.

"Who the hell are you?" My father looked between me and Rich, an obvious misinterpretation of who he was forming in his furrowed brow.

"Richmond Preston, sir." Rich stuck his hand out, but my father just looked at it.

"I'm a friend of Teresa and Tom. Dropping off a casserole for the new parents."

My father ignored him. "And where is Tom?"

"He's working, Daddy. He'll be home around six."

Alice cried from the curtained off bedroom. "Michael, why don't you help me with the baby?" I pulled his sweater toward the crying.

I yanked the curtain around us and picked up Alice. I changed her diaper and then held her out to Michael.

"Will I hurt her?" he asked as if she were a piece of delicate china.

"She's sturdier than she looks. Just make sure to support her head." I arranged Alice in Michael's arms, making sure to put her head in the crook of his elbow. On the other side of the curtain, I could hear my father giving one word answers to Rich's questions about the optometry business.

"Tell me why Daddy is here instead of Mom?" I whispered, aware that a thin curtain didn't provide us much privacy.

"You know them," Michael whispered back. "I told Mom and she told Daddy. He said he would come and maybe she should come later. He said he was protecting her. And you know Mom."

"She didn't argue," I said, quiet as a feather falling.

"She didn't argue," Michael mouthed back.

I undid the curtain and paraded Alice into the middle of the living area. Rich and my father were sitting in utter silence now. Rich lounged on the sofa. My father stood by the window looking out at the view of a brick wall across the street.

"Do you want to hold Alice, Daddy?"

My father nodded and sat in a chair opposite the sofa. As I placed Alice in his arms, she made a tiny gurgle and I saw it. A crack in his armor. An almost imperceptible smile. He relaxed into the chair as Alice squirmed and his arms softened around her.

"Your mother will adore her, Teresa. Were you thinking of my mother's aunt when you chose the name Alice?"

"It was actually Rich's suggestion." I said, feeling slightly guilty that I did not remember my great aunt Alice.

"That one was all the Lord. I was praying for a safe delivery for this little one, and God spoke to me the name Alice. They called not five minutes later asking for advice, and I simply shared what the Lord had put upon my heart."

My dad gave a little snort and didn't respond. I detected an undercurrent of anger, and I was determined to keep this a happy occasion. I asked Michael about school to change the subject. Michael started to speak, but my father cut him off.

"I'm grateful for all the help you've given my daughter, but she's going home now and she will no longer be in need of your services."

I froze. "Daddy?"

"Michael and I have come to bring you and the baby home. Your mother is getting everything ready. That's why she's not here today."

I looked over at Michael but the surprise and anger on his face told me he wasn't in on my father's plan. I went over and took Alice gently from my father's arms.

"Daddy, this is my home. My home with Tom. We're not coming back. But you and Mom are welcome to come and see Alice any time."

"This isn't a home, Teresa. This is a hovel. And if this is the best that Tom can provide you, then he's proven himself to be more of a failure than I thought."

Anger surged through me. I patted Alice as I scrambled for something to say. My eyes met Rich's across the room. He didn't say anything, but I felt some of my anger sputter out in his gaze.

"Daddy. I'm not going with you. Tom and Alice are my family and this is my home. And it's more of a home than I've known in some time." My words found their mark. My father was out of his chair before I finished speaking.

"Teresa Anne, I do not know what has come over you, but you are going to go home with me today and leave this godforsaken place whether you like it or not."

"I'm not going, Daddy. And I think you should leave. You're upsetting the baby." I rocked Alice in my arms and looked at the door.

"Come on, Dad. Let's go. Come on." Michael put his hand on my dad's arm and tried to steer him toward the door.

"Teresa." My father's voice sounded as though he were syllables away from screaming. "I'm going to say this one more time—"

"She heard you the first time, sir, And she gave you your answer. Seems like it's time for you to go."

Rich was standing toe to toe with my father now. Michael froze by the door and looked at me. I continued to rock Alice, unsure what to do next.

"I don't know who you think you are, but you have nothing to do with me and my daughter." My father's voice dropped to a deadly quiet.

"I'm a friend of Teresa, Tom, and Alice. And more importantly, I'm a servant of the Lord. Your daughter has made it perfectly clear that she's not leaving with you. And now I'm making it perfectly clear that you need to leave." Rich's voice still had that easy-going tone as if he was chatting with someone at the laundromat, but his eyes flashed with a menace I hadn't seen before.

My father lost his last grip on his control, and then things seemed to happen in slow motion. He swung his fist and Michael jumped forward to keep him from striking Rich. Rich ducked the blow in a lazy swing of his lanky body and pulled his arm back for a swing of his own. Then everything fast-forwarded and my father was laying on the floor, blood flowing from his nose. I screamed and looked up at Rich. He seemed unbothered. He strolled to the kitchenette and rummaged around while my father scrambled to his feet. My father looked too stunned to speak. He glared at me as he held his nose to stop the bleeding. Rich sauntered back over with a kitchen towel full of ice. He handed it to my father, who took it without a word or look in Rich's direction.

"I'm mighty sorry it had to come to this Mr. Andersen, but I've got a flock to protect."

I wanted to say I didn't need protection from my own father. I wanted to say he was swinging to hit Rich, not me. I wanted to say I appreciated the gesture but I was capable of standing up for myself. But I didn't say any of that. I was angry and grateful and the emotions were too tangled to sort out.

"Teresa, if I leave this place right now, I'm not coming back, and you'll no longer be welcome in our home."

"This is my home, Daddy. I told you that already."

"Good girl," I heard Rich whisper behind me, and my indignation flared brighter than my gratitude.

Without another look at Alice, my father walked toward the door, pulling Michael along after him. Michael turned back once more. His face was a mixture of bewilderment and sadness. He mimed calling me on the phone and the door closed. Rich seemed to sense my fury because he only said, "I'll see myself out. Enjoy the casserole. Jennifer says you can keep the dish."

Then he was gone and I was alone in the apartment. Alice started to cry again, so I carried her to the sofa to feed her.

*****

Rich knocked on our apartment door that night. "Good evening, Tom. I'm sure Teresa has told you what happened."

I tensed. I hadn't told Tom anything yet. I was still trying to wrap my head around it.

"About the altercation with her father?" Rich looked at me. "I'm sorry. I've overstepped. I've been doing that a lot today."

To my astonishment, there was a catch in Rich's throat, like he was about to cry. He sat down on the edge of the sofa and ran his hands through his hair. "I don't know what came over me. I could just see how difficult your father was making things, Teresa, and I wanted to help. Growing up, one of the ways I learned to help people was by hurting the people who hurt them. I'd get between my mom and dad when he started knocking her around and that kind of just stuck. When someone hurt someone I loved, I hurt them. I know that's wrong now, and that's part of why I got right with God. To find other ways to help people."

"I thought your mom was alone when she had you?" I said, remembering his story from the sandwich shop. "Her boyfriend, I meant. She had a few who pretended to be my dad. Anyway, I just wanted to come by and say I'm sorry. What I did was wrong, and I hope you know I was just trying to help."

"Sure, Rich. We understand. Thanks for coming," Tom said.

Tom walked over to the door as he spoke. Rich picked up on the cue to leave and followed him. When he was gone, Tom rounded on me.

"What happened while I was at work?"

I told him.

"So he punched your dad? Knocked him flat on his ass? And you're just now telling me?"

I nodded. Tom sighed, but it caught in his throat at the end, like he was about to cough.

"I'm sorry I didn't tell you. I thought—" But I couldn't finish the sentence because Tom had thrown his head back in laughter. Loud and booming. It woke Alice and she gurgled from her crib. It almost sounded like a giggle, even though she was too young for that.

"It was actually kind of scary, you know," I said, my mouth already cracking into a smile.

"I know. I'm sorry, Teresa," Tom said between gasps for air. He was bent over now, one hand on his knee and the other held up in front of him like a stop sign. "It's just every time I picture your dad, Dr. Andersen, Mr. I'll-pull-my-door-off-the-hinges-before-I-let-you-marry-my-daughter, flat on our floor and I think of the look on his face, I just—" Another spasm of laughter rocked his shoulders.

"There was blood!" I said, but laughter burbled in my throat as I spoke. I scooped up Alice from the crib and she cooed.

"Phew," Tom said and wiped his eyes. "I guess he'll have quite a story to tell all the other deacons on Sunday."

That did it. Laughter tumbled out of me. I bounced Alice on my shoulder, and her drool made a dark patch on the shoulder of my top.

-9-

ALICE

Edwin is already on the porch when I open my front door a few days later. I know he will be there before I've even gotten out of bed. It was always like that when we were kids. I would get this feeling while eating my breakfast and Edwin would be waiting for me outside when I left for morning chores. I could feel him in the air. Brother Richmond was always telling us to lean into the vibrations from God, but Edwin's were the only ones I ever felt. He turns to face me when the screen door clangs shut behind me.

"You put on quite a performance for those reporters out there the other day."

His face flushes pink. "I was trying to get rid of them. Get them to stop pestering us. Maybe show a few folks the light in the process. They're all so hung up on so many people gone. They can't see the bigger picture."

"Don't sound so modest. You could have bested Brother Richmond up there."

His eyes go wide. "Coming from you, I won't take that as a compliment."

I motion for him to sit on one of the chairs on the porch while I lower myself into the other. "You were good. Really. Seemed like you had them all well in hand. What are they expecting to find out here?"

"Magic? Wizards, maybe?" he says.

I smile but it fades when I think about how I'm still not sure what I believe myself. "And? What do you think happened, Edwin? Do you think they really went to paradise? It didn't happen last time. And if it did happen this time, why leave some of us behind? Was there not enough room for everyone the first time?"

"I don't know, Alice. I have the same information you do." His voice has a hard edge.

"Really? You always seem to be one step ahead of me. Like Brother Richmond's always given you the notes for what's going to come next. You're telling me you didn't know about this whole 'join me in two months' thing?"

He laughs, but it sounds hollow. "Me? Yeah, right. I feel like I've spent most of my life trying to catch up. Trying to make Brother Richmond see I could handle more responsibility, but he always seemed to pass me over."

"Is that why you stayed when your parents left?" I'm surprised to hear the question come out of my mouth. That was so long ago. We've never talked about it. I shiver and wish I'd brought a sweater out with me. I start to tell him never mind, he doesn't have to talk about it, but he speaks first.

"Partially. He'd already told me they were leaving, so I had time to think about it, even before they told me. I wanted to show that I was capable of taking that big step he was always saying we needed to look for. I wanted to show that I could make a stand when Mom and Dad felt too called to the world. But it wasn't just that..."

I know the rest. I know the other reason he stayed was me. "I know, Edwin. We were best friends. I would have done the same." I don't know if it's true, though. I'd wanted to leave the Farm for so long. I'm not sure I could have bypassed a gift wrapped opportunity to walk away with my parents. He wouldn't understand that though. I don't have to ask to know that his one-on-one meetings with Brother Richmond were very different from mine.

"Were best friends?" Edwin asks.

"Are. We are best friends. But you know Jason and I got married, and things sort of..." I don't finish the sentence.

"Sort of what?" That edge in his voice is sharper now.

"Sort of lapsed, I guess? It's my fault. I never apologized for what happened after. We shouldn't have asked you to help us. That was too much. And then what happened after, it was all awful. I'm sorry, Edwin."

"I wanted to help you. You know that." Now his voice is hushed.

I don't say anything. I can't tell Edwin I think about that night all the time. Jason and I pacing back and forth in the storeroom. Clinging to each other and an imagined future where we could be together. I wanted to leave right then. To run away and never come back. But Jason was too wrapped up in everything. Too new. Too devoted. He wanted to obey, but he loved me. I know he did. Edwin showed up at some point, desperate to let us know he hadn't been a part of Brother Richmond's plan. He knew I'd always gone to the storeroom when things got to be too much. I knew he'd find us, even as I prayed no one else thought to look there. Then the three of us were sitting in the dust on the storeroom floor, tossing out ideas. I don't remember all the options we batted around, but I know Edwin was the one who said, "Ask for forgiveness, not permission," and I'd laughed because that was usually my line. I didn't know what it would cost him then.

Edwin clears his throat. "Well, I better get going. Gotta prepare for Evening Table." I blink, unsure if I've heard him correctly.

"Evening Table?" I manage.

"Someone's gotta lead it. It's good to keep traditions in times of crisis. It helps people feel secure."

"I don't know if people really need—"

He stands and interrupts me before I finish my thought. "I know that you may not care about our traditions anymore, Alice, but you're not the only one who was left behind." The sudden harshness in his tone startles me, and I'm speechless as he walks away.

I'm still sitting on the porch, wondering about Edwin's sudden turn and why he didn't say anything to me about the baby—I've stopped trying to hide it at this point—when a woman I've never seen before walks down the path in front of my house. She sees me on the porch and raises a tentative hand in greeting. She's tall with golden brown hair tied up on top of her head. She looks familiar somehow, but I can't work out where I've seen her. She walks toward the porch, but I stand, my protective instincts kicking in for this baby, the girls, and, God help me, this place.

"I've already talked to the police. I don't have any new information for you. And if you're a reporter, then you should know you're trespassing on private property."

She looks confused and then shakes her head. When she speaks, her voice is hoarse, like she's been crying or sick. It's so raspy I can feel the rattling in my own throat.

"I'm not with anyone. I'm looking for Sarah Stafford."

"If you're not with the police, then what business do you have with Sarah?"

"I'm her aunt. I know she's here. You can't keep her from me. Not anymore."

I'm skeptical, so I leave her on the porch and walk backward into the house, locking the door behind me. I wake Sarah and explain the situation. I'm just about to tell Sarah we can send this woman away, that she doesn't have to talk to her, when I see why the woman looks familiar. Her face and Sarah's face are almost identical. I stop mid-sentence and change tactics.

"Would you like to talk to her?"

Sarah nods. She's still got the rumpled sleepy look about her, but her eyes are alert. In the bed beside her, Bekah looks terrified. I nod and head back toward the front door to let the woman in.

Bekah comes into the living room first. She sits on the chair furthest from the woman and doesn't say anything. Sarah comes in after her, and it's clear she's made a stop in the bathroom as her cheeks look flushed with washing and her hair has been smoothed down, that same golden brown as the woman sitting in my living room.

"Sarah," the woman says.

"Aunt Lily!"

"Oh, I was so worried," Lily says. "I saw your mom's name on the news. Did she say anything to you before she went missing? She must have left a clue, a note. I know that man brainwashed her. Brainwashed them all. It's all the news can talk about. It's on every channel. I was terrified I'd lost you, too."

They embrace, and Sarah cries as she buries her face in the woman's shoulder. Feeling as though I've intruded upon an intimate moment, I pull Bekah into the kitchen with me to make some coffee. We don't speak as we load coffee things onto a tray. Stray scraps of conversation filter in from the other room. *These people. Scared. Crazy. Come home.* I guess I didn't consider how the outside world would take the news of the disappearance. We've always been taught to discount the world's opinion, so it didn't cross my mind that what happened to us would be a big deal to them. Bekah's hands tremble as she carries the sugar bowl to the tray, and I know she's listening just as hard as I am. Sarah's her best friend, and I know it will destroy her to lose that last bit of security. I put the creamer on the tray and turn toward her.

"Bekah. I'm here. I'm not going anywhere. Ok?" She picks up

the tray and nods.

When we enter the living room, Sarah and her aunt are sitting side by side on the living room couch.

"Coffee, anyone?" I say.

"Sarah says you've been taking such good care of her since her mother's disappearance." Her voice is restrained but I can hear the anger thrumming under the civil tone.

"She's been taking care of me as much as I've been taking care of her. They both have." I look at Bekah. "Really. It's been difficult for all of us."

"Yes, I imagine so," Aunt Lily says. There's something in her tone I can't quite make out, but it sounds accusatory and fearful at the same time.

"Aunt Lily's been worried about us for a while now." Sarah says it like an apology, and I stiffen. I'm not about to get stuck answering for all Brother Richmond's sins.

"I'm not sure what you've heard, but I—"

"Oh, I've heard plenty. My sister cut me off and cut me out of her and Sarah's life once she joined this place." She looks around my living room like it's the birthplace of all the Collective's transgressions.

I have a desperate need for this woman to know that I'm not like the others. To know that I wasn't supposed to be here. That I had other plans. "You should know—"

"I know all I need to know. And now that my sister is no longer with us, I'm taking Sarah home with me. I don't know what you people have done with Audra, but I'll be back when the police find her." She turns to Sarah. "They will find her, Sarah. They will. She didn't disappear into thin air."

Bekah makes a little murmur from her spot on the floor. I can see I'm not going to get anywhere with the aunt. I turn to Sarah.

"Is this what you want, Sarah?" Oh god. I sound like Brother Richmond in one of those playacting rituals where he would make everyone think someone was staying of their own free will.

Sarah nods. "You've been so great, Alice, but—" I hold up my hand to stop whatever she's going to say. I know that whatever it is, it's not true. I've been anything but great.

"You don't need to say anything, Sarah. I'm happy you've got a piece of your family back."

Bekah stands from her spot on the floor. "Bye then. Have a nice life, I guess."

"Don't be like that, Bekah. You know I never wanted to come here in the first place. Making friends with you was the only good thing that happened to me here. I talked to Aunt Lily." Sarah looks at her aunt for encouragement. Lily gives her a wide smile. "You can come with us. We'll help you track down someone in your family. Not everyone was here. There's got to be someone out there, and with all those reporters covering the Homegoing, it shouldn't be hard to find them."

For a moment, Bekah considers this. She takes a small step toward Sarah and my heart contracts. Then Bekah speaks, "No. This is my home. This," she points emphatically to my living room carpet, "is my family." She turns and walks out the door. Sarah starts to go after her, but I stop her.

"She just needs some time. It's a lot to process."

"But I need to say goodbye. She's my best friend." I step aside, and Sarah heads out the door after Bekah.

I'm alone with Aunt Lily now. I offer her more coffee, but she shakes her head. I speak quickly, before she can stop me again.

"I know the stories of this place. Hell, I've lived most of them. I want you to know that I am not like that. I love Sarah and have done all I can to help her during whatever this is. I've been trying to leave this place all my life, so I'm glad you're here for her. I really am."

"It seems to me," she says as she sets her mug on the coffee table, "if you were that desperate to leave, you would have done it by now. I'll wait for Sarah out on the porch. We need to get on the road before it gets too late."

This stings from a woman who doesn't know me. She doesn't know what this place is like and what it can do to a person. A million retorts spring to mind, but I don't say any of them because I know they wouldn't help. I watch Sarah's aunt walk onto my porch, and then I pick up the tray of coffee and cups and creamer and carry it into the kitchen. I stand still for a moment, suddenly unsure what to do with my hands, and then I throw the tray into the sink. One of the mugs cracks, and I watch spilled coffee collect in little beads along the jagged edge.

Sarah returns, alone. She whispers to me that Bekah is in the library but that it's all ok now. Sarah takes her aunt into the room she shares with Bekah to collect her things, and I offer to make lunch. I want Sarah to be with her family. I want her away from this place. Of course I do. So why am I dragging my feet? They say there's no time for lunch, and Sarah hugs me. Lily watches from the door with a look that says I'm responsible for every bad thing that's happened to Sarah. I think maybe she's not wholly wrong. And then I'm watching from the doorway as they walk away. I can't face the mess in the kitchen or the empty house, so I walk toward the library to find Bekah.

Tabitha is outside hanging clothes to dry when I walk by her place. The sky looks like rain and there's a distant grumble of thunder.

"Hear that?" I gesture at the clouds and then at her clothes on the line, all white and bright against the pewter sky.

"If they get rained on, they get rained on. I like the smell of rain, and they'll dry in time."

"Sarah just left. Her aunt came to get her." I brace myself against the strong wind. It whips Tabitha's clothes around her line like little kids trying to pump their legs hard enough to swing up and over the bar.

"I know. I let the aunt in. She was ranting and raving at the side gate about how she knew we had her sister in here somewhere. Took me close to an hour to get her calmed down enough to send over to your house. Tried calling to give you a warning, but no one answered."

"I was out on the porch with Edwin. The girls were sleeping."

Tabitha nods. "Sarah's not the only one with people coming down. Jeff and Cadence had family show up for them after they saw it in the papers. Jeff didn't want to leave without finding Mary, but Cadence left. We're big time news, it seems."

I feel something like fear curl up my spine. Tabitha continues hanging clothes on the line with that persistent normalcy that makes me crazy.

"Tabitha. Can you just stop for a moment? And look at me?"

"What do you need, Alice?"

"I don't know. This is ridiculous. How can you just stand there hanging clothes when police and reporters and relatives are all beating down our door? Did they tell you at the police station that the FBI is involved? Bekah is heartbroken about Sarah leaving, and now I've got to pick up the pieces. How am I supposed to do that? And on top of it all, Brother Richmond is supposedly coming back for the rest of us in less than two months?"

"Have you talked to Edwin?"

"What good will talking to Edwin do?" I recall the coldness in his voice when he left my house yesterday.

Tabitha shrugs. "He's good at reading people. And I heard you two were thick as thieves. Aren't you friends?"

"We are friends." I hear how defensive I sound, and I bite my lip. I don't say that a year apart changes a friendship or that guilt eats up whatever's left when it was your fault. Tabitha wasn't here that year, though. She won't get it.

The rain spits a few drops and then peters out. I wonder if it will pass. Instead, the sky breaks open and rain whooshes down on us in a great sheet. Tabitha and I are soaked before we can make it onto her porch, but we scurry up the steps anyway and sit in the wooden rocking chairs. Rain comes in at the open edges and hits our feet, but we are mostly protected. I inhale the smell and push my wet hair out of my face.

"Did you really believe everything? Everything Brother Richmond said, I mean? I know they're all gone, but we're still running on the porch to get out of the rain. It's still raining. Doesn't there seem to be a disconnect there? I know, I know. Second Homegoing. Two months. Blah. Blah. Blah. But I'm not planning to lead any second Homegoing. So, what then? Does the world keep turning like it is now? Do we get zapped whether we want to or not? And what about all the other stuff he got wrong? All the wrong he caused?"

Tabitha wrings out the rain in her black hair before she answers. It patters onto the wood and runs in a zigzagging stream down the angled floor of the porch. "I've only been here three years. I don't have all the same baggage as you. I came in clear-eyed. I moved here because I needed something new in my life. I joined the Collective because I saw a group of people working together to bring about some good in the world. I needed that kind of community. All the religious stuff? I was never too sold on that. I thought that maybe I could just sidestep it all, sing along, but not let it affect me too much." I hold my breath. This is the most straightforward answer Tabitha has ever given me and I'm afraid to move in case it breaks this spell.

"When I finally started seeing what was below the surface, I was already in too deep. Then I thought I could help to fix some of the worst stuff. I'm not sure I did much of anything besides make a fool of myself now. So, when your mom came to me, I knew I had to—"

She stops speaking and stands up, like someone has just called her name. Her chair pivots sidewise with the sudden departure but continues to rock an invisible occupant. My heart leaps several extra beats at the mention of my mom.

"I better get those clothes in. They are getting soaked," she says and dashes off the porch.

"Tabitha, wait. What do you say about my mom? She came to you? Why?" I trail after her, but she marches without pause toward the line and starts ripping down clothes. The wind has died down, but the rain's brought cold autumn air with it. I shake in my clothes as a garden of new questions blooms in my mind. Why did Mom go to Tabitha? I can't recall them ever speaking to each other beyond checking in about deliveries to the farm stand or compliments about the bread at Evening Table.

"Tabitha! What are you talking about? What did my mom say?" She turns toward me, arms full of sopping laundry.

"I shouldn't have said anything. It's freezing out here. You need to get yourself inside. That baby won't like it if you catch your death in this cold."

She jogs back to her house, the pile of clothes flapping wet in her arms. I'm about to go after her when I see Bekah sprinting through the rain toward my house.

-10-

TERESA

When Rich called a meeting on a Wednesday, we knew something big was going on. Meetings were held Saturday evenings. It kept us out of trouble to be surrounded by fellow believers instead of out galavanting, Rich always said. Wednesday was a work night, so whatever he had to tell us must be important. We hoped it was something good.

Everyone was already at Rich's apartment by the time we showed up, little Alice tucked under two blankets to ward off the cold. Edwin ran up to us in that precarious toddler way that made me think he would topple over at any moment.

"See the baby?" His little face turned to me in expectation. I lowered our little bundle and pulled the blanket back from Alice's sleeping face.

"Love the baby," he said in a tiny whisper that could have melted an ice cap.

Rich rushed over to us. His eyes were scrunched together, and he had a deep crease between his eyebrows. "You're late. If you're not committed to the cause, then why bother even showing up?" The agitation in his voice wasn't new. I'd seen him grow impatient with others in the group. He once told Angelica he didn't know if she was mentally fit enough to be in the group when she asked three times what page he was reading from in Bible study. This was, however, the first time that frustration was turned on me or Tom and shame flushed my cheeks.

"Sorry," I said. "Getting out of the house with a baby is still new for us. We'll try to be ready earlier next time."

"It's really my fault," Tom chimed in. "I was late getting home after work. Teresa was a saint getting everything ready without me." He squeezed my shoulder, and I was grateful for the support.

The crease between Rich's eyes vanished and his teeth showed through his mustache as his smile broadened. "Babies are tricky like that, aren't they? I'm just really anxious to get everyone here so I can share the news." He clapped his hands together like a little kid who has just been told they could have candy for breakfast.

My shame dissipated. We were ok. It was all ok. Rich headed toward the front of the room, and we settled on the floor. Edwin wedged himself next to me. Jennifer rose from her seat across the room and made her way toward Edwin, but I waved her away. I liked that Alice had a little friend before she even knew the word.

"Hello friends! Thanks for coming out on this blustery night. I know this was a bit unusual, so I'll get right to the point. My uncle died recently."

A round of sympathetic mumbles traveled the length of the room.

"Thank you. He was 97 and lived a good life. And I know he's in a much better place now than this sick and tired world. But through death comes life, Amen?" Eager 'Amens' peppered the room.

"C.S. Lewis once said that people who believe strongly in the next life, do the most good in this one. And we are a people who believe in doing good in this life, Amen?" The 'Amens' were louder and more energetic. "And we are a people aching for the joy and paradise of the next life, Amen?" The 'amens' were a little more apprehensive this time. Rich usually skirted around mentions of the afterlife, preferring to focus on our efforts in the here and now.

"Well, my uncle Arthur was a believer. And, even though he never joined us in the body, he's always been here in spirit. That's why I believe he left me a little something in his will. So, in order to do the most good in this world while we're here, I've taken Uncle Arthur's gift along with some of the generous donations to our cause, and I've bought us a building!"

People murmured amongst themselves. I wondered what kind of terms he was on with his family to be the son of a woman thrown out of the family and to still be mentioned in his uncle's will. Alice stirred, and I handed Tom her pacifier without missing a beat. We were getting the hang of this parenting thing.

"This new building will be a place where we can all live in comfort together. Well, mostly all of us, I'm not made of money after all," Rich said. People shifted in their seats. I heard whispers behind me. Clearly, it was the first time most of us were hearing about living together.

"We can also achieve more progress in— Hey now!" he said, seeming to notice the discomfort in the group for the first time. "Don't look at me with those shocked little rabbit faces." He grinned and pointed at a few people in the room. They chuckled nervously.

"Why do we need to live together? Hell, why do we need a building? It seems like those funds could be better spent on extra food and supplies for the sack lunch program and the laundromat coin giveaways." Jennifer's voice cut through the nervous laughter. I loved that she was always willing to speak her mind. It made me feel a little braver.

"Now, this place isn't the Ritz," Rich ignored Jennifer and

continued talking. "It needs some work. But I know we have some carpenters in the group, at least one electrician, and a whole slate of folks who don't mind getting their hands dirty. If we put in a little elbow grease, I think it could be just perfect."

*****

Some folks left the group when they realized Rich was serious about us living together, but he won most of us over in the end. The building turned out to be an old rambling Victorian on a shabby downtown street. Rich had painted too rosy a picture when he said we'd just give it a little 'TLC'. The house needed rewiring throughout and there were bats in the attic. I almost twisted my ankle walking over the caved-in floor of the back bedroom, and the kitchen was just a couple of mice-infested cabinets and an ancient fridge that didn't work. Even still, you could tell it had been lovely and grand at one point. "Like this world," Rich said. "Before we mucked it up."

We felt like a real family getting that place up and running. Every weekend and evening we were at the house working. Tom helped pull down walls and hammer in new beams in the attic. I watched Alice and Edwin and made sandwiches for the work crew. We stayed late into the night and drank coffee out of a green thermos I found at a thrift store. We strung up lights through the bedrooms and called our work sessions parties. In the end, we put four small apartments on the first and second floor. Each had a bathroom, a small living area, a tiny efficiency kitchen, and most importantly to me, a telephone. The attic was converted into several bedrooms and a shared bath for singles. We knocked out the existing walls of the basement and turned it into one large space with a stainless steel industrial kitchen and a seating area with long wooden tables and chairs. There was a carriage house out back that Rich took for his living quarters and the offices for the Collective.

A few folks grumbled about Rich living apart from the rest of the group, but most didn't mind since he'd largely footed the bill.

Life was good in the old Victorian. Our apartment wasn't much bigger than the moldy one we'd left, but we'd put effort into it, so we felt like it was ours. It wasn't, of course. No one paid rent in the Victorian. Instead, we all contributed a percentage of our earnings toward maintenance of the house and the ministry. Jennifer and Anthony kept track of everyone's dues and income. Still, I was so excited for Michael to visit the Victorian and see our new space.

I hadn't seen my father again, but Michael continued to visit off and on. He was always wary of Rich, but he adored Alice. He brought her books and toys and took her on long walks hoisted up on his shoulders. Occasionally, he brought my mother. I knew she loved Alice, but she always seemed unsure how to act. I never thought for a second that she had my father's permission to be there, and she confirmed it with her countless looks over her shoulder toward the door. She seemed worried he would appear around every corner. We'd never been terribly close, but her paranoia made me anxious and resentful. We never talked about what happened between my father and Rich. We talked only of Alice and Michael and the weather. I always planned to ask her more or share more on our next visit, but I never seemed to get around to it.

When Michael finally made it out to the new place, he had news that overshadowed our new apartment. He was going to college a year early.

"That's wonderful!" I said. "I'm not surprised though. "I knew all that nerdy studying would pay off."

He lifted eighteen month old Alice into his arms. "I'll be leaving in a couple of months, and I won't be able to visit quite as much."

"Of course. But you'll get breaks, right? And it's not like University of Rochester is in Siberia or something."

"I'm not going to University of Rochester." I noticed then that he was looking at Alice, lifting her above his head, tickling her under her chin, but he wouldn't make eye contact with me.

"But you've always talked about going there. Where else would you go?"

"I got into Stanford. It's a full ride scholarship." He said it like he was telling me my dog died.

"Stanford? Like California? Michael! That's on the other side of the country!"

"I know. It's far. But I'll be home on longer breaks, and you guys can visit me there. Haven't you always wanted to travel?"

"Wow, Stanford." The shock of it made me feel numb, but I tried to put on a happy face so I wouldn't spoil Michael's excitement. "Of course we'll visit. I'm so happy for you, Michael."

I was happy for him, but I knew we wouldn't visit. Not all the way to California. We couldn't afford it. The Collective needed us. I knew as well that he wouldn't come home on breaks if he could help it. He was going to college early and on the other side of the country to get away from our house, and I knew, from experience, how easy it was to forget the place existed once it was in your rearview mirror. Without Michael, my mother would never be brave enough to visit on her own. Two losses in one.

We arranged for Michael and my mom to visit once more before he left for school. I refused to call it a goodbye, but I knew that's what it was. This would also be the visit where I would hash things out with my mom, I told myself. Really set things right. I didn't know when I'd see her again without Michael there to play facilitator.

The day of the visit, my mom and Michael were late. That was unusual, but I was busy trying to make the perfect farewell meal, so I didn't pay it too much attention. I fussed over the soup I was making, adding a little more spice, tossing in a bit more garlic, and putting the bread in the toaster oven to warm. Tom played with Alice in the living room. When lunch was ready and they still hadn't shown up, I decided to call. The phone rang as my hand touched the receiver, as if it knew before I did.

"Hello?"

"Teresa." It was Michael, but his voice sounded like he'd gargled rocks before calling me.

"Michael? Have you not left the house yet?"

"Teresa, it's Mom."

"What about Mom? What do you mean?"

"She...she...died, Teresa. She died. This morning." His voice broke off and I could hear now how hard he was trying to keep from crying.

My head spun. "What are you talking about? She's coming here with you today. I'm making soup. The bread's in the oven."

"She was vacuuming the living room and collapsed. They think it was an aneurysm. Dad came home to get a file from his office and found her. They rushed her to the hospital, but there was nothing they could do."

I felt like I was out at sea, and I'd forgotten how to swim. The phone hung limply in my hands. If Michael was still talking, I couldn't hear him. Tom crossed the living area in two strides.

"What is it?"

"My mother. She died. This morning. Aneurysm." Saying the words out loud took every ounce of energy I had. I sank to the floor. Tom dropped down to his knees and wrapped his arms around me.

"She wasn't sick. It doesn't make any sense."

Tom didn't say anything, he just hugged me and stroked my hair. I was motherless now, and even if I hadn't felt particularly mothered in a long time, she was, at least, there. There was always the possibility we'd patch things up and make a go of it again. But now she was gone. Forever. At some point, Alice toddled over, bored with her toys. She looked at us with her head cocked to one side like she was trying to figure out what her parents were doing there bunched together on the floor.

Tom and I pulled her into our arms. I breathed in deep the smell of her. I wiped the tears from my eyes and kissed the top of her head.

*****

The funeral was scheduled for the following Wednesday morning. I was supposed to be on duty in the outreach kitchen that day. I knew I'd need to clear the switch in shifts with Rich.

"And what, may I ask, is more important than serving the Lord?" he asked. There was a twinkle in his eye. I hadn't yet told him or anyone about my mother.

"My mother died. Yesterday. We need to go back to Dover Springs for the funeral."

"Oh, Teresa. I'm so sorry. Was she ill?"

"No. It was sudden."

"A sudden loss is hard even for the faithful among us. I'm so sorry."

"Thanks."

"So the switch? For the kitchen?" Tom asked.

"Teresa," Rich said, ignoring Tom. "I understand you're grieving, I really do. And the Lord wants to comfort and bind up the brokenhearted, as you well know. And I am the last person who would want to add even an ounce of pain to your suffering, so please know that I say this in love: I don't know if it's the best idea for you to go back there. I know that I made a mess of things with your father when he was here, but it was clear to me that his negativity is toxic to anyone in his orbit. I don't want that for you, Teresa. And you have a family here. They need you."

I tried to speak, but I couldn't. Tom cleared his throat and spoke again.

"I'm going with her. You don't need to worry. Besides, her father is grieving his wife. I don't think he's going to be any trouble. I'm sure you can find someone else to serve the lunch. She needs to be with her family right now. She needs to be there to say goodbye."

"The stardust of our souls is separated from our bodies just as easily as water spills from an overturned bucket." Rich said. He did that sometimes. Spoke in obscure scriptures or quotes or puzzles that made the rest of us feel foolish for not knowing.

"We don't really have time for riddles just now," Tom said, irritation lacing his words.

Rich kept a smile on his face. "It's no riddle, Tom. Simply some wisdom the Lord has seen fit to share with me in my own private prayers. I'm surprised you don't see the relevance here." He turned back toward me.

"Jennifer offered to take over my duties at the outreach lunch," I said.

"Teresa. Your mother's soul is gone from this world. Her body has perished and is no more. You cannot say goodbye to something already gone. But there are souls and bodies right here and right now who need your attention. And again, your father's energy will only draw you into a negative headspace. You have purpose, Teresa. The Lord has plans for you. I don't want to see you or anyone else derail them."

"That's enough. We're going to the funeral." Tom was almost shouting now, and I put my hand on his arm to steady him.

"I appreciate your advice. But it's not just my mother. I need to be there for my brother. Help him get sorted out for college.

I'm not interested in getting drawn into anything with my father. I need to go for myself and for my brother. Jennifer will take my shift at lunch. We'll be back as soon as we can." I took Tom's hand and we turned to leave. As we reached the door, Rich said,

"Tom. Teresa. I'm telling you once more. Don't do this."

*****

We arrived early on the day of the funeral in case there were any last minute arrangements to help with. Michael met us in the driveway.

"The ladies' auxiliary is taking care of the food for after the service, and Mrs. Hamilton from next door has been dealing with all the flower deliveries. They're all inside. I came to warn you in case you wanted to slip in the side door."

I looked past my brother toward the darkened doorway.

"Dad just mostly sits in the living room with the lights off and drinks."

"And you? How are you doing?" I wanted to wrap Michael in a hug, but I felt stuck to the cracked concrete beneath my feet.

"I'm doing ok. I feel like we really connected these last few months. Mom and me, I mean. She actually laughed the other day when I told a joke. She was teaching me to garden. Said she couldn't wait to come visit me in California. Said she wanted to ride down the coast in a convertible."

I tried to imagine my mom in a convertible. Her hair tied up in a scarf like an old time movie star. Her head thrown back in laughter. Her eyes closed behind her sunglasses with the ocean in the distance. I couldn't do it. All I could see was her in our living room, nodding at whatever my father said. Her in church, her hand resting on my father's arm. Her watching the door while she tried to play with Alice. Her looking askance at the broken lamp in our apartment.

"Well that's really nice for you, Michael. I'm glad you had that time together." It sounded just as sarcastic as I meant it, and I regretted speaking at all.

"Teresa—"

"I'm sorry, Michael. I don't mean to sound petty. I'm glad she opened up to you. Really." I squeezed his hand and tried to smile.

"She was proud of you, you know."

"What?"

"She told me. After our last visit to your place. She said she couldn't believe you did all that on your own. That you had done what you wanted to do, no matter what. That you were making it work with Tom and Alice. She was really proud, Teresa."

Now he squeezed my hand, and I blinked back tears. I said, "I'm going to see if the ladies in the kitchen need any help. Why don't you take Alice to the park with Tom?"

There was no way I was going to walk into that kitchen and let all the ladies I'd grown up with size me up and pass judgment on me, but I knew I couldn't stand there any longer without breaking down. So, I went in the side door and sneaked upstairs. My parents' bedroom door was open at the top of the stairs, and I ducked in.

The air still smelled of her perfume and I swallowed again, determined not to have to redo my mascara before the service. The chair in front of her vanity was pulled out, as if she'd been sitting there and just stepped away. All her makeup and perfumes and lotions and creams were organized and lined up against the mirror, arranged from largest to smallest. The light from the hallway caught in the colored glass of one of the bottles as I picked it up. It was lighter than I expected, the liquid inside almost gone. When did she last pick up this bottle? Did she use it the day she died? Did she leave this world smelling of roses and lilac? Of course she did. She wouldn't go to the gas station without checking her makeup twice, so she surely wouldn't go into the next life without smelling her best.

Rich's words about the soul being gone from the body knocked around in my head. They made sense. My mother wasn't in the casket at the funeral home. If any part of her was still in this world, it was here, among the things that made her who she was. I set the bottle down and lowered myself into the chair. I tried to look past my own reflection in the mirror and see my mother's face, the way I remembered it as a little girl, when I would watch her get ready from the bed. I ran my hand along the edges of the mirror, willing that reflection into existence. Only my own stubborn face looked back at me. I stood and began to push the chair back under the vanity when I heard footsteps behind me.

"Are you happy?" My hands fell to my side and I turned to see my father standing in the doorway. His words slurred together and he was holding an empty highball glass.

"Daddy. I was just checking to see that everything was in order for the service. Do you need anything before we go?"

"I asked you a question. Are. You. Happy?" He swayed on the spot and I took a step back, afraid for a moment he would topple forward, felled like a tree from whatever had been in that glass.

"Daddy, I'm devastated. We all are. I miss her."

My father laughed then. A cold stuttering laugh, and Rich's words echoed in my head. "You never came to see her. You never brought her grandbaby here for her to love."

"You made it clear that I wasn't welcome here the last time I saw you, Daddy."

"Since when have you listened to anything I've ever said? If you'd been here this wouldn't have happened."

I knew he wasn't really talking about her death, but I still lost my temper. I'd tried to hold it together for Michael, but I couldn't manage any longer. I no longer cared about the ten women from church bustling about in the kitchen, or about Mrs. Hamilton fussing over the flowers.

"Maybe this happened because of you," I said, my voice low and angry.

"What did you say to me?" My father's eyes glinted with clarity for an instant, but it was too late to put the words back.

"You heard me. She was always afraid of you. Did you know she came with Michael to see Alice but she couldn't even enjoy the time she had with her because she was afraid you were going to find out? She was always looking over her shoulder. You're the reason she didn't get a chance to love Alice. If it's anyone's fault this happened, it's yours."

I gripped the edge of the vanity chair. It was all that stood between us, a shield. But my father didn't shout or come towards me. He crumpled. A crushed weed more than a felled tree. His face dissolved into wrinkles and sloppy wet tears followed the creases down his face. He let out a sob. I stood rooted to the spot, stunned and a little panicked. I'd never seen my father express any emotion but anger, and I didn't know what to do. Another strangled cry escaped his mouth, and he dropped the glass he'd been holding. It hit the carpet with a little thud, tumped over on its side, and rolled across the floor toward me. I bent down and picked it up. I took it into the ensuite bathroom and filled it with water. I sat the glass down next to my father and then edged my way past him into the hallway. I was halfway to the front door when I heard the glass shatter against the wall of my parents' bedroom.

I went straight to the park. I would have to call Michael later to explain why we didn't make it to the church, but I knew I couldn't do it. I couldn't sit in the pew next to my father. I couldn't talk to all the church members who wondered where I'd gone, who wanted to coo at Alice while she blinked up at them, unaware of who they were. When I got to the park, I only saw Tom and Alice. Michael must have gone back to the house already. Tom's back was to me. He was pushing Alice on the swing. Her squeals of delight echoed in the empty park and the sunshine framed them both in such a way that it made my eyes well up. Michael was going to California. My mother was gone. My father was lost. Tom and Alice were all that mattered now. Tom and Alice and the life we'd created with our chosen family. I walked toward them as Alice saw me and squealed, "Mama!" I ran the short distance to the swing and hugged her, her chubby legs still dangling from the baby seat.

"Mommy loves you so much, Alice."

Tom put his hand on my shoulder. "Is it time to go to the service?"

I shook my head.

*****

Alice never liked riding in the car and the ride home was more than she could handle. She screamed the last forty-five minutes back, and I couldn't wait to get her into bed and then collapse myself. Tom stuck his key in the lock on our apartment door and fought with it for an inordinate amount of time.

"This girl isn't getting any lighter, Tom." I heaved Alice onto my shoulder and tried to see what was going on with our front door.

"It's not working."

"What do you mean it's not working?"

"Exactly what I said. My key isn't working."

We left our bags in front of our door and climbed to the next floor where Jennifer and Anthony had a spare key to our place. I rapped gently on their door. Jennifer opened it a crack. She looked worried.

"Hey, sorry, our key doesn't seem to be working. Could we get our spare from you?" I stepped forward, anticipating that Jennifer would open the door and let us in. She looked pained, but didn't budge from the crack in the door.

"Um, just a sec, ok?"

"Ok." I stepped back into the hallway as she shut the door in my face. I turned to Tom. "That was weird, right?"

Tom nodded as the door opened again and Rich stepped into the hallway.

"Tom. Teresa." He looked us in the eye, but there was no welcome, no smile there. His eyes looked gray and distant. A deep sense of foreboding brewed in the pit of my stomach. Tom said, "Our key isn't working. We came up here to borrow the spare."

"There is no spare, Tom."

"Yes, there is. I just gave it to Jennifer a few weeks ago," I said.

"There's no spare because the locks on the apartment have been changed."

"Rich, we've got an exhausted baby and we've just been through hell, so can you give us the new key?"

"There's no new key. The locks have been changed so you cannot get in."

"Come on, Rich. Quit messing around and give us the goddamn keys." Tom's voice was strained, and I wondered if we just should have stayed in Dover Springs for the night.

"The apartment is mine, Tom. You lived there at my leisure," Rich said. Tom started to say something, but Rich cut him off.

"Oh sure, you pay a little money here and there, but you and I both know that it doesn't cover half the upkeep on this place. We are a shared community and I've shared the apartment with you and now I'm not sharing it with you. I warned you against going to that funeral, Tom. And you did not listen. You knew better than me." His eyes lingered on me just long enough to make me feel he could see what happened with my dad written all over me. Then he spread his hands wide.

"Actions have consequences."

"Wait." I shifted Alice to my other shoulder and she made a little hiccuping sound in her sleep. "You're telling me that you've barred us from our apartment because we went to my mother's funeral? Where are we supposed to go tonight? Where are we supposed to take Alice?" I whispered.

Rich winced. "I hate that Alice is all caught up in this. You are welcome to leave her in Jennifer and Anthony's apartment until this has all been sorted out, but no one here will allow the two of you into their homes tonight. I told you that funeral would only bring you suffering, and it seems it has, in one way or another." His eyes caught mine again before I buried my face in Alice's hair. I couldn't look at him. I couldn't think, I couldn't speak, I couldn't even cry. All I could do was hold my daughter and continue standing upright.

Tom scooped Alice out of my arms and ushered me toward the stairwell. Rich stayed in the hallway watching us. I looked back just before we descended the stairs, and he was wiping a tear from his eye.

"Where are we going to go, Tom?"

"The only place we can," Tom said.

-11-

ALICE

Bekah makes it to the house before me. She's sitting on the steps like a half-drowned kitten as I come panting up the stairs. I'm winded from the run and the baby pushing against my lungs. I'm sopping wet, starving, and still reeling from what Tabitha said. I didn't even know my mother spoke to Tabitha on a regular basis. What could she have told her? What did she know? But I don't have time to process these thoughts because I see that Bekah's eyes are wet and I know it's not from the rain. I put my hand out and she takes it.

At the kitchen table, in dry clothes, a plate of cinnamon bread between us, I try talking.

"How are you doing?" I ask.

"I'm ok." She doesn't look at me. She picks at a spot of dried food on the wood table.

"Are you sure?"

"Yes, I think so. I'm glad Sarah's aunt found her. I know it was good for Sarah. It's just..." She stares out the window behind me.

"Just?" I repeat to her, hoping she'll finish the thought.

"It's just that I didn't even consider that." Her voice has a dreamy quality to it, like she's sleep talking.

"Consider what?" I wonder if being pregnant is making my

brain work slower.

"Consider that she had other family. That there was someone out there looking for her. My whole family was here. So, when everyone went away, I just assumed we were alone now, all of us. But at least we were alone together."

"Oh, I see." I say, something like understanding stirring in my brain.

"I went to the library to get some perspective."

"And did you?"

"Maybe? I calmed down a little at least. And Sarah came by. We said goodbye. I haven't really been in the library much. It's quiet. A good place to think."

"Did you know I helped build the library?"

"You?"

"Don't sound so surprised. I guess you're too young to remember when we built it. They let anyone help who wanted to."

I remember thinking the library was going to be a new adventure, a chance to see the world through books, to loosen up. I threw myself into the work whole-heartedly and then, like everything else on the Farm, it turned out to be a mirage.

"I used to see Jason coming and going from there, but you were never with him," Bekah says.

"Yeah, well. Maybe I got a little sick of it over the years. Jason spent a lot of time there when he was writing pamphlets or counseling someone."

Jason had been so excited when Brother Richmond made him communications director after we got married. He said it showed recovered trust in us and he was determined to be found worthy of that trust. I played along at first. Being with Jason made you want to believe. It renewed a long dormant zeal in my life for the mission of the Collective and for our life on the Farm. But it was a fast burning flame. A sparkler. Quick to flare and quicker to go out. While I was fading back into ambivalence and distaste for the Farm, Jason grew more devoted.

"These people, Alice. They are begging for the truth. They are longing for a better way. And to think we can show them that way? To think we can lead them to the truth? It's so awesome," he would say, his enthusiasm bubbling over into wild hand gestures. It was endearing in the beginning, but soon my smile grew strained and even when I said something encouraging out loud, I felt like I was dying inside.

"Jason was so committed," Bekah says, and it brings me back to the kitchen table. The kitchen table I shared with Jason.

"Mmmhmm," I say.

"And that's the other thing I don't get about Sarah leaving. There's the principle of the thing, right? I mean we all made a commitment to be here. To serve here. Even if we were born here. It's part of the mission. Brother Richmond never said it would be easy. There were always going to be sacrifices. But because he's gone for this brief time, should we just abandon everything we believe? Time is so short until his return."

Her voice is no longer sleepy. Righteous indignation seems to give her confidence, and she sits up straighter.

"Well," I start, with no plan of where I'm going. "Not everyone has your..." I turn various words over in my mind. "Not everyone has your faith."

She scans me up and down, like she's seeing me for the first time. "What do you mean by that?"

I really don't want to have this conversation right now, but I guess we've opened this can of worms, so we'll have to plunge forward. "Just that the Farm and Brother Richmond and everything here, it hasn't always been easy for everyone. Some people have had a rough go of it."

"What, like my life is so easy?"

I remember my own terrible stubbornness at her age. "I'm not saying that, Bekah." I wrack my brain for something to help her understand. "Ok, take me for example. I've been in the Collective my whole life, but then this baby comes along and suddenly I'm not so sure what's going to happen to me. We're not supposed to have a baby, right? But this one is coming whether I like it or not. So maybe I don't feel too sure about my place here on the Farm knowing that I'm probably going to get in a whole heap of trouble. That kind of thing might make someone doubt their place here. Does that make sense?"

Bekah studies me. "Why didn't you just go to Brother Richmond? He always says that the Lord likes to surprise us. That His ways are not our ways. It seems like telling him and then letting him help you would have been the easiest thing."

I want to shake her and scream that when Brother Richmond said our ways were not his ways, he was referring to himself, not God. I take a deep breath and try again. I think of Sarah sitting in my living room saying 'Brother Richmond is a bad man' and how many things she could have been referring to, and I decide I'm tired of being delicate.

"Bekah, look. Brother Richmond was not always the perfect leader. He did bad things. Things that hurt people. Things that hurt me. You've got to know that. That's why some people wanted to leave. That's why I wanted to leave."

Bekah is quiet. I look out the kitchen window and watch the rain while she processes my words.

I remember another rainy day. I was standing outside the meeting house while everyone was at Evening Table. I'd just been put on my first Separation. My mom snuck out to sit with me outside even though no one was supposed to talk to me. I was supposed to sit out there that first night, so everyone would know I was being punished. My mom didn't talk, she just sat with me. Once we heard the scrape of chairs on the concrete floor and knew people were about ready to head outside, I told my mom to go. I knew how much trouble she'd get in if Brother Richmond caught her out here with me. But Brother Richmond was in front of us before we could even stand. He had a small plate piled with bread, corn on the cob, and thick slices of turkey and ham. He held it out to me. I was so hungry, and Brother Richmond looked like an angel standing there with that food. I reached for the plate, but my mom caught my arm.

"Alice knows her punishment."

"Even those who must bear the consequences of their sin need to eat. Consider this an acknowledgement of your wrongdoing and a pledge that you'll complete your Separation without incident."

People spilled out of the meeting house and gathered around us, despite the rain. I heard a few comments about Brother Richmond's generosity, but others seemed more hopeful for a confrontation. My mom and Brother Richmond seemed to be in some kind of standoff, but finally she let my arm drop and nodded toward the food.

"You wanted to leave? What was so bad that you wanted to leave your home?" Bekah's accusation cuts across my memory.

"There were a million little things and a million more big things. I can't even remember them all." In truth, I remember everything that Brother Richmond did and said to me. Every grace, every punishment, every ridiculous rule, every day I wasn't allowed to speak to my parents, to Edwin, to anyone. I remember it all. But I'm so tired, and I just can't bring myself to pull all those memories to the surface right now.

"And Jason?" Bekah looks as though she's about to cry again and for a moment I feel bad for springing all this on her after she's already lost so much.

"Jason didn't want to leave at first. He was very committed, as you said."

"What made him change his mind?"

"The baby. Worrying what Brother Richmond would do when he found out."

That's not the whole truth. That's what made Jason finally agree to make a plan. But he became more open to the idea of leaving when I'd told him what had happened all those nights in Brother Richmond's office. He'd held me when I cried. He'd stroked my hair and promised me that things would be ok. That we'd find a way forward. That he loved me more than anything else. Still, I should have known that Brother Richmond would come first for him. Brother Richmond always came first.

"But you didn't know what Brother Richmond would do. You didn't know how he would react." She is incredulous, and I recognize the self-defense. I spent a long time reacting the same way to anything that felt too big or difficult to surmount with the remnants of childhood faith.

"Bekah. Please. It's been a long day. Things aren't always what they seem here on the Farm. Surely you must know that by now. You've lived here your whole life. And now that Brother Richmond is gone, we've got a chance to do things differently. To leave, if that's what will make us happy. Can't you see that Sarah was happier with her aunt than she would have been here?"

Bekah's face is impassive, but she gives a minor nod of her head. Then she stands up and turns to walk toward the bedrooms.

"Bekah—" I start to call her back but stop. I'm too worn out to argue anymore.

*****

I'm walking to Tabitha's house the next day when Edwin finds me on the path. I'm planning to talk with Tabitha about restarting the farm stand. I'm draining what little money I have fast, and baking is really the only thing I know how to do. Plus, it will give me a chance to ask her about what my mother said to her.

"Alice," Edwin calls after me. "Alice. Wait up."

"Hey." I still feel the awkwardness of our last encounter rubbing like sandpaper against my skin.

"I'm sorry. I know I was kind of abrupt the other day. I just feel responsible for the group and I—"

"Why do you feel responsible?"

"Because Brother Richmond...because I...because we need someone to take charge," he says.

"Why?" I ask again. He looks tired, but I can't seem to let him off the hook.

"Why what?"

"Why do we need someone to take charge? Brother Richmond left us here. Seems like that's as good a reason as any to be done with him and this whole illusion that we're one big happy family."

"Alice. You don't mean that. What about the second Homegoing? It's getting closer every day." He's looking up in the sky, like Brother Richmond is going to smite me for talking bad about him behind his back.

"I'm through with pretending, Edwin. I've been doing it for so long. Sarah left yesterday. Her aunt came and got her. Other people's families will probably come too. There's an ongoing investigation into the disappearance. And you can't keep those reporters at bay for too much longer. They're going to keep coming. It's too much. Besides, even before all this, you know the problems we've had." I look hard at him, willing him to make eye contact with me.

To see, in my eyes, that when I say "we" I mean "me." He runs his hands through his hair and picks at a branch that's hanging over the path.

"Every family has troubles, Alice. In his last message Brother Richmond said you and I should be the ones to lead the others into the second Homegoing. I'm trying to do my part. All I'm asking is that you meet me halfway."

I groan and sit down on the bench that's off to the side of the path. I remember sitting here with my mom when I was little so we could watch the bees buzz around the flowers. That feels like a million years ago now.

"I'm not going to help bring about a second Homegoing, Edwin."

"Alice. That's direct disobedience of Brother Richmond's wishes."

"So what?" I say. "Who cares? Do you think he's going to come down here and put me in Separation? Everyone is gone and the world hasn't ended. Why would it end in two months? Maybe we should all move on. I've got a baby coming in case you didn't notice."

"Then why are you still here?"

"What?" His question catches me off guard.

"Why are you still here?" he asks again. "If you don't care about Brother Richmond, if you don't care about the second Homegoing, then why stay here? Why not leave and make a new life far away from this place that has caused you so much trouble?"

"Bekah is here. Jason took our money. The detective told me to stay." I rattle off all the logical reasons I'm here, but I know they sound flimsy. So I finally say the thing that keeps me up at night. "I don't know. I can't seem to leave this place, no matter how much I want to. I worry about what will happen when that Second

Homegoing arrives. I wonder if maybe I'll see my parents again if it's true. I don't want to lose the few people I have left. I'm scared, okay? Is that what you want to hear? I'm scared, but I can't pretend we're all a happy family anymore."

"You didn't want to leave when Jason was here." There's no jealousy in Edwin's voice, just a statement of fact.

"That was different. I was young and stupid enough to believe that our love could fix all the problems here."

"You never even told me what drew you two together. You were always so guarded when I asked about it." Edwin looks down, and I feel a longing for the friendship we used to share.

"He seemed so pure. He believed in everything so deep in his heart. He wasn't going along with whatever Brother Richmond said out of fear. I felt like I could maybe get back on track if I was near him. And that morphed into love along the way."

I see Jason standing in the sun with his family during the membership ceremony. His broad smile lighting up his whole face. I think about what it felt like when that smile was turned on me. When he said, "Alice Moffat, I think I'm in love with you." And then I think about how his face twisted into agony when I told him I was pregnant. How he'd seemed so tortured about our plan to leave, even though staying could mean losing our baby.

"Morphed into love? What does that even mean?" Edwin asks.

"What do you want me to say, Edwin? That I never should have married him in the first place? Is that what you want to hear?" I know that I'm responding to myself as much as to Edwin, and I see shock in his face as the words tumble out.

"Alice, No. I—"

"What about you?" I say.

"What about me?" Edwin says.

"After Jason and I got married, you didn't exactly want to hang out anymore either. I mean, after the Separation. After we could have all hung out again." I sound like the world's most ungrateful brat. I try again. "You just seemed extra devoted to Brother Richmond after everything. It surprised me. But now that I think of it, I guess it was really after your parents left that you and Brother Richmond started getting closer."

"I don't want to talk about that."

"I just meant it wasn't as easy to convince you to break the rules." I try for a grin, but Edwin doesn't return it.

"I said I don't want to talk about it. You don't know everything, Alice." There's that coldness again, like a flipped switch.

"I'm sorry," I say. "This baby is making my brain malfunction. I don't want to fight."

Edwin's face softens and his eyes linger on my swollen belly. "It's fine. Hey, I know you're kind of done with all this, but will you do me a favor?"

"What?

"Will you come to Evening Table?" Just tonight? Just come and see if you're sure it's something you're ready to give up." He smiles, and I feel that rush of friendship again. The years that tether us together, like some invisible binding. We've never been good at telling each other no.

"Ok, fine. I'll come once. I won't promise anything else."

"Great. Remember that one thing Brother Richmond always said?"

I laugh. "There were a million things that Brother Richmond always said."

"'Community is built together. No one is an island alone.' I don't want you to be an island alone, Alice. I'll see you tonight." He turns and walks off toward the library and I'm left to find my way to Tabitha's alone.

*****

Evening Table has always been the centerpiece of life on the Farm. Before the world turned upside down, we held it every night. Families would prepare a dish to bring to the pavilion next to the meeting house. Brother Richmond would bless the food and we'd all eat in community. After dinner, he would offer some kind of devotion and give out that day's announcements and news. After a while, those announcements just became bulletins about who'd found favor with Brother Richmond and, more often, who had screwed up.

A few times a week, my mom and I, along with whoever else was on kitchen duty, would bake fat loaves of bread for the meal. We'd be covered in flour and sweating from the constant heat of the ovens, but those baking sessions were the happiest times of my week. My black hair would be bleached gray by a fine sheen of flour, and my mom would tease me about looking like an old lady. I'd counter that my loaves rose better than hers. We'd laugh because no one baked better bread than Teresa Moffat. The smell of yeast and dough would linger on my clothes for hours afterward. Bekah and Sarah had slipped easily into our rhythms when they joined the baking duty, and the best days were when it was just us four women baking bread. It was as if we could pretend the rest of the Farm didn't exist for those few hours.

It's startling walking into the cavernous pavilion now. In the past, there'd be an entire row of tables on the back wall piled with food. The smell of roast corn and potatoes would be enough to induce a food coma, and the murmur of people catching up on that week's gossip would fill the big space with a thrumming that reminded me of a beehive. Now, Bekah and Angelica fuss over two narrow tables placed with food, and the fifteen or so people gathered speak in halting tones that echo around the ceiling and clang into the support beams like the lone bell in a church tower.

Bekah stands by the food table, a swipe of flour still visible across her forehead. I should have known she was the one baking the bread. She'd left the house without a word hours earlier. I picture her in that hot kitchen, measuring, kneading, and sweating alone, and it pulls at my heart. I should have helped her bake the bread at least. Even if I wasn't going to take part. I shouldn't leave her to face that big kitchen alone. To work those countertops laden with so much laughter and so many tears.

"The bread looks terrific, Bekah," I say by way of greeting. She tugs a loose strand of hair from her ponytail, a sheepish grin pulling at the corners of her mouth. "I'm sorry you had to do it alone."

She takes a step back and seems to trip over her own feet. Her face reddens and she busies herself with retying her hair. "I didn't do it alone," she says quietly.

Surprise mixes with something akin to indignation in my chest. Who did she allow into our kitchen? I chide myself for feeling protective over the space. It's not mine. Or my mother's.

"I helped her. Couldn't have her baking all that bread alone." Edwin materializes by my side. "Glad you came, Alice."

"You helped bake bread?" I allow myself an eyebrow raise.

"I watched you and your mom do it enough when we were growing up, I figured I could handle it. Plus, I had a good supervisor." Bekah's face flushes and I worry she'll stumble over her own feet again, but she manages to stay steady.

"I'm glad you had help," I say, and I mean it. Maybe Edwin is right. Maybe I need to be here, in community again. Maybe things will be ok now that Brother Richmond is gone. Maybe that was all that was ever wrong with this place. If I can just get the Second Homegoing out of my mind, it all feels possible.

Bekah and I find seats at the half dozen tables lined in neat rows in front of the small pulpit at the front of the pavilion. Angelica sits down on my other side and pats my shoulder.

"Your parents would be proud of you, Alice." I start to say thanks but am unable to get the words out before Angelica continues. "Look around. We're a smaller group than were left after the Homegoing. Others have run away or gone back to worldly family members. But we," she spreads her arms wide at the small gathering, "are the true faithful. The ones who've known hardship and have passed the test. I know you've had your mistakes," she looks down at my stomach, "but we will reap the greatest reward in the next Homegoing, and your parents would be proud to know that you'll be right at the front, leading the charge."

I guess Edwin converted her after all. She pats my shoulder again and arranges her napkin on her lap. I shift in my seat. The hard metal is digging into my back, the baby is pressing against my bladder, and the temperature must have risen a degree for every word that came out of Angelica's mouth because I am sweating. I haven't told anyone but Edwin and Tabitha that I don't plan on leading any kind of second Homegoing, but now I see that my coming as good as cements it for the faithful gathered here tonight. Did Edwin plan it that way? As if he knows I'm thinking about him, Edwin stands and moves behind the podium in front of the tables.

"Before we begin our meal tonight, I'd like to say a few words."

Angelica has slipped out of the seat next to me and is now sitting behind Edwin, slowly strumming a guitar. I'm surprised her gnarled fingers can still find the chords, but I recognize an old hymn, *Where He Leads Me*. My mom used to sing it to me as a lullaby. I feel sleepy as the words come back to me.

I can hear my Savior calling.
I can hear my Savior calling.

I can hear my Savior calling.
Take thy cross, and follow me.

"I know a lot of us didn't know what to think when Brother Richmond took that first Homegoing up to glory. We felt left behind. We felt worried. We felt, dare I say, betrayed."

A few people nod.

"It's ok, friends. It's ok to name our feelings. I think Brother Richmond knew we'd feel these things, and that's why he left us a message." Bekah is staring up at Edwin like he's hung the stars. I whisper, "Psst, Bekah!" to get her attention, but she doesn't seem to hear me over the guitar strings.

"He left us a message of hope. He left us a message of love. He left us a message of eternal significance." The nods are more vigorous now, and I can't help but think that Edwin made a shrewd choice having Angelica play behind him. Music always riles people up, heightens emotion and gives weight to whatever is being said.

"I believe he left us that message not so we could hide in our homes until the Second Homegoing. No, thank you. I believe he left us that message so we could forge ahead, eyes open, and hearts set on what's to come. But..." He looks at me and my stomach sinks. The aroma of dinner that was, only moments ago, making me salivate, now makes me nauseous. When Edwin stretches his arm out toward me, my appetite evaporates. This is new. I can always eat through anything.

"I'm only a helper, folks. Alice Greene. She's the real beacon of light here tonight. She's the one who is going to lead us home this next go around. The time grows short, and I think we need to support her, help her, love her, and lift her and this new life she's carrying up as we march toward our final goal. What do you say folks, will you make a covenant with me to help Alice as she takes on this mantle of leadership?"

A dozen expectant faces turn their nods toward me this time, and I want to sink into the floor. Anger boils in my ears. Edwin knows how I feel about this, and still he lured me into this trap. There's no other word for it. He smiles at me from the podium, as if it will erase the betrayal that has doused the timid renewal of our friendship. I don't say anything as everyone mumbles their agreement with Edwin and smiles at me. Angelica is still playing that wretched guitar and the next lines of the song twist around my brain like a virus.

I'll go with him through the judgment.
I'll go with him through the judgment.
I'll go with him through the judgment.
I'll go with Him, with Him all the way.

I slip out the side door as everyone starts eating. Twilight stretches to the hills and the cold air is a reprieve in my lungs. I hear someone else coming out of the door, but I pick up my pace instead of turning back. I hear Edwin call my name, but still I keep walking. I can't have it out with him right now. Not tonight. I walk toward the old gate where Detective Cameron brought me home. I'm not sure where I'm going, but I can't stay here.

-12-

TERESA

We pulled into Vivian's driveway just as the last light was fading from the sky. She rushed out onto the porch and her eyes lit up like lanterns when she saw us.

"Tommy! Teresa! What are you doing here? I figured you'd be staying at your daddy's after the funeral. I thought I'd see you at the church, but I couldn't find you. I'm so sorry, Teresa. Your mother was a good woman."

She wrapped her arms around me, and I sank into the faded floral print of her dress. She smelled like cinnamon, and she was soft and warm, and I would have stayed in that hug forever if I could have. I didn't know what we were going to tell her.

"We just figured we'd come for a visit since we were back here anyway. Hope it's ok we didn't call first," Tom said.

Vivian shooed away Tom's words with a wave of her wrist. "Of course! How's that great grandbaby of mine?"

"She's great," I said and focused on getting our bags from the backseat.

Once we'd gotten Alice to sleep in Tom's old bedroom, Vivian stuffed us with cookies in the kitchen. We both ate too many, even though I knew neither of us was very hungry.

"How's the new place? Did I hear right that your brother's

going to school early? When are you two going to give me another grandbaby? I'm not getting any younger, you know." Vivian bubbled over with questions, and I wracked my brain to remember when we'd last called her with an update.

We filled in Vivian the best we could, sidestepped the questions we couldn't answer, and finally collapsed onto the pull out couch in the living room. The metal bar in the middle of the bed dug into my back. I sighed and looked up at the dark ceiling. I could feel Tom fidgeting next to me.

"He was right, you know," I said. "Rich. He was right. It was a mistake to go to the funeral. What happened with my dad, not making it to the service, dragging Alice back and forth like this. It would have been better if we'd just stayed."

"It doesn't matter if he was right. He locked us out of our apartment. That's not how you handle disagreement." I put my hand over Tom's on the lumpy mattress as he spoke. "I feel like we're back at square one. What are we going to do now, Teresa? Our whole life is in that apartment."

I knew he meant more than just our belongings. That apartment was where we fit in. It was where we were making our new start. Our better life.

"I don't know. Your grandma will let us stay here until we can figure out what's next and then..."

Tom pulled his hand out from under mine and sat up. The thin frame gave a whine as he did so, and I winced, worried the noise would wake Alice or Vivian or both. "We can't stay here. You know that as well as I do. We can't let Alice grow up in the shadow of your father's rage. Granny would love it, but we need our own life." I could feel Tom's exasperation shifting to anger. I sat up.

"Wait a second. Are you mad at me?"

"No. It's just, I'm not mad, but I wish, I don't know, Teresa.

I thought we had cracked the code, gotten on track, and now it seems like we've flown so far off course, and we can't go back to the apartment and let Rich dictate our lives, but you're over there talking about how he's right. It's just a lot."

"He was right, Tom. I'm not saying he was right to lock us out of our apartment, but he was right about coming back. You know that as well as I do. He can be right and wrong at the same time."

Tom laid back down on the bed. "It's late. We're both exhausted. Let's get some sleep and we'll figure things out tomorrow."

Things didn't look much better in the morning, but by the grace of God, Alice slept in, and Vivian made strong coffee. We were drinking our second cups and Vivian was talking about taking Alice to the zoo when there was a knock at the door. She left us in the kitchen to answer it. The next moment, I heard Rich's deep voice laughing from the hallway. Tom and I looked at each other. My mouth fell open, speechless at the audacity. Before we could make a plan or even set our mugs down, Rich was strolling into the kitchen, laughing about something with Vivian.

"Look who I found!" She beamed up at Rich and he beamed right back.

"Tom. Teresa. I'm so glad you were able to visit your grandmother. Family is so important." He smiled up at Vivian. Alice cried at that moment, and I jumped up to go get her, but Vivian insisted I stay and visit, and she would tend to Alice. Rich nodded like he was planning and executing this whole dance.

"What are you doing here? How did you even know where my grandmother lived?"

"You'd be surprised what I know, Tom. But that's beside the point. I'm here to bring you home."

"You threw us out. Locked us out of our apartment with a baby asleep in our arms. What on God's green earth makes you think we're coming back with you?" I asked.

"'He went looking for a road that doesn't lead to death. He went looking for that road and found it.'"

"We don't have to play your games anymore, so you can save that one for someone else," I said, watching Rich through the steam coming off my coffee. I may have thought he was right when I was lying on Vivian's lumpy sofa, but I didn't have to give him the satisfaction of knowing it.

"I didn't kick you out. I merely exercised my influence as the leader of our group to exert some discipline. That line is from a book by Ursula K. Le Guin, by the way."

I rolled my eyes.

"Poetry is its own form of prophecy, wouldn't you say?" Rich continued. "The line says 'A road that doesn't lead to death.' You found that road with the Collective. You found a family and a home and I'm willing to bet that even one day away has been sufficient for you to realize just what you're missing when you're not among us."

Tom and I fidgeted with our mugs. Part of the appeal and the irritation of Rich was his ability to somehow know your innermost thoughts. Sometimes even before you did.

"Look." Rich steepled his fingers on the table. There were dark circles under his eyes I hadn't noticed when he came in. "I know I can get a little hyped up sometimes, but I only have the best intentions for you and all the group. I was up half the night thinking about you guys. I'm new to this whole leadership thing. It's not what I want, you know that. I'd love to pass along this role to someone else, but I'm trying to trust the Lord and do what's right. And I meant what I said before you left. You have purpose. Both of you. And there are souls at home who need you. I need you."

Rich stood and held his hands out toward us. It seems absurd now, but at that moment I felt his sorrow. It's hard to explain feeling that way, but it's what happened. I can see now that he never actually apologized or accepted responsibility for the fact that he'd turned out a young couple with a baby. But at the time, bleary-eyed, staring into my coffee, it felt like the apology I needed, even if the words weren't all there.

"I realize you two may need some time to think about it, but I hope to see you both at home soon."

"You're right," I said. "We need to think about it."

Tom nodded, but I think we both knew we'd go back before Rich left the kitchen table.

Years later, after Rich had abandoned his game of quizzing us on obscure quotes, I looked up the Le Guin quote. I had dreamed the night before of that morning in Vivian's cramped kitchen and woke up with a need to know where the road had led, if not to death. The line was from a book called *Always Coming Home*. After he found the road that didn't lead to death, the man in the poem turned to stone. He never went anywhere else again.

-13-

ALICE

It is almost completely dark by the time I reach town. When I see the police station up ahead, I am panting and sweat beads on my forehead despite the chill in the air. My legs feel as though they will give out any moment, and the baby grumbles inside me, furious that I didn't eat anything at Evening Table. I just need a minute to catch my breath, but then I see Detective Cameron walking toward me and there's nowhere to go. I try to shrink into my jacket, but the baby is making that difficult these days.

"Mrs. Greene?"

"Hi, there. Nice night for a walk." I hope this bit of small talk will be enough to get me out of further conversation. It isn't.

"Probably one of the last few nice ones we'll get. I was just on my way home. Are you headed down Main Street? I can walk you to your car."

"I didn't drive. I walked." I'm feeling faint, like I've just stood up too quickly, and I lean against the storefront next to me to rest a moment. My breath is fast and ragged, and I can't seem to take in enough air.

"Are you alright? You don't look so good." Detective Cameron grabs my elbow just before I slip down the wall.

"I think I'm just hungry."

"Come on," Detective Cameron steers my elbow toward the street. "We're getting you something to eat." I don't protest. I allow myself to be led to his car, the same car he drove me home in. It's only been a couple of weeks since that day, but it feels like a lifetime ago.

I don't pay attention to where we are driving, and I don't talk. Detective Cameron seems to understand because he doesn't try to talk on the drive. He makes a phone call at one point, but I must be slipping in and out of sleep because I do not remember who he called or what he said. It is completely dark when we pull up to a small yellow house. The shutters are green and there are tidy bushes and flower beds in the front yard.

"I thought you said we were getting something to eat."

I can barely form words and I'm astonished at my stupidity for walking all the way to town. I've done it a hundred times, but never with a human life growing inside me, depending on me to make the good decisions it can't. I think I might cry but then realize I'm too tired to do even that.

"We are. This is my house. I called my wife on the way over. She's just getting dinner ready." I must look horrified at the idea of meeting Detective Cameron's wife because his face breaks into a sympathetic smile. "If you tell her I said this I'll deny it to my grave, but she's not that great a cook. She is, however, a terrific nurse. A labor and delivery nurse. Retired. She'll take a look at you, if you're ok with that. I had a feeling you wouldn't take too kindly to the hospital if I took you there."

"I've never been to the hospital except when I was born. We always managed things at the Farm."

"I figured. I think it's meatloaf tonight, and that one is usually pretty good. You're lucky you didn't come on a Thursday."

"What's Thursday?"

"Leftover Surprise." He makes a face like he's gagging and opens the car door. He comes around to the side and opens my door as well, watching me closely as I step out onto the driveway. My legs seem to be working again. I make it up the front walk and to the door, but I can feel Detective Cameron at my back, and I know his arms are probably outstretched, ready to catch me if I fall.

Inside, the light is warm and orange in the little living room just off the front door. There are soft armchairs and an array of jewel toned pillows with phrases like "Stay Awhile" and "i love us" stitched in looping script. Lamps twinkle on each side table and there's music, low and jazzy, playing in the background. Photographs of Detective Cameron with a short woman with close cropped black hair dot the walls. In one, she smiles and leans around his shoulder from behind. Two young women stand on either side of them. They're throwing fall leaves into the air with expressions that say, "We can't believe you made us do this," but the twinkle in their eyes says they're actually enjoying themselves. I look at this photo for a long time. Brother Richmond was never a big fan of photographs. He said they were just another form of vanity. Still, we had a few. Quick snapshots my mom took of us around the Farm. None like this. None where the whole point was to be seen and be seen having fun no less. I can see Detective Cameron watching me out of the corner of my eye as I study the photograph.

"I know, I know. It's a cheesy pose, but Lorraine thought it would be cute."

I stop scrutinizing the portrait. "No, I love it. You all look like you're having so much fun." I try to keep from sounding too wistful.

"Is that you, Brad?" Mrs. Cameron's voice carries like a melody down the hallway off the living room, and I like her before I set eyes on her. She is shorter than she looks in the portraits on the wall, and she has to stand on tiptoes to give Detective Cameron a kiss on the cheek. She turns toward me.

"You must be Alice. So happy to meet you, dear. I'm Lorraine."

"Thank you for having me. I hope it's not too much trouble."

"Nonsense! You're the cutest thing Brad's brought home in years. And he's brought some folks home, let me tell you."

I smile but feel another wave of faintness come over me and reach out for the nearest chair.

"Listen to me just babbling on. Brad said you were a little worse for the wear. Walking five miles! Exercise is good for a mama, but let's not overdo it, huh? Let's get some dinner in you. Then, if you're ok with it, I can give you a once over. Maybe we can even find that little one's heartbeat, if you want." She beams at me. A ray of sunshine personified. I can see why she must be a great mother and baby nurse. I would want her around my baby.

"You can hear the baby's heartbeat?"

"Sure, sure. I have a little portable doppler. Got it when my oldest daughter was pregnant. Of course, I trusted her midwife completely, but you can't blame a grandma for wanting to hear that little one's heartbeat if I could, ya know? But if you'd rather not, then say the word."

"No, that would be nice. Thank you." I stand and follow Lorraine down the hall toward the kitchen.

Detective Cameron needn't have warned me about the meatloaf. It was just fine. Perfect, even, after not having eaten most of the day. After we're finished with dinner, Lorraine takes me into the sitting room off the kitchen.

"You've already gained a lot of your color back. There's not too much that can't be cured with some food and rest, I always say. Would you like me to see if I can find the baby's heartbeat? Have you been to the doctor at all?"

"No. There are some midwives on the Farm, and they usually handle all the births, but no one was really supposed to know about this baby, so I didn't go to see anyone."

"Oh, that's fine dear. I've dealt with babies that weren't supposed to be here many times. Does the father know?" I am taken aback by her suggestion, but then I realize how my explanation must sound to an outsider.

"Oh, the father is my husband. It's just that the two of us weren't supposed to have a baby."

"Ah. fertility issues?" I decide to leave it alone and not say anything more, but Lorraine must see something off in my face because she persists.

"Not fertility issues? I don't mean to pry. Just my nosy nature and it's always good to have more information from your patient, but you don't have to tell me anything else. I'm sorry. My daughters always tell me I'm too pushy. Don't mind me."

"No, it's not that. On the Farm, Brother Richmond decided how many children each family should have, well he said God told him how many children each family should have, and Jason and I weren't supposed to have any. Kids that is."

I look away from Lorraine, aware how crazy this all must sound. It was an unspoken rule on the Farm that you should take care to keep your family size at whatever Brother Richmond said it should be. There were a few doctors in the Collective who still practiced outside the Farm, mostly for the money they brought the group, and they supplied birth control to anyone who needed it. No one was supposed to actually test out Brother Richmond's prophecies. I'd done the dutiful thing. I'd visited the doctor. I was still trying then. For Jason. But after Andrea White announced she was having her fifth child, with Brother Richmond's blessing,

I couldn't do it anymore. I buried the pills in an unused field. If Brother Richmond's prophecy was gospel, then we wouldn't have any kids. Why did I need to make sure it was fulfilled? Wasn't that his responsibility? A few months later, I missed my period, and I knew. I kept the news to myself for a couple of days, enjoying the secret I carried around. I eventually told Jason after Evening Table one night. I watched the color drain from his face and wished that I had kept it to myself longer.

"Alice, what have you done?"

"I didn't do this on my own, Jason."

"You know what I mean."

"This is a good thing." I said, my voice pleading and shrill.

"Brother Richmond won't see it that way."

Jason sounded scared, and his fear lodged a kernel of an idea in my mind. When Brother Richmond found out about the baby, there could be any number of consequences. He may put us in Separation, exile us, or worse, take the baby and give it to someone else. It was rare, but it had happened. To Jessica Matthews. She already had the two children she was allowed. Baby number three had been taken from her hours after birth and given to John and Samantha Barry. Jessica ran all over the Farm ranting to anyone who would listen about her stolen baby. She threatened to take her remaining children and leave. She threatened to go to the police, but in the end, she did none of that. She stopped ranting and continued raising the children she had left. I never could wrap my mind around giving up like that, but I knew Brother Richmond had many methods of persuasion at his disposal. I was certain I would never let it get that far. I would leave long before taking my baby was even a possibility. Still, the thought of leaving without Jason put a pain in my chest. I thought I could use such an unthinkable consequence to finally convince him to leave.

"So, this baby's not supposed to be here, but here we are anyway," I say to Lorraine to avoid heading any further down memory lane. I pull at the ties that hold the cushion on the wooden chair next to me. I know how bizarre it all sounds, and I brace myself for scorn, pity, or bafflement. But when I dare peak up at Lorraine, she is grinning from ear to ear.

"I'm sorry, dear. I don't mean to laugh! Really, I don't." But even as she says it, I can hear the laughter behind her words.

"It's just dreadful all the rules that man put in place for you all, but you and your husband are a fine example," she says, her eyes misting over with mischief.

"A fine example of what?" I say, still missing the joke.

"A fine example of what happens when you tell folks what they can and cannot do with love. Love's going to find a way. It will push its way through, every time. And here you are. Carrying that love around with you, and soon she'll be on the outside giving that love right back to you."

Her words stick in my head like a chorus. Love pushes its way through. I've been so bogged down by grief, loss, fear and confusion, but these words float above all that, light as a kiss on the forehead. I turn them over and over in my mind looking for some stain on them, some poison that will twist and mangle them. And then I hear the second part of her statement.

"Wait, can you tell? If it's a she?"

"Oh, no. We can't do that here in the house. It's just a hunch. But I'm often right about these things. I guess after so many babies you get pretty good at guessing. I've been right on all three of my grandbabies."

Now she is waving around a gray box with a small black screen. The box is attached, by what looks like a telephone cord, to a little wand that is flat on the end. I'm sure I've seen one before at other births on the Farm, but it's never been pointed at me, so it looks a little grander, a little holier than I remember. She adjusts the knobs on the box and directs me to lift my shirt.

"This may tickle a little." She squirts a blob of clear goo on my belly and puts the wand in the center of the goo. It makes a sucking sound, like it's sealing itself to my skin. She pushes it around on my stomach. An erratic static fills the room. For a while I don't hear anything else. Lorraine has a look of utmost concentration on her face as she moves the wand back and forth.

"A stubborn little thing. But we'll find her."

I hadn't thought about the heartbeat of this little creature until Lorraine mentioned it, but now I want nothing in the world except for her to find it. I can hear my own heartbeat getting louder and faster and I begin to panic, thinking this love has been lost to me too. But then, from beyond the static, there's a whooshing. A *wompwompwomp* that sounds like nothing I've ever heard. It's fast and hard and strong, and tears prick my eyes before Lorraine tells me what I'm hearing.

"Ah, there it is. Nice and clear. Sounds perfect, my dear."

I am transfixed. For a moment I can't breathe, but then I realize it's because I've been holding my breath to keep any other sounds at bay. After what feels like too short a time, Lorraine shuts off the machine and hands me a tissue for the goo still on my stomach.

"Thank you," I manage through my tears.

After Lorraine finishes my impromptu checkup, she leaves me in the living room to run to the pharmacy for vitamins. I'm still basking in the thrill of that little *wompwompwomp*, when Detective Cameron appears in the doorway carrying a tray with a chocolate frosted cake.

"Would you like some cake? Our daughter Haley's in marketing and one of her clients owns a bakery in Cooperstown. She sent this one over yesterday." He sets the tray on the table between us and sits down in one of the chairs opposite me. He looks a little odd in the bright green chair, squashed between the pillows like a giant squeezing into doll furniture.

"I happened to like the meatloaf very much," I say.

"I'm glad. You certainly needed it. I know you must be exhausted, but was there any particular reason you felt the need to walk all the way to town tonight? Did something happen out on the Farm?"

I have almost forgotten going to Evening Table and the mess Edwin made of everything. I hadn't planned on confiding in anyone, but in this cozy room, with the baby's heartbeat still ringing in my ears, I feel my guard slip.

"I just couldn't stay. They were having Evening Table and— Oh, sorry. Evening Table is like our nightly service."

"I'm familiar with the term, Mrs. Greene. I am surprised to hear that meetings are still going on with Preston gone."

"Please, call me Alice. Yes, Edwin is determined to carry on. He thinks..." I'm unsure how to continue. "You should know..." Am I really going to do this?

Detective Cameron doesn't rush me or interrupt. He waits while I gather my thoughts. I think again of the gift Lorraine gave me with the heartbeat monitor and I feel my defenses fall away. "Ok. I was planning to leave the Collective. With my husband. Jason. We had it all planned out. We were supposed to leave during the Homegoing. But then everything went topsy turvy."

"So, your husband was planning to leave and still disappeared with the rest of the group? Do you think he was taken against his will? This may be important information." Detective Cameron sits up straighter.

"No. He didn't go against his will. He changed his mind."

"I'm sorry, Alice. On top of everything else, I can imagine that's the hardest."

"Thanks," I rush on, so I don't have to think about it too much. "So, I'm not even supposed to be here, that's important. I'm only here because you asked me to stay." I wonder, as I say it, if he can see that it's only half true, that there are so many other things I didn't anticipate keeping me here. "After everyone disappeared, Edwin read us a letter from Brother Richmond saying there's going to be a second Homegoing in two months. There was a video as well, but the VCR ate it, but Edwin said it contained our instructions. He wants to carry on as before, but we can't carry on like we did before. Everything is different. And even if it wasn't, I don't want to carry on. That's why I was leaving. There was too much—"

"Wait, Preston left documentation saying this would happen again?" Detective Cameron interrupts.

It takes me a moment for me to realize that he's talking about Brother Richmond when he says 'Preston' and a further moment to realize maybe I've said too much.

"I mean..." The warmth of the house, the low light, the food, my exhaustion, it's all coalescing in my stomach and I can no longer think straight.

"Alice, if there's a video, then that's important evidence. We can get a warrant for something like that."

"The video was all messed up. We didn't even get to see it."

"We've got tools that can pull data from a damaged tape."

"I don't think..." But that's it. There aren't any more words. My brain has spun out all its resources.

"Stop interrogating this poor girl, Brad. Can't you see she's exhausted?" I didn't hear the door open, but Lorraine is now by my side, a small plastic bag from the pharmacy dangling from her arm.

"You're right. I'm sorry, Alice." Detective Cameron looks

chastened. "I can get a little carried away sometimes. Honestly, there's been very little to work with on this case, but I shouldn't have overwhelmed you with it all when you're a guest in our house."

I feel a nudge at my knee and a giant golden retriever pushes her nose against my leg.

"Gracie!" Lorraine says to the dog. "She's been outside in the garage because she can't always be trusted during dinner. Can you, Gracie? Hope it's ok I let her back in. Go on, girl. Leave Alice alone."

"It's ok. She's fine. Really." The dog presses her sympathetic face right up against my stomach now. "You're a good dog, aren't you, Gracie?" I stroke her head again and she looks up at me with eyes that seem to say yes, she is a good dog, and thank God someone finally noticed.

-14-

TERESA

The first night on the Farm, we ate dinner in the meeting house because the pavilion wasn't built yet. Rich welcomed everyone as the sun set. There weren't even enough tables for everyone, but no one cared. People spilled onto the floor and pushed their backs up against the windows. I loved that building. Its ceiling went up forever, pine beams stretching up to the clouds and windows opening down the whole back wall to let in the sun. Through those big windows, I could see the stars starting to make splotches of light in the darkening sky.

"Welcome, friends," Rich said. "This is a time to enjoy the fruits of our labor and be thankful to our God! Amen?" A flutter of giddy amens went up around the room. The air was thick with celebration and the bated breath of the hundred or so of us who couldn't believe we were here, that this was our home now, that Rich had once again pulled a rabbit out of a hat and found us another sanctuary from the world.

After dinner we sat around a bonfire until late in the night talking about all our big plans. The warmth of the flames lulled Alice to sleep on my lap. Heat radiated from her tiny body, but the cool of the night was at my back, and I leaned against Tom and felt content and full. Everyone was there, even those who were staying on at the old Victorian until the closing, which was still a few weeks away. Several members gave speeches. Even Angelica, in her grumpy way, described how we'd come so far by sticking together, by trusting the Lord, and by giving to others when we could have kept for ourselves.

That last note prompted a tiny stirring in the back of my mind. I wondered how exactly we'd afforded all this if we were in the business of giving things away. Anthony had walked us through a presentation on how we'd invested some proceeds from the sale of the old Victorian and how Rich had generously donated funds from his radio show to the purchase of the land. Still, as I watched the flames climb and tumble over each other in a constant cycle of reinvention, a pinprick of doubt lodged in my mind like a grain of sand I couldn't quite rub out of my eye.

But then Rich got up to speak. The firelight stretched his smile wide. Flames pulsed in his eyes. I don't remember exactly what he said that night, but I remember feeling calmed by it. I watched him talk next to the blaze of the bonfire and thought he was much like the fire himself. A little dangerous at times, but he was our center. And when we all gathered around him, he was good and constant and warm. And he'd brought us all here. He'd led the way and made a space for all of us when we were rejected in so many other ways and places.

*****

It was that first night on the Farm that Tom and I started trying for another baby. Tom was promoted at the garage. We had all the space we could want on the Farm. We felt secure. I couldn't wait to see Alice dote over a baby brother or sister.

When I wasn't pregnant by the time Alice started school that fall, Tom said not to worry, it would happen in time. I tried to keep my hopes up, but it was hard. Heather, one of the midwives on the

Farm, told me to just be patient. I was young and healthy. It would happen.

I couldn't be patient. I couldn't sleep, I lost my appetite, and I was prone to bursting into tears at the drop of a hat. Every time I saw a pregnant woman out shopping or someone announced they were expecting, I had to fight back a wave of misery and nausea. I plastered a smile on my face and hoped they didn't see through the cracking facade. Even Alice knew I was feeling blue about not having another baby. One night, after I'd been crying over someone else's pregnancy announcement, she came into the living room and sat next to me.

"Mommy, I don't need a brother or sister. I have Edwin. Plus, I don't want to share my room."

I laughed through my tears and pulled her close to me. I inhaled her little girl scent of soap and outside air and crayons and something sticky sweet that told me she had probably been sneaking cookies from the kitchen. I told her I loved her very much, but I still felt grief each month knowing I couldn't give her a sibling. I thought a lot about my brother in those days. I wanted to call him, but I didn't know what to say. He was busy in California. We'd written a few times after he left. I'd told him about the move to the Farm, and he described the new life he was building for himself. We called each other every once in a while, but we were living in different worlds and rapidly losing enough common ground to justify all those long distance minutes.

*****

A year later, we had a farm stand up and running every week for the Saturday farmer's market. We were gaining a reputation and people were coming from other counties for our pies and bread. My specialty was a rhubarb pie with a crumble topping, made with rhubarb grown right on the Farm. I was even taking a few midweek orders from some families and a couple shops in town. All money from the farm stand went back into the Farm. I was, however, allowed to keep some of the money from these side ventures, as long as Rich approved of them. Pin money, he called it. An old fashioned joke, but I think he really did see things that way. He, the benevolent father, and me the faithful daughter who he indulged when he could.

All was going well, but still I held space for another baby. One night, after another false alarm, I cried on Tom's shoulder and asked him if he was as upset as I was with our inability to get pregnant.

"I would love another baby, but I'm also very content with you and Alice. We've got the Collective, we're both busy with work. I think our lives are really full, and that makes me happy. But I can see that you're not."

"Great observation," I said, and then felt guilty for the childish remark.

"You don't have to take out your frustrations on me, Teresa. We're supposed to be on the same team here."

"I know," I said, without further comment. I felt bad for lashing out at him, but I was also irritated that I was carrying the weight of longing alone.

"Maybe we should go talk to Richmond about it," Tom said. "Maybe he could give us some counsel on how to get through this dark cloud." I resented being referred to as a dark cloud and told him so. He protested that he wasn't referring to me, which only made me more upset. We went to bed angry but got up early the next morning and went to Rich. He told us that his heart was with us and to come back in a week so he would have time to pray about it. When we went back the next week, we met in his newly finished office at the back of the farmhouse.

"Tom and Teresa. You two have been loyal to God and to the

mission of this Collective. I couldn't ask for better friends in this journey called life. I can see that you are both hurting. And that makes my heart hurt. I love you guys. I want you to know that I fasted and spent thirty hours in prayer this week over your situation. God spoke to me in those hours with a message for you."

I'd seen Rich do impossible things, make impossible predictions, so if he said God gave him a message, then I believed him. Tom put his hand on my knee and gave it a little squeeze. We both waited.

"God showed me your family. The two of you and Alice. And the sun was shining on you, and you were happy and healthy, and Alice was growing into a strong young lady with a heart for the work of the Collective. In that vision, God told me your family is complete and perfect as is, and that you should not worry about trying to expand it. I know this may not be what you want to hear, but God works all things together for good, including this."

I should have been crushed. I should have broken down right then, but I didn't. Rich's eyes welled up with tears. He leaned in close toward us, put his hands on our hands and told us again about the light he saw around Alice, how beautiful it was. How pure. The sting of knowing I wouldn't have another baby was still there, but Rich's words softened it. I thought Rich's vision was grace, love, and a way to move forward. I didn't yet know that he would use those intimate and comforting tones and our private grief to play God in the families of others in the Collective. That he would use my own tears and thanks as proof that his visions were gospel truth. I didn't know it was all beginning to crumble around us.

-15-

ALICE

I remember stroking Gracie's fur until it was warm silk beneath my hand. I remember Detective Cameron offering me another slice of cake and Lorraine bustling around cleaning things up. I remember the light growing dimmer as lamps clicked off, and Detective Cameron and Lorraine talking behind me. I remember sinking into pillows, soft and close around my face. And then I am awake in a four poster bed and sunshine is seeping in at the edges of my eyes. I sit up and try to piece together the evening. I must have fallen asleep. It's strange. I haven't spent a night away from the Farm in all my adult life. I get up and make my way to the kitchen.

"Good morning. Brad's gone on into the office, but I'll drive you home when you're ready. After you've had some breakfast, of course."

"I didn't mean to fall asleep," I say, as Lorraine hands me a glass of orange juice.

"Oh hush, dear. You couldn't help it any more than a bird can help flying. That baby needed sleep and so did you. You weren't in any state to go home. What's the point of having a guest room if you don't get a guest every now and again?"

I let Lorraine drive me back to the Farm, but ask her to stop at the back gate, so I can walk the rest of the way. The sky is an indecent shade of blue and the sun is brilliant yellow white, but the air has already turned cold and the leaves on the trees betray the coming season. Smatters of red, orange and brown tinge their edges. I can tell it won't be long before snow is on the ground, and even sooner the second Homegoing will arrive. I shiver as Lorraine navigates the car right up to the path.

"I really wish you'd let me drive you all the way to your door, dear. I hate you traipsing off without anyone to watch after you. And with all those reporters constantly camping out at your front gate. Brad said he was going to send someone over to make sure they kept their distance, but I still worry."

"I've taken this path a million times, Lorraine. And I haven't seen anyone inside the gates who wasn't supposed to be there. I know the Farm like the back of my hand. Last night was actually the first night I remember ever being away. I was only five when we moved out here."

"You never went on any trips away with your family or anything?"

"No. There was a time we were supposed to go on a mission. People did that occasionally, went off to try and start another branch of the Collective or to raise money or to recruit new members. We were supposed to be gone for three weeks, but the night we were supposed to leave, the mission was canceled."

"Why?"

"I never found out. My mom said something ridiculous like it was bad weather, but I never knew why we didn't leave the next day. I wish I could ask her now."

I wanted so badly to be away from Brother Richmond and his lessons as we packed for that trip, but I was terrified to be away from our home. Three weeks felt like an eternity. I'd filled about half my bag, and my parents were speaking intently in the kitchen.

Then I heard it. The *plink, plink, plink* of pebbles hitting my window. I was supposed to meet Edwin. I rushed over to the window, keeping one eye on my door. I opened the window, and the smell of damp leaves filled the room. The trees were wet and glossy, and a halo of mist shown around the porch lights of the other houses in the Village. Edwin was standing a few feet from my window, pebbles still in his hand.

"Where were you? I was worried." He glanced behind me at the suitcase on my bed. "Why are you packing? You're not thinking of running away, are you? We've been over this. You'd get caught before you even got off the Farm."

"We're going on mission for Brother Richmond. Three weeks. Super-Secret. My parents just told me about it tonight. I couldn't get to the pond. Sorry."

"You'll miss the Harvest Festival." His voice was too loud.

"Shhh. I'm not supposed to be talking to you. To anyone. Like I said, it's a secret."

"Why would a mission be a secret?" he said.

"Who knows the ways of the father?" I grinned and Edwin did the same. It was a serious mantra we'd recited a hundred times as kids, but somewhere along the way, we'd adopted it as our own private motto. I heard my parents' voices getting closer. "I've got to go. Tell me everything that happens at the Harvest Festival, ok?" I reached through the window and pulled Edwin in for a hug. The pebbles fell from his hand and clattered against the siding of the house as he hugged me back. I'd yanked the curtains closed just as my mom came in to check on me.

"Sometimes," Lorraine says, bringing me back to the present, "our parents' actions don't ever make sense, even when we can ask them." She squeezes my hand, and my throat aches.

"You promise me you'll come for dinner on Saturday? We're

having hamburgers and baked beans. That baby needs the iron. I'll be here at six to pick you up. I won't take no for an answer. Ok?"

"I can bring a pie."

"Oh, you don't have to bring anything," Lorraine pauses, "but I'm sure Brad won't say no to pie."

I climb out of the car and the air bites into the space between my sweater and my neck. I close the door and pull open the rusted fence. Lorraine waits until I'm inside the fence before she pulls away.

When I get back to the Village, Bekah and Tabitha are waiting on my porch.

"Thank God you're alive," Bekah shouts as soon as I get to the front steps.

"I'm fine. I was at a friend's house."

"A friend?" Tabitha looks at me quizzically.

"Alice, we thought you'd, you know, disappeared. Edwin came by to check on you. He looked really concerned." Bekah looks like she hasn't slept much.

I pull my sweater tighter around me and wish things could be easier with Edwin, like they were when we were kids. The warmth and ease of Lorraine's kitchen feels like a distant memory already.

*****

Avoiding Edwin turns out to be easier than I expected. My growing stomach makes it feel like an effort just to walk across the house, much less the Farm. Nevertheless, I keep true to my word and get up Saturday morning to start a pie to take to the Camerons' for dinner. It feels almost rebellious and even wrong to be baking a pie and going to a friend's house for dinner when there's so much unknown looming before me. But they were good to me, and I want to bring them something sweet and tangible to express my thanks. I make the pie crust and stick it in the fridge to chill. I realize I don't have any rhubarb in the house, so I waddle down to Bekah's room to ask if she minds running to the storeroom to bring me some. There's a note on her door that says she's gone to the library to read. I'll have to get the rhubarb myself. As I round the corner to the storeroom, Edwin steps into my path, blocking the door.

"What, have you taken to rationing the supplies now?"

"It seems to be the only way I can talk to you these days, Alice."

"I don't have many words for you right now."

"I know I kind of blindsided you on Wednesday—"

"That's putting it mildly," I interrupt.

"I just thought if you were back in the pavilion with everyone, and with the music, and you could feel how things used to be, then maybe you would—"

"Oh, yeah. Nice touch with the music. It wasn't enough that you had to call me out in front of everyone and make them think I'm going to do something impossible, but you had to throw in my mom's favorite song to seal the deal. Do you get how manipulative that is, Edwin?"

"You must have felt something, or you wouldn't have stormed out. Bekah said you went to a friend's house? In town? You've got worldly friends now?" I answer his questions with one of my own.

"Bekah told you? She's vulnerable right now, Edwin. She was really upset when Sarah left. Don't go putting ideas in her head."

"I'm just trying to be a good shepherd. I didn't ask for this role."

"Oh, please. You just loved jumping up in front of everyone and taking charge as soon as Brother Richmond was gone. I could see it on your face."

"You don't know what you're talking about, Alice." He takes a step forward as he says this, and I see more of Brother Richmond in him this time.

"You sure like to say that a lot, Edwin. And I'll admit it's true. I don't know what I'm talking about most of the time, but what makes you think you do?"

"I know what Brother Richmond wanted. He told us plain as day. You and I are supposed to lead the second Homegoing. Together. We don't have much time left, so one way or another, I'm going to make it happen."

"Good luck with that," I say, and push past him into the storeroom.

*****

Lorraine is waiting for me right at six at the back gate. I carry the pie in one hand and use the other to hold my dress out of the muck on the ground. The fall rain is here, and everything is cold and soggy. I climb into the car and set the pie on my lap. It's still warm, and it feels like comfort on my legs.

After dinner, we settle in the cushy chairs in the living room with tea and slices of pie. Detective Cameron has been called into work, so it's just the two of us. It's nice.

"This pie!" Lorraine closes her eyes and tilts her head back toward the ceiling. "It's heavenly."

"I'm glad you like it," I say and sip my tea.

"You ok, dear?" Lorraine asks.

"Sure, why?"

"Well, you're quieter than you were on Wednesday and then you were half-starved and suffering exhaustion."

"Oh, it's nothing." Lorraine gives me a look that says I better try again with that excuse. "It's just," I bite my lip. Lorraine is solace and warmth and every good thing I've been missing since my parents left, but I don't really know how much I can trust her. We've only just met.

"Edwin just seems to be getting more agitated about things on the Farm and it has me a bit worried."

"Agitated?"

"I don't know. It's hard to explain. He's going on about this second Homegoing and what Brother Richmond wanted. I don't know."

"What does he say Brother Richmond wanted?"

"He said he wanted me and Edwin to lead the Collective, but I'm not interested. Not that Brother Richmond ever concerned himself with what I or any other girl wanted." Lorraine makes a murmur of concern and sets her pie down on the side table, and I realize I've done that thing again where I speak out loud without working through the consequences of what I've said.

"What do you mean he was never concerned with what you wanted?" The question she wants to ask is obvious, it's just hanging there, unspoken, between us.

I, too, set my pie down. I remember how heavy the door to Brother Richmond's office felt when I pushed it open. I remember how the carpet was thick and squishy under my feet, so different from the threadbare rugs in our house or any other. The Farm was, at least from the outside, bright, airy, of the earth, sunshine and light. But Brother Richmond's office was wood paneled and dark. There were no windows. I pick up my tea cup and take another sip to steel my nerves. Then I plunge forward before I can change my mind.

"He met with girls on the farm a lot." I tap my fingernails against the ceramic mug. "Including me. The first night, he asked me to come in and lock the door. I can still hear the clicking sound as the metal bar slid into place. He told me the Lord had much to teach me and so had he. Others had it worse. I know that."

Lorraine raises her eyebrows. "It wasn't so bad for me. He

made me sit in front of him on the floor while he sat behind me in an armchair. At first, he just recorded me reading all these science fiction novels. He said my voice soothed him. We weren't allowed to read novels, but he had a whole collection in the bottom drawers of his desk. Then one night after I finished a recording session, he pushed himself right up against my back, and he started rubbing my shoulders and arms and down over my chest. Eventually, he had me take off my shirt and bra and he rubbed oil all over me from my head down over my arms and chest and stomach while he moaned some words I couldn't understand. Then he had me do the same to him. He said it was anointing. He said it was cleansing. That was it. It never went further. Like I said, I know others had it worse. It was probably my fault anyway. If I hadn't always been getting into trouble, then he never would have called me into his office in the first place."

I shake my head, trying to get rid of the smell of the massage oil, the rhythmic click of the recorder, and the heat of Brother Richmond's hands in my hair. I try to shake it all away.

My tea cup is rattling against the saucer in my hand, so I set it down and lean as far forward as my belly will let me. Dark marks appear on my dress as the tears fall. Lorraine puts her hand, feather light, on my shoulder. Her voice is soft but stern. I imagine it's the voice she used when she was helping deliver babies. Gentle, but authoritative enough to make you pay attention.

"Alice. I want you to know that what happened to you was not nothing. Do you understand that? I don't know what happened to those other girls. But what happened to you was wrong. That man touched you in ways that were not ok. He made you do things that were not ok. It was wrong. All of it. And none of it, and I mean none of it, is your fault. Look up here, dear." She lifted her hand and pointed with two fingers to her eyes. "You look right here in my eyes." I obeyed. "None of this was your fault. None of it."

I lean into her and cry. Lorraine wraps her arm around me and lets me cry for as long as I want. When I've calmed down, she asks, "Did you ever tell anyone what happened to you?"

"Jason. And I think my mom knew, at least some of it. She saw me coming out of Brother Richmond's office once. Judging by the way she reacted, she thought it was the first time. I could tell she knew that bad things went on in there. Everyone did. She tried to get me to talk, but I was afraid she would smell the massage oil or feel it on my skin still and I felt so ashamed. That was actually the last time I was in his office. I don't know what happened, but he didn't call me again."

-16-

TERESA

The first time we were called for a 'family meeting,' I had no idea what it was about. Alice and I met Tom on the walk to Rich's office. People were starting to call him Brother Richmond by then, but I never did. He'd been Rich when we met him, and I didn't see why I should call him anything else. Tom and I hadn't seen each other in almost two days between his work schedule and mine. I asked if he knew what was going on.

"Haven't a clue. I was just with Richmond this morning, and he didn't say anything."

Alice walked between us. Twelve and already beginning the surliness of the teenage years. She didn't say anything.

We made it to Rich's office huffing and puffing. It was set up on a little hill, the rest of the Village sloping down, like a fiefdom. The view was spectacular. As I caught my breath, I counted my blessings that we called this place home, despite its challenges and Rich's occasional erratic behavior. I reminded myself that he had been there for us when no one else was. My heart still beat like a hummingbird's.

The door was already cracked, and it fell open at my touch. The orange sunset spilled into the room, illuminating Rich's desk. He was leaning against it, dressed all in black. That was unusual. In those days, he favored brightly colored sweatshirts.

"What's going on? Is this a funeral?" Tom tried to lighten the mood, but I could see from the mournful expression on Richmond's face that it wasn't going to do much to lift the gloom.

"Teresa, Tom, Alice. Please, come in. Have a seat." He gestured to three metal chairs arranged in a semicircle around his plush red wingback. Its imposing height and dark upholstery made me feel like a child waiting outside the principal's office as I settled into the small folding chair. Alice sat next to me and Tom on the other side of her. Three ducks in a row.

"Tom, Teresa, I consider you two of my closest friends, so it pains me to bring this to your attention."

He pulled a book from behind his back. He held it out in two fingers, like it would bite him. It was a library book. A well-worn edition of *Jane Eyre*.

"*Jane Eyre?*" I looked at Tom for clarification, but he looked as puzzled as me. Alice fidgeted with the zipper on her sweatshirt next to me, and I was once again aware that my daughter was approaching adulthood faster than I could keep up.

"Have you read this book?" Accusation dripped from Rich's every word.

"Of course I've read it. I think everyone had to read it in school, right?" I looked at Tom, who nodded.

"Is that where you were forced to read it, Alice? In that dung heap the town likes to call a school?" Rich had changed his tone. Now it was sympathetic, like he was an understanding uncle. Alice continued to look at the floor without saying anything. I was still confused.

"I'm sorry. Forced to read it? What's going on, Alice?"

She spoke for the first time. "They didn't force me to read it at school. I got it from the library because I wanted to read it."

Now that she'd decided to speak, she stopped fidgeting with her sweater. She looked Rich square in the eyes. She was forceful and determined. I had prayed countless times for Alice to be able to stand on her own two feet in this world, for her to not fall prey to charlatans or let anyone push her around. And here was the answer to my prayer. I sensed the storm brewing, but I was also proud of my daughter for being so direct. Richmond made a 'tut-tut' noise and turned back toward me.

"This book highlights everything we stand against in this family. Focus on the individual, wildly improper use of Scripture, infidelity, lack of obedience and respect, need I go on?"

I was bewildered but had a flashback of his reaction to *The Little Engine That Could*. I'd gotten a copy to read to Alice and Edwin and Rich had seen it and ranted about how selfish the children in the story were, how terrible they were for breaking down the little engine in their greed for toys. I remembered the hurt look in Alice's eyes when I told her we couldn't read the book anymore. It all felt so long ago and like it had happened yesterday. I racked my brain now and tried to recall what my ninth grade English teacher had said about the themes in *Jane Eyre*.

"Rich, be reasonable. I think the book deals with all of those things to help us understand them. Besides, it's just a story. It's not real."

"Teresa, are you so small-minded as to not realize that stories impact us? They shape our reality whether we want them to or not. This book is dangerous, and I'm shocked you would allow your child to read it. Perhaps Alice would do well to spend a few weeks with another family, one who can instill a better set of values in her."

Alice grabbed my arm. "I don't want to go anywhere else. I want to stay at home with Mom and Dad."

"Richmond, there's an easy fix here. We'll return it to the library. Alice will not check it out again. Not a big deal. There's no need to go threatening things."

I was grateful for Tom's calm demeanor at that moment. I was ready to fly off the handle, shout at Rich about all Tom and I had done for him, but I knew that wouldn't end well, and Tom knew me well enough to step in before I made a mistake I couldn't take back. Rich stood up.

"See that it is returned today. And, Alice? I don't want to see you with a book like that again."

"Yes, Brother Richmond." Alice said the words, but I could still see the defiance in her eyes. It worried me.

*****

"Folks, we're going to build ourselves a library!"

Richmond made the announcement to cheers. The library would house a multitude of books, he said. Those he'd written, those containing the household codes for Collective members, and stimulating and interesting works for all Collective members, he said. We could, he announced in that almost whisper voice he used when he wanted to to really make a point, write books and submit them to the library panel for publication. If chosen, those books would be bound and housed in the library for anyone to check out. He touted it as a gift to the community. He would personally provide the funds for the books, and he would be taking sign ups for those who wished to help with the building project or those who had book ideas.

Alice threw herself into the preparations for the library. She and Edwin both signed up for the building team, and every day after school they worked at the site until Evening Table. They carried buckets of nails, moved wood, helped clear up, and anything else the library crew told them to do. They showed up to Evening

Table flushed with hard work. Pink cheeks and big smiles. One night after dinner, they begged Jennifer and me to come see their progress. We walked a few yards behind them toward the half-finished building.

"I think Alice and Edwin are going to be disappointed when the building crew doesn't put their names on this library when it's finished," I joked.

"I'm glad the kids are having fun with it, but I'm not so sure about this library," Jennifer said. "Once it's finished, Richmond will say we don't have a reason to go to the library in town. I'm worried he'll want to build a school out here next."

"Well, maybe that wouldn't be so bad. You and Anthony could lead it."

Jennifer rolled her eyes and dropped her voice. "Even if Richmond let us lead a school, we'd only be allowed to teach what he wanted us to teach. He's getting more paranoid by the day. He thinks the whole world is out to get us. When is the last time we hosted a community dinner here? It's worrying. Anthony and I have been thinking—" She broke off suddenly, as if she only realized at the last minute what she had been about to say. But she didn't need to say the rest. I knew they were thinking about leaving. I could see it on her face. I changed the subject. It was too depressing to think about Jennifer leaving.

In the end, the library was a squat and unattractive one story building, only about as large as two tool sheds put together. The concrete walls made it stand out from the clapboard siding of the rest of the Village. Still, Alice and Edwin marveled at it. And Rich made sure to point out their contributions at the opening ceremony for the building.

"Alice and Edwin have gone above and beyond. They've been on the build site every day since construction began. While the world's young people are obsessed with fulfilling selfish desires, our young people are here, helping to build something that will outlast them. Helping to build something for God and for this community. Let's give them a hand." Everyone clapped and cheered. Tom gave Alice a little fist bump as she went up on the stage and she looked happy. Really happy. I thought the tough times were behind us.

*****

"Ok, last time we were surprised going into this. Any idea what's going on today?"

Tom shook his head. Alice looked over at the door. She was fourteen. We'd been called in for another family meeting, and I was determined that we wouldn't be blindsided in this one.

"Alice? Do you know something about why we're here?"

Alice reached into her bag and brought out two *Nancy Drew* books.

Just a week before, Rich had sent Marian's son, Eric, to live with Angelica for two months because of some undisclosed sin. I shuddered at the thought of Alice spending two months with Angelica, but I didn't really think Rich would take her away. We'd been with him almost since the beginning. We were loyal and true and never missed a meeting. Still, he'd threatened to do it last time, and that was before the library. Before he'd brought Alice up on stage and touted her as a model young person. Since the library had opened, Rich had, without actually saying it, forbidden any reading material he didn't approve of. I was certain that *Nancy Drew* was not on his list.

He wasn't in the office when we arrived. Frank Smith ushered us into the metal chairs. Frank never spoke much or smiled, but whatever Rich wanted done, he did. He'd taken over that role from Anthony after he and Jennifer's disagreements with Rich started churning up the Collective rumor mill. When Frank started appearing with Rich to collect the monthly sum everyone was required to pay the Collective and stood next to Rich during his devotions, there was no announcement, no speech. Just a bereft Anthony sitting at a table in the back with Jennifer and Edwin. I tried to talk to Jennifer about it after that first night that Frank sat up on the stage with Rich, but she just shook her head at me and walked away.

Frank went out of the adjoining door that connected to the rest of the house. We sat there for over an hour. Rich wielded time like a weapon. The longer he could make you wait, the better. He came in all in a rush. He wasn't wearing black this time, but a cheerful shade of yellow with dark green jeans. He looked like a manic sunflower.

"I trust you all know why you're here this time?"

"Richmond, Alice is just a kid. Kids make mistakes," Tom said.

Rich continued what was obviously a prepared speech. "So, you know why you're here. Alice refused to take the grace offered her after her last indiscretion."

"Richmond—" Tom tried to cut in.

"No, Tom. The time for you to talk is over. It's clear that you're not letting God lead in your parenting, so we need to make a change for a time. Alice will go to stay with Frank and his family for one month. You will not be allowed communication with her during this time, but trust that all her basic needs will be met." He turned and spoke directly to Alice. "Alice, I hope this will be a learning opportunity for you. Otherwise, we may have to resort to more drastic measures. Someone will be around to your house to collect you tonight before Evening Table. Pack only the most basic necessities. Remember, God works all things together for good. Even this."

The business-like tone of his voice made my head spin. Separation happened to other people. Not to us. As we left his office, I clutched Alice's hands. Tears left track marks down both our cheeks. When we got home, Alice went into her room to pack a bag and I paced the living room.

"Tom, maybe we should..." He knew where I was going with the thought.

"Where would we go, Teresa? The house isn't ours, the cars all belong to the Farm. Your work is here. Since The Collective bought the garage, I can't even count on my job. Granny's not even around to take us in this time. We've given everything we've got to this place."

'I know all that, Tom," I snapped. "But we're just supposed to let him take our daughter away from us because she wanted to read a stupid book? Jennifer said—"

"I don't care what Jennifer said." Tom rarely shouted, but when he did, it stopped me cold, whatever I was doing. In that way, I was almost grateful when he raised his voice. It gave me a chance to regain my composure and refocus my thoughts. "I hate it. I hate it so much. But she's not going to be far. She's just going to be on the other side of the Farm. I know that Frank can be a little intimidating, but Susan is sweet, and you know she'll take good care of Alice. It's just a month. We'll get through it. And when it's over, it's over. We can move on and put this behind us. She'll be home. I don't think we need to be reckless about this. Emotions are high. Let's take a minute to think."

"And what if she wants to read a book again, Tom? What then? What are the 'more drastic' measures Rich mentioned?"

"I don't know, Teresa. I only know what we know now. That Alice broke the rule. Yes, it's a stupid rule," he raised his voice as if he could predict I was about to interrupt, "but it's still a rule.

Like it or not, we've submitted ourselves to Richmond's authority. I think he still has the best intentions at heart, but he's gotten off the path a bit. He'll come back. He always does."

Memory of our return to the Collective after Rich threw us out all those years ago hung in the air between us. I went into the kitchen and started scrubbing dishes to avoid thinking about what could have been if we'd made a different choice that night.

When Alice came back to the kitchen with her bag, I hugged her and told her that we would get through it. That God really did work all things together for good. Then I went into my bedroom and unlatched the box under my bed. I took out all my emergency chocolate and brought it to Alice. "Wrap these up in your underwear and put them in the bottom of your bag. When you're missing home or you need us, have one of these to get you through and know that we are thinking of you and praying for you and wanting you home every minute."

Alice's eyes were swimming in tears, and I hugged her tightly. I wanted to tell her I was sorry. I wanted to tell her that things would get better, but I wasn't so sure anymore.

That night at Evening Table, I felt Alice's absence at our table. Those on Separation had to sit outside the pavilion the first night, so everyone would know that they had done something to merit punishment. On subsequent nights, they sat with the family they were assigned, but were forbidden from speaking to anyone.

Jennifer, Anthony, and Edwin sat across from us. They didn't say anything, but Jennifer locked eyes with me as she passed a dish across the table. Edwin handed me the larger of the two rolls left on the plate between us. I thanked him and took it, even though I couldn't eat anything. Everyone knew expressing too much sympathy for me or Alice or Tom could get them on Separation themselves.

Rich twisted the knife during his evening announcements. "Let's give a round of applause for these parents, Tom and Teresa. Taking the hard but righteous road of parenting to bring their daughter back into the fold. They are doing God's work, folks."

I pushed my plate away and went outside.

*****

Rich first started looking at Alice in *that way* just after she finished her Separation. He called her up to recite Scriptures the night she was released to us, and I saw the way the focus in his eyes changed. My stomach lurched. I knew from Jennifer that he'd already been asking Lacey's daughter to visit his office a few times a week after Evening Table. Lacey said it was for enrichment lessons, so she could take on a bigger role within the Collective now that she was in high school, but it didn't sound convincing, not after what happened with the waitress.

Just before we moved to the Farm, Rich was spotted leaving a hotel with a waitress from the diner in town. She was seventeen. Rich said he thought she was eighteen and thought that he'd found a new recruit for the Collective. He said it was all a big misunderstanding. Said nothing happened but prayers and discipleship. The girl's parents threatened to press charges, but then it all went away. Jennifer told me Anthony arranged a meeting with the girl's family and paid them a suitcase of money. She said, at the time, that it was for the best. That we needed to keep any negative light off the group. I wondered if she would say the same thing now that Frank had taken Anthony's spot as Rich's right hand man.

Rich hadn't had any issues since the waitress, but every so often, a younger girl in the Collective started receiving the extra 'lessons' that Lacey's daughter was getting. They usually led to some kind of higher position within the Collective when the girl graduated. I tried to tell myself that these lessons were actually lessons, that the girls were almost all of age. I tried to tell myself so many things that I'm ashamed of now. Tom was ready to pack a bag and carry Alice out on foot, if need be, when I shared my concerns with him.

"You said we couldn't leave before. What changes things now?"

"Everything has changed, Teresa. Why aren't you already packed?"

"Nothing's happened. It's just a feeling I have. We shouldn't act on emotions. You said that, remember?"

Tom seemed to contemplate for a bit and then said, "We can figure it out. We could go to California. See your brother."

"Tom, Michael and I have barely said ten words to each other the last couple of years. Plus, how would we even get out there?"

"Well, what do you suggest?"

"Let me talk to Rich. That man we met in the laundry room is still in there somewhere. You said so yourself. This is our home. We helped build this place. I'm not willing to abandon it without a fight anymore. I'm sick of being scared. The only way we'll make things good again is by changing things from within."

I went to see Rich after Evening Table. The wood paneling and the rug in his office were roughly the same color and made it hard to see where the floor began and the wall started. I wondered why he didn't have any windows in this room.

"Teresa! What can I do for you?"

"I want to talk to you about Alice."

"She's doing well. No more issues since her last Separation, right? She and Edwin did that lovely little musical number at the Easter festival last month. I think everyone really enjoyed it."

Facing him, all my suspicions shrank within me. But I couldn't leave without some kind of reassurance. "I noticed you seemed to be taking an extra interest in Alice lately, and I wanted to..." The words died on my tongue. I needed to be strong for Alice, but I couldn't find the right way to approach it.

"Yes, Teresa?"

"I just don't want anything to happen to Alice. I don't want her to get any extra lessons. We can manage those at home, I think. I don't want you to, I don't want her to be..."

Under his concerned gaze in that darkened office, my words faltered. I stepped back and collected my thoughts. This was my daughter and she had no one to protect her but me.

"You once told Tom and I that you always wanted us to be honest with you. To tell you the hard truths that others may try to smooth over in the name of pleasing you, right?"

"Of course. That's what I value most about you and Tom. You've always been my honesty barometer. I know if you bring something to my attention that it needs my focus as soon as possible."

I relaxed a little at those words. I knew he was in there, that man that we decided to follow. "Ok, then. I don't think it sets a good precedent for you to be alone with young girls in your office. We're always trying to teach our girls modesty and purity and even the appearance of something untoward can affect your authority and credibility, so I think these extra lessons should take place in an open group setting. And I don't want Alice to participate." The words came out in one long breath, and I felt dizzy when I finished speaking.

"I hear your words, Teresa. And I can see that they come from your soul. I can tell you've carried them a ways. They're weighty, like stones on your back, and they've been dragging you down."

I nodded.

"You have my word. I will not let any harm come to Alice or her reputation. I will make sure that things are above board with all the young girls in this family. I want only the best for them, for you, for all."

"Thank you, Rich. Thank you." My voice cracked and Rich handed me a handkerchief on my way out. I went home to Tom overwhelmed with emotion at the confrontation and so happy that we could still call this place home. I was convinced that Rich truly was the leader we believed him to be. I had brought him a concern and he listened and vowed to make a change. Things were going to be ok.

-17-

ALICE

It's been a week since my dinner at the Camerons' house, and I'm feeling better and worse at the same time. Dinner with Lorraine was a balm, but Detective Cameron and several agents searched the Farm and still haven't found the video tape. Everyone is on edge after the search. I go in for questioning again. Detective Cameron is there, but an FBI agent is the one doing the interview this time. She's got red hair and a long, angular face. *Yes, I saw the physical tape come out of the VCR mangled. No, I didn't see what was on it. No, I don't know what happened to it after we all watched it that first day. No, I haven't been in Brother Richmond's house since.* Over and over with the same questions. Her exasperation and exhaustion reveal themselves in the fine red lines that spiral out from her irises and the way she keeps licking her already chapped lips. I know Edwin must have done something with the video after he told us about it, but I can't figure out what, and I've got a pain in my back that I can't seem to shake, so I leave without offering anything helpful.

I remember my mom once telling an expectant mother that walking helps with the back pain, so I go out to wander the Farm. I try to bring Bekah along. I've been working to keep more of an eye on her lately, but she's left another message taped to the door about going to the library. I make a mental note to stop by there on my way home. My feet carry me, without consultation from the rest of me, to my parents' house. I haven't gone inside since they've been gone. I go around to the back door and see the notch in the door frame where my dad measured my height when I was nine years old. I remember the disappointment I felt when I stepped away and saw the notch.

"I'm only that tall?"

"Don't worry," my dad laughed. "You're going to keep growing. We'll come out here and measure you each year and then when you're a grown up lady, you can come home and see how small you once were."

We never did come back out here to measure again. Time got away from us, I guess. But here I am. A grown up lady. Only I don't feel grown up. I feel like that same little girl, small and unsure of myself. I want my dad to tell me not to worry and to show me how much I've grown. I run my fingers over the notch in the wood, and flinch. I bring my hand back to my mouth and taste the new penny bite of blood. There's a splinter sticking out above the skin of my ring finger. I reach toward the door handle before I know I'm doing it. It's unlocked.

The house still smells of lavender and pine wood soap, but I can see that things have been moved around. The drawers are all pulled out of the buffet table in the dining room. Cushions are lopsided on the couch. I'd made sure to be at the Camerons' house when the police searched the Farm to look for the video, but they'd been careful in my house. Everything was put back as I'd left it. It seems they weren't so delicate with the other houses. The clock my dad gave my mom for one of their anniversaries is tipped over on its side, the glass cracked across the face. I breathe in and out. My breath pushes a puff cloud of dust into the beam of sunlight shining through the back door. I'm angry, but I'm not sure where to direct that anger. They destroyed my parents' things, but it was me who sent them here.

The sting in my finger reminds me of why I've come in, and I make my way to the bathroom where I know my mom keeps tweezers. I open the medicine cabinet. It all looks so tidy compared to the rest of the house. No tweezers, but my parents' toothbrushes rest on the bottom shelf. Green for dad and pale purple for mom. Always the same colors. I poke at one of them with the tip of my finger and recoil as if I've touched a dead animal. It feels too intimate, too invasive. These are my parents' things. Maybe they'll be back for them, and they should find at least one room in their home in order. The splinter pulses under my skin, and a tiny drop of blood drips into the bathroom sink. I try to pull out the splinter with my teeth, but I only wedge it deeper. I know there are tweezers here somewhere.

I look in the basket on the back of the toilet. There's *The Collective Code* and a notebook with a few hastily scrawled prayers. I laugh out loud, and my voice fills the empty room. Only my parents would be scratching out prayers while sitting on the toilet. Faithful to the end. What's wrong with me? Why has my own faith been so fickle? Why couldn't I just be satisfied? I slump on the bathroom floor, the tiny ruffled rug under the sink providing a small cushion to the ever growing weight of my body. I'm probably not far from the end now. The thought alone sends a little shiver of fear down my arms. I lean against the cabinet. The amount of pain this splinter is causing feels irrational. I should just go back to my own house, where I can picture tweezers in the drawer next to my bed.

I open the cabinet I've been leaning against and root around. A few cleaning supplies, some extra toilet paper, an old makeup compact. That's odd. My mom never wore makeup. It's always been looked down on in the Collective. The delicate silver case is solid and cold against my palm. I open it. It's a perfect circle of pressed blush. A rose is embossed in the middle. Its edges shimmer in the bathroom light. I run a pinky against the edge of the rose, and it smudges. I snap the compact shut, afraid of damaging it more. A little puff of pink explodes into the air when the two pieces of the compact collide, and it smells like our garden in the summer. As I turn it over in my hands again, I notice "J.M.A." carved in a delicate, whirly script.

I put the compact in my pocket and reach toward the back of the cabinet to feel around for tweezers one last time. I feel the toilet paper stacked against the back wall of the cabinet and am about to concede defeat when my hands land on something soft and leathery. For a moment, I think I've brushed against some small animal that has taken up residence here in my parents' absence, and a wave of nausea rolls over me. When nothing darts out of the cabinet's darkness, I reach my hand back in. The object is sturdy, unmoving. I close my hand around it and pull it out. It's a journal. The cover is soft leather, worn with age. It's dark green and has those same initials, J.M.A., stitched on the front. I open it and see my mother's careful handwriting.

I've only read a few words when I hear shouting outside. I stuff the notebook into my inside jacket pocket and switch off the light in the bathroom. I creep back down the hall and out the back door. The noise seems to be coming from out front, near the Village path. I step quietly around the edge of the house.

People are running down the path. They're shouting, and some are crying. It looks like everyone on the Farm is moving in the same direction. Confusion seems to course through the group like lightning. I look for any familiar faces and finally see Tabitha. I run toward her, grabbing the edge of her sweater. I've forgotten about my splinter, but the tiny cut is obstinately bleeding, and a red stain blooms on the white knit as she turns toward me.

"Tabitha, what's going on?" I'm already out of breath, even though it's only taken me a minute to cross the Village path and catch up to her. Uncertainty flits across her face. "Tell me. What is it?"

"He's come back. I think they've all come back." Her words feel like they're traveling a great distance to reach me, like she's said something from underwater and I'm meant to decipher it on the surface.

"What? What? What?" I keep repeating the question, hoping I'll find more words. Tabitha looks as bewildered as me, but she takes my hand.

"Edwin's called everyone to meet him at the old barn in the north field. He says they're all there." I drop Tabitha's hand and run. I see Bekah as I run past the storehouse, hear her calling to me, but I know I've only enough energy and breath to make it if I don't stop, so I keep running. To my parents. To Jason. To say it's ok they went. To say we can start again.

When I make it to the barn, I am winded and panting. I reach for the door, hands trembling, the splinter in my finger long forgotten. There are others coming up behind me. I can hear them, but I need to get in first. I need to see their faces first. I open the door. Someone has strung up twinkling lights in the rafters and I blink twice in the dusty light and look around. The barn is empty save Edwin. He's standing in the center of the room. His arms are stretched wide. I deflate like a balloon. I want to cry, but rage surges past the tears, and I gulp in another breath and shout at Edwin across the barn.

"Everyone thinks they've come back."

"Rumors are nasty things. I only asked for a gathering here in the barn. I said I had a message from Brother Richmond. I received it in a dream. Nothing more. Someone must have misinterpreted."

I hear the door of the barn creak open on its hinges behind me, hear the hushed silence that follows as everyone realizes they've misunderstood, or been lied to, or tricked, or all of the above. I turn to push my way back through the crowd, but I hear Edwin call after me, his voice earnest and low,

"Alice, please stay. I think you'll want to hear this."

He sounds so genuine, so much like the friend who's shoulder I cried on and got into trouble with. My heart breaks all over again, and I let my shoulders sag. I can't escape this place. Is that my true punishment? To be unable to break free of its orbit, even when Brother Richmond isn't around to hold me here? Bekah runs up and stands next to me. Her face is shining, but I'm not sure if it's sweat or devotion. I stand with her, resolved to leave the minute Edwin finishes speaking. His voice booms out over the group, no longer the folksy tones he used with the reporters, but the baritone of a new leader taking charge over his flock.

"Hello everyone. It seems there has been some confusion. No one has returned. Why would anyone come back from paradise?" He laughs too hard at his little joke, holding his stomach for effect. I expect them all to turn on him now. To call him traitor and storm out of the barn. To my amazement, others join in the laughter.

"No," he wipes his eyes, and now he's serious. "I called you all here rather than the meeting house because I've been given a message from Brother Richmond in a dream, and he was specific that we should meet here in this barn. You know, this was one of the only buildings on the property when it was purchased for the Collective."

I remember the boy I used to know and wonder how he could seem so different now. Maybe we're both different now. I think of all the happiness I've experienced on the Farm and all the fear and pain and grief I've found here as well. I can't let go of the happiness or I'll drown in the sorrow, so what to do?

"Brother Richmond, he came to me in this dream to remind me that we are not just working to make the world a better place. We are working to leave the world a better place, because we are leaving it behind, amen?"

A flurry of amens goes up around me. Bekah looks rapt, and I try to see Edwin through her eyes for a moment. When all the world feels precarious, Edwin has a plan. When no one is left to carry the torch, Edwin says, "I'll do it." I wonder, were I in her shoes, would I be so taken in with him? I might be.

I hear piano strains behind Edwin, and I crane my neck to see Angelica sat down at a piano as ancient as herself. She's pecking out a tune I don't quite recognize this time. Somewhere in the other shadowy corners of the barn I hear strings join the piano, plaintive and mournful. Edwin doesn't mention the music, but his tone of voice changes. His cadence rises and falls in rhythm with it. I feel a pain wrap around my middle, and a sense of foreboding creeps up the back of my neck.

"We are homegoing people, not earthbound people. And I don't know about you, but I'm feeling weary. This world is feeling weary. Things are reaching the end. We're only ten days from our final Homegoing and I sure don't want to hang around and see the fiery conclusion, amen?"

I do the math. Ten days? Yes, that's right. How have I let time get away from me? I can't be here to watch those I have left vanish again. I can't do it. I turn toward Bekah, anxious to get her out of this barn with me. She is swaying in time with the music and her eyes are closed. I tap her on the shoulder and make a sign that says we should leave but she barely opens her eyes. She waves my hand away and turns her attention back to Edwin. He's talking with his face turned up toward the ceiling, like he's in conversation with someone in the rafters.

"Now, Brother Richmond came to me in this dream, and he said it's time to get ready. I said, 'Brother Richmond, are your people really ready to join you in paradise?' And he tells me, 'Brother Edwin, they're ready but they may need a little persuading.' He says you might be a little too comfortable in this world. He says you may resist." He presses his tongue down hard on the 's' so it sounds like the hiss of a snake. "He says you may want to stay in this world with all its problems, with all its woes, because you don't know what's waiting for you. And I say, 'Brother Richmond, how can I make them see?' And he says, 'I'll help you, Brother Edwin. I'll help you show them the light.'" Edwin looks back out across the tops of our heads. "And is there anything more you could ask for than a little help in this world? Don't we all need a little help?"

People are chorusing 'amen' up and down the room even though Edwin's not really making sense. Angelica is banging the keys with an intensity I wouldn't have thought possible from her frail frame. The unseen strings are reaching a fever pitch. Bekah's got her arms up in the air, and I feel heat rising in my body. The air is pressing in on me, the oxygen is leaching from my lungs, like Edwin's proclamations and all the swaying bodies around me are sucking it out of me. I look for Tabitha, the only one I know isn't taken in by all this, but I'm crowded in now, and I can't see her. I want to get away from this place, but the door seems so far away. Edwin is pacing back and forth on the podium at the front of the room. He jumps as he reaches one end and turns around, droplets of sweat fall to the floor and he looks up into the lights again.

"Brother Richmond, I've gathered our people here. If you're there, please give us a sign that we are ready for our next Homegoing."

Everyone stands still and looks up at the lights along with

Edwin, as if Brother Richmond is going to float down on a cloud. I'm swaying on my feet, and I notice others looking at me approvingly. No, I want to shout. I can't breathe. I'm too hot. This, whatever this is, it's all smoke and mirrors. There's no second Homegoing. But I'm starting to doubt myself. 138 people disappeared in the blink of an eye. And Brother Richmond made that happen. *Why can't you just believe?* A small voice in my head questions me, and I realize it's always been there, as long as I can remember. I look up into the lights with everyone else.

The tiny bulbs sway. They seem a little brighter than when I came in, and I wonder if my mind is playing tricks on me. But no, other people are whispering and pointing now. Bekah grabs my arm.

"The lights, Alice. Look at the lights."

They are almost impossibly bright now, it's hard to look at them. I wonder how they can be shining this hard without blowing out, and, in answer to my question, they all blow out at once. Tiny shards of glass rain down on us and people scream and cover their heads. We're left in almost total darkness. A single lantern, hung high up in the loft shines down on Edwin. Glass shards sparkle in his hair and his face is in shadow. He holds his arms up to the ceiling and speaks softly now, his eyes closed.

"Thank you. Thank you, Brother Richmond."

The heat is unbearable. It's churning my stomach in low pulsing beats. I wipe sweat from my forehead and ram my way toward the door. I've got to get out of here. I'm almost to the door when I hear Edwin shouting again.

"Who is ready to go forward into the light?"

People cheer and surge forward toward the stage. I force myself against the sea of people and make it to the back of the room. I push the heavy door open and welcome the rush of cool air as I walk toward home.

-18-

TERESA

There was a terrible storm the night before Anthony and Jennifer left the Collective. The local weather authority put out a warning, but since we didn't heed the warnings of the world, we paid no mind. Half our corn crop was destroyed, and extensive repairs were needed to the new barn and the chicken coops. The old barn in the north field somehow made it through. Later, Rich would say the destruction was a sign from God. That it was a warning of the bad fruit in our midst. But the morning after the storm he didn't have any such predictions. He just rolled up his sleeves and started the cleanup.

Everyone was exhausted by the end of the day. We hoped there would be no devotions after Evening Table and we could all go home and collapse on our beds. But Rich had other ideas. His devotions that night were tied to a few Proverbs about wisdom but mainly focused on an opinion piece he'd written for the local paper on the problems with the school system and the lack of say parents had in what their children learned. The fact that Rich had no children didn't seem to matter. Eventually, he found his way back to the idea of opening a school at the Farm. I could feel the tension ratchet up at our table as Anthony and Jennifer listened in silent frustration.

By the time of the storm, Jennifer and Anthony were in family meetings at least once a week. "They have a problem with authority and obedience," Rich had said. That didn't gel with the Jennifer and Anthony I knew, but I also knew there were only so many times I could 'speak the truth in love' and I felt I'd used up most of those chances on my speech about Alice. As Rich finished his devotions and asked if anyone would like to share anything, I knew Jennifer would not be able to stay silent.

"We don't have the resources or necessary personnel to run a school," Jennifer said.

"You and Anthony can run it. I know we have other teachers in the group. I really don't see what the problem is. With our own school we can be in control. We don't have to worry about the garbage the world is feeding them. We can make sure our kids are being raised in the right way."

"It might not be such a bad thing for them to be exposed to some other ways of thinking," Anthony spoke in an almost whisper. Even so, it surprised me to hear him say something like this to Rich, much less in front of everyone.

"What did you say, Anthony?" Rich said.

"He said that it might not be such a bad thing for our kids to be exposed to the outside world." Jennifer's strong and grounded voice was such a contrast to Anthony's apprehensive comments.

"What is that supposed to mean?" Rich's voice took on a menacing tone.

"We're isolated here. The kids need to know what the rest of the world is like if they are going to live in it."

"The outside world offers nothing but depravity, isolation, and depression. Is that what you want, Jennifer? Is it?"

"We're isolated here, Richmond. Don't you see that?"

"I see two people who don't recognize the favor of the Lord

in their lives and therefore may not deserve it. I see two people weak to the ways of the world. People, who, as the book of Jude tells us, are 'wandering stars, for whom blackest darkness has been reserved forever.' I see people who don't yet understand how weary this world is. That it is passing away before our very eyes. It's not long until we'll be standing at the edge of the end."

Jennifer seemed temporarily stunned by Rich's speech.

"It doesn't matter, Jennifer. Not to us. Just leave it." Anthony's mousy whisper may have gone unnoticed by most in the room, but Rich never missed a word.

"What do you mean it doesn't matter to you?"

There were blue shadows under Jennifer's eyes and her hair was pulled back into an untidy bun on top of her head instead of her usual loose waves. I could tell she was trying to steel her nerve for whatever came next. My own pulse quickened as she straightened up to her full height and spoke again.

"We're leaving, Richmond."

I looked back at Rich, expecting to see surprise on his face, but he was smiling. Something must have gone wrong if Rich was smiling.

"Are you? Leaving? Well, we don't keep people here against their will. Go. Join the world and don't say I didn't warn you when that world you love so much turns its back on you."

Jennifer and Anthony began to gather their things. Edwin, who had watched the argument between his parents and Rich like a ping pong ball bouncing back and forth across a net, sat still.

"Come on, Edwin." Jennifer motioned for him to follow, but still, he didn't move.

"Oh, Jennifer. You didn't think you were taking Edwin with you, did you? Unlike his parents, Edwin lives in truth and doesn't want the world's corrupting influence in his life." Richmond's smile turned into a sneer, and I felt sick. This wasn't how we solved things. Edwin was only seventeen.

"You can't do that, Richmond. He's a minor. He's our child." The threat raised Anthony's voice an octave or two. Rich's smile grew comical at Anthony's comment, but he didn't speak again. Instead, he looked at Edwin.

"Mom? Dad?" Edwin looked terrified and kept glancing toward Rich for reassurance. "I want to stay. I need to stay. I want you to stay as well. It's our home. Please."

"Edwin, let's talk about this at home." I could hear the fear creeping into Jennifer's voice and saw on her face the sudden realization that she was on shaky ground here in the middle of everyone. Edwin's voice, meanwhile, was becoming stronger with every word and approving glance from Rich.

"No. I'm not going. If you don't let me stay today, I'll just come back here tomorrow. Brother Richmond already said I could stay with him because I belong here. With him." Edwin paused and looked between his mother and Brother Richmond, clearly trying to clue in his mother to something he wasn't willing to say out loud. "This isn't just some stupid kid thing, Mom. It's about life and death. It's about our very souls."

The color drained from Jennifer's face, and I watched a million insults for Rich form in her eyes. She didn't say anything. Instead, she turned to Edwin.

"Edwin, I said we'll discuss this at home." Edwin looked once more at Rich, who gave the smallest nod, and then Edwin followed his parents out of the pavilion.

Tom was called to look at the ailing dishwasher after the service, so Alice and I walked home alone from Evening Table. She hadn't gotten into any trouble lately, but I could feel her pushing and poking at the boundaries of our world, looking for the next place to slip through. It was getting harder to make her see that our life here was better than the one she imagined in the outside world. I wanted to tell her that I would throw myself in front of a moving train if it meant protecting her. I wanted her to know all the ways Tom and I had tried to make the Collective, this world we'd helped to create, a better place for her. I wanted her to know that it was sometimes physically painful to think about the depths of my love for her. Instead, I asked her if Edwin had mentioned his parents leaving. She spoke with her head down, her hair curtaining her face.

"I mean, Edwin's been spending a lot of time with Brother Richmond ever since we worked on the library, but he never said anything about leaving. Did you know?"

"No, I didn't know."

"That was a pretty shitty thing for Jennifer to do."

"Alice. Language. Wait, why is Jennifer the bad guy here?"

"Just springing it on Edwin like that. Telling him she was taking him away from the only home he's ever known in front of everyone like that. I would die if you did that, Mom. Die." She stopped in the path and looked at me for the first time.

"Jennifer is just trying to do her best to keep her family together. It's hard to be a mom. Besides, I thought you hated it here."

"I thought this," she gestured to the hills around us, "was our family? Figures you would side with her." I silently counted to three and tried to calm the quick flash of anger that welled up so frequently when I talked with Alice in those days. I looked up at the sky and tried to count the clouds stretched thin across the sky. When I felt the anger dim, I spoke again.

"Your dad and I don't have any intention of doing anything like that. Ok?"

We walked in silence, and I thought the conversation was over.

But just before we reached the Village, she spoke again. "Maybe I hate it here, but it's still my home." With that, she turned and ran the rest of the way to our house.

Later, I snuck over to Jennifer and Anthony's house. Frank was sitting on their porch, no doubt guarding against anyone sneaking off with them, so I went around to the back door and tapped as quietly as I could on the kitchen window. Jennifer came out with red eyes ringed with tears.

"Jennifer—"

"He's going to take Edwin from me, Teresa. He's going to take my baby."

"He can't take your child. There are still laws, Jennifer."

She stood wringing her hands in front of me until I opened arms. Then she put her head on my shoulder and started to cry. "He can take him, Teresa. He can."

"Why do you keep saying that?" She raised her head and wiped her eyes with the back of her hand.

"Do you remember when we met? That first time in the diner after the laundromat? And you asked me if Rich and I had any other kids?"

"Yes," I said as a growing sense of dread built behind my eyes.

"It wasn't totally truthful what I said. I said Rich wasn't my husband. That part was true." Jennifer stared at me, willing me to connect the dots.

"Edwin is Rich's son? Oh my god," I said.

"That's why I can't take him. That's why Rich will keep him," she sobbed.

"Does Anthony know? Does Edwin know?"

Jennifer nodded. "Anthony's always known. Rich introduced us, remember? I was already pregnant then. Rich said he couldn't raise a child and a movement. He said Anthony was willing to serve. To make us a family. Richmond told Edwin when he found out we were thinking of leaving. That's why he's so insistent on staying."

I leaned against the door jam. The revelation washed over me in waves. "Why tell everyone he was Anthony's?"

"Richmond said it was better to present ourselves as a fully-formed family and not an unwed mother. He said Anthony and I would be contributing to the greater good and he would always take care of us."

I pulled at my sweater. Jennifer's tears had left a wet patch, and it was cold against my skin in the night air. Finally, I said the only thing I could think of.

"Why don't you stay then? He can't take Edwin from you if you're still here."

"We can't stay. You know that." Her eyes were pleading, but I wasn't ready to give up.

"Jennifer, you're the one who taught me that we have to change things from the inside. It was one of the first community dinners we had. You took me to the front of the room and told me to look at all the people's faces. You told me to see how they changed with a little kindness. You said that change started on the inside. So, take your own advice. Stay here, keep Edwin close, make this school the best school you can make it. This is your home. I'll help you."

"I can't, Teresa. There's been too much. It's all too much. It's not just the school and Edwin. Even after Anthony and I got together for real, Rich would still call me to his room at night. I felt like I didn't have a choice, but then he stopped, and I thought things were finally changing. That's when everything happened with the waitress and the 'private lessons' for the older girls. And I know you know he's swindling those poor people who call into his radio show. Selling them vials of 'holy' pond water and telling them their donations are funding the 'ministry'. That's not what I signed up for."

My heart seized at the mention of the private lessons, but I forced myself to focus on one thing at a time. "But if you go now, you'll lose everything, Jennifer. And I'll lose you." Somewhere in the conversation, I'd started crying as well.

"Remember the day we met you and Tom? And he told you about his mom being kicked out of her house because she was pregnant with him when she was a teenager?"

I nodded, remembering how that connection had helped cement our friendship.

"It's not true."

I pulled back from Jennifer, another shock freezing the tears on my face. "What? How do you kn—?" "Because he told me his mom had committed suicide when we met. And he told Anthony his dad lived with them but was an alcoholic. He's a liar. At the time, I excused it because it seemed innocent. It helped you feel better and got you to join. I told myself that it wasn't that bad because it was for the good of the group, that it would bring folks closer to God. But Teresa, excusing Richmond's lies has become my whole life. I've let things get worse and worse because it's Richmond and he's always got the best of intentions, right? Isn't that what we tell ourselves while we're looking away from whatever terrible thing he's doing? If I don't leave now, I'll never get out."

"But what about Edwin?" I searched my mind for even a scrap of me that would leave Alice with Rich, even if she was his child. I couldn't find it.

"He's seventeen years old. I can't buckle him into a car seat and drive him away and make him forget he ever met Richmond. He knows the truth now, and he's got to figure out what he's going to do with that information. Look out for him, will you? He's always loved you and Alice."

*****

That winter, after Jennifer and Anthony left, the worst flu season we'd known raged on the Farm. For a time, it seemed everyone was sick. Still, we gathered. Even as we turned pale and feverish, we dragged ourselves to the meeting house to hear Rich rant about our sin, our pride, and our fear.

"'The Lord will keep you free from every disease. He will not inflict on you the horrible diseases you knew in Egypt, but he will inflict them on all who hate you,'" Rich quoted from Deuteronomy. He loved that verse because he hadn't gotten sick, so it was clear the failure was ours.

Around that same time, he installed a large metal gate at the front of the Farm. He locked it at night and wore the key around his neck when he preached. It glinted against his throat as he shouted. "You think I do not see into your sinful hearts?" he barked at us. "I see what brews there. The Lord sees." The gate was never hard to climb over, and there were other ways off the Farm, but Rich wanted us to know we were betraying him if we left. Families slipped away in the night anyway.

When Tom and I got sick, I sent Alice a few doors down to the Whites to try and keep her well. I knew she was friendly with Andrea White, and I knew Edwin would find his way over there. Alice needed friends in those days. Neither Tom nor I could get her to talk to us. Something seemed to shift in her when Jennifer and Anthony left, and she was always getting into trouble. Mostly small things. Taking more than her portion at Evening Table, neglecting her Farm chores, speaking out of turn during devotions. But sometimes her anger flared in a fit so verbose it felt like my daughter had been replaced by a stranger. Everything I said to her was wrong.

Everything I thought I knew, outdated. I held out hope we'd find our way back to each other, but I was feeling less sure by the day.

It took me a week to get back up on my feet after the flu, but the first day I could, I went to get Alice and bring her home. The Whites weren't yet home from Evening Table, so I walked toward the pavilion. I saw Andrea on the path and asked about Alice. Andrea wouldn't make eye contact with me, so I knew something was wrong. I placed my hand on her chin and tilted it just enough to bring her eyes level with mine.

"Where is Alice?"

"I heard that Brother Richmond called her to his office after Evening Table." Her voice was filled with sympathy and fear.

I rushed toward Rich's house but stopped short about fifty yards away when I saw Alice coming out of the side door that led to his office. Even at a distance, I could tell her she'd been crying. I rushed toward her, wanting to sweep her up in my arms, but she turned and walked in the opposite direction. I touched her shoulder and she jumped.

"Alice, are you ok? What were you doing in Rich's office? Why are you crying? What happened? Are you ok?"

She looked terrified. "I'm fine, Mom. It's fine."

"Alice, honey. You can talk to—"

"I don't want to talk about anything. Ok, Mom? I don't want to talk to you or anyone about anything." Her shoulders shuddered as she spoke, and she looked past me, toward the hills.

I pulled her into my arms, and she collapsed into me. She didn't make any noise, but her sobs shook both our bodies. I let her cry. Wary of prying eyes, I wrapped one arm around her shoulders and steered her toward our house. Once home, I put her to bed and stayed next to her until she fell asleep. I called Lacey and told her we were grateful for the hospitality, but Alice had caught the flu anyway and would be recovering at home. Tom had been much sicker than me and was still sleeping off his infection. I knew he was in no state to handle the task at hand, so I left him a note telling him Alice was home and I was going out to get some medicine.

I burst into Rich's office in a rage. I had pushed past Frank at the door and knew I was on dangerous ground, but I didn't care.

"You promised," I shrieked, before I even saw him. "You promised me that you would leave her alone."

Rich appeared at the internal door that led to his house. He looked like I'd just stopped by for a cup of tea. There was not a hair out of place, not a single facial muscle registered the screaming mother in front of him. "I said I wouldn't let any harm come to Alice. No harm has come to her," he said in that infuriating calm voice of his.

I ignored him. "You can't do this, Rich. She's my little girl." His eyebrows raised, but the tone of his voice remained calm, bored almost.

"You should be more careful how you speak, Teresa. I won't be told what I can and cannot do in my own home. And really, you don't know what you're talking about. I've simply offered Alice the additional instruction she is so sorely lacking at home."

"I don't care whose house we're in. I won't let you hurt her. I'll take her and we'll leave." A look of irritation crossed his face but was quickly replaced by a smile. He sat on the floor, crossed his legs, and looked up at me.

"Teresa. Think about what happened with Jennifer and Edwin. Our young people make up their own minds about their beliefs and their place in this family. You think it will be so different with Alice?"

"Alice is different."

"Oh?"

"She isn't yours, for one." I knew it was a risk to let him know I knew about Edwin, but I had to try. Shock and surprise clouded Rich's face for a moment. Then he stood and we were once again facing one another.

"'The prudent keep their knowledge to themselves, but a fool's heart blurts out folly,'" he said.

"Proverbs 12:23," I said under my breath, a reflex of all those Bible lessons when I was a kid.

Rich smiled. "So? Are you a fool, Teresa?"

I faltered for a second, fearful of the menace in his voice. I could see from the glint in his eyes that he knew he'd won this round.

"I suggest you go home and pray about this matter. Give it to God. I think you'll find that with some prayer things will become clearer. This is Alice's home. And yours. We can't have a mass exodus here. People will get the wrong idea about us. Now, you go home and pray, and we won't mention this little outburst of yours to anyone, hmm?"

I started to speak again, but there was a shadow to my left, and then Frank was pulling me toward the door by my elbow. I jerked my arm away from him as we crossed the threshold and turned back to face Rich again, but the door was already shut. I heard it bolt from the inside. I walked home at as normal a pace as I could manage, aware that Frank was watching me. I didn't want to give the impression that I was still worked up, but inside I felt as though I were about to fly to pieces. I looked back across our time with Rich searching for the wrong turn, looking for the place we went off the rails.

When I got home, Tom was sitting at the table, an uneaten piece of dry toast on a plate before him.

"Where's Alice?" I asked.

"She's down at the creek with Edwin. She said she felt fine. I took her temperature. No fever, so I let her go. Told her to be back before it gets completely dark."

"We have to go, Tom."

"Go where? I thought you were getting medicine."

"I didn't want to worry you. I saw Alice coming out of Rich's office tonight. She was crying and..." I struggled to get the rest of the words out. To name, out loud, my failure as a mother felt outside my grasp. So, I sat at the table and put my head in my hands instead. I heard Tom move the plate of toast and felt him drumming his hands on the table top. It was a nervous habit, and the gentle vibrations brought me back to myself enough to sit up and look at him.

"That bastard," he said softly as he ran his hands through his hair. "We should have left when we had the chance."

"You think I don't know that, Tom? You think I don't wish I could reverse time? You think I don't know this is my fault?" My failure crackled between us, a barrier that set us at odds.

He sighed. "Ok, then. We'll go." We sat still in the knowledge of what leaving meant for a long moment. Fear layered itself over the silence, and I spoke just to keep it at bay.

"Rich knows we want to leave. I told him as much. He didn't like hearing it. He won't let us just walk off the Farm. Not after Jennifer and Anthony."

Tom wrapped his arm around me. We were allies again. With his other hand, he reached up and switched off the kitchen light, so we were sitting in the almost darkness of twilight. The purples and indigos of the hills were silhouetted against the fading light outside the kitchen window. It was a lovely view. Then the screen door banged, and I could hear Alice clattering out of her boots in the front room.

"We'll figure it out," Tom whispered.

*****

We waited three weeks before we made our attempt at leaving. I wanted things to feel smoothed over. I stayed away from Rich at Evening Table, but I was pleasant enough when I couldn't avoid him. He cornered me once, as I was leaving the meeting house.

"Good morning, Teresa. Have you prayed about what we discussed?"

"I have." I fiddled with the button on my dress to keep from looking at him.

"And what has the Lord revealed to you, Teresa?"

"I haven't received a clear word from the Lord. I'm still troubled by the matters we discussed, but I do know that God works all things together for good, even this." I'd been rehearsing this little speech in my head for just such a time as this. I held my breath as I finished.

"Good girl."

I kept Alice by my side as much as possible in those next few weeks. I met her at the school bus stop and took her straight to the farm stand with me after school. Every time there was a gap in our time, I filled it. I had Alice and Edwin help me with the bread baking on Wednesday nights. Angelica needed someone to help her beat her rugs? Alice and I were happy to oblige. The rocking chair in our living room needed to be recovered? What a great chance to learn the valuable skill of reupholstering. I ignored Alice's annoyed eye rolls. I let Edwin come along whenever he wanted, partly to avoid any complaints from Alice and partly to keep my promise to Jennifer. I hadn't heard from her since she left. I hoped she was ok.

I was sure Rich knew what I was doing, but because I was no longer arguing or defying him publicly, he seemed to allow this little respite. He'd also refocused his attention on Joselyn Myers. I invited Joselyn over to play cards a few times after Evening Table when I saw Rich's gaze lingering on her, but I was careful not to draw too much attention to myself. I knew I should do more to protect Joselyn. She was only nineteen and had come to the Collective on her own. She had no one to look after her or keep her from Rich's advances. I told myself I was doing all I could, but I knew in my heart that I would have let a hundred nineteen year olds wander into Rich's path to keep my daughter from it. I hated myself for this knowledge.

While I was playing nice with Rich, Tom was able to convince a friend at the garage to help us. This in and of itself was a small miracle since the Collective owned the garage and employed only a few outside workers. Josh was one of those rare outsiders who held goodwill with Rich without being required to join the Collective. We figured he was our only shot.

It was a Monday afternoon when Tom came home early from work. Alice, Edwin, and I were packing up some orders for the farm stand.

"Teresa, the new microwave you requested for the main kitchen just arrived." That was our signal. I nodded and continued labeling the boxes for the pies.

"I think we've done enough work for today. Thanks for your help, kids. Edwin, could you take these boxes over to the kitchen after Evening Table tonight?" Edwin took the boxes without a word. One half of my heart contracted in sorrow that I'd have to leave him. Tom and I had agonized about finding a way to bring Edwin with us, to find Jennifer and Anthony and reunite the Belfry family, but in the end, we decided that if he wouldn't go with his own parents, there wasn't much chance he would go with us.

That night, after Evening Table, we rushed Alice home. Once we got in the house, I locked the door and pulled the shade.

"Alice, I need you to pack a bag for a trip." I tried to make my voice conspiratorial and excited, but I could hear the tremor as I spoke.

"A trip?" Alice already sounded suspicious, but teenagers always did. "We never leave the Farm."

"We've been assigned to go on mission for the Collective," Tom said, taking over for me. "We're traveling to recruit new family members, but it's a selective mission. Only we're going. No one else can know about it. And we must leave tonight. We got a good deal on tickets, so we can't miss our window." I almost mouthed the words along with him. We'd practiced so much.

"It's a secret? Why?"

"Jealousy. Everyone wants to be chosen for mission and there's only so many to go around. Brother Richmond doesn't want any rumors that we're getting special treatment."

Alice looked uneasy at these words. "How long are we going to be gone?"

"We're not sure yet. Maybe three weeks, maybe a month." I spoke quickly, anxious of our need to get going.

"A month? Why are you just now telling me this? I haven't even had a chance to get ready. I need to tell Edwin. He won't know where I went. I promised to help him with his algebra homework tonight. This isn't fair. You always talk about how I can tell you everything, but you never tell me anything." Alice threw herself on the couch in dramatic teenage fashion, but I didn't have time to indulge her. We needed to go.

"There's no time to go see Edwin. Your father will get a note to him, so he knows we've gone. This is important, Alice. I know it's short notice, but we've been given a very special opportunity here."

"You promise you'll get a note to Edwin?"

"Scout's honor." Tom held up his hand above his heart and did a salute with the other.

"You're so lame, Dad," Alice said, but she grinned at Tom as she headed back to her room to pack. I breathed a sigh of relief and went into the kitchen. I washed the few dishes in the sink, placed them on the drainboard, and arranged the kitchen towel over the handle on the stove. Satisfied with the kitchen, I went back into the living room and scrunched up a blanket on the couch. I opened the Collective hymnal and placed it open on the coffee table. If any of Rich's spies happened to drop by for a visit, then I hoped the scene I set would give the impression that we were having a normal evening at home.

The clock above the mantle hit eleven o'clock, and I jumped. It was now or never. The plan was for us to hike out to the cow path where the fence was being repaired. Once we got off the Collective property, we'd have less than a mile to the main road and Josh would meet us with his car. He'd take us back to his place for the night. From there, we'd be on our own.

We were packed, backpacks on, lights off, and about to head out the kitchen door when the knock came. It was so soft I wondered if it was the wind. Tom started to walk toward the door, but I held my hand up. I wanted it to be someone who was just looking for a chat, who would think we weren't home and then head back to their own house. But there it was again. That knock that I somehow knew was for me. Tom headed for the door again. I whispered to him from across the room.

"Don't. I'll get it."

Alice looked bewildered but didn't say anything. Tom ushered her into the kitchen while I headed to the door. I took a deep breath and opened the door.

"Teresa! I wasn't sure you'd be home tonight. Glad I caught you." Rich looped a finger through the backpack strap over my shoulder. "Going somewhere?" His smile could have curdled milk, and I shuddered before stammering out our excuse.

"We're just taking a family prayer retreat. Thought we'd go to the south fields for the view of the stars. Closer to heaven, closer to our hearts." My smile was too tight, and my voice was too high.

"Have you checked the weather?"

I was expecting a yell, a shout, a simmering lecture, but idle chat about the weather threw me off my prepared script. "The weather?"

"I've taken the liberty of checking for you. It looks like rain."

"We're not made of sugar."

"Are you sure about that, Teresa? I'd hate to see any of you hurt."

"Thanks for the concern. I think we'll be fine. Have a good night now. We'll see you at morning prayers." I edged back toward the door.

He made a *tut-tut* sound with his teeth and looked past me toward the kitchen. "Don't make this harder than it has to be, Teresa. Frank is around the back of the house. No one is going anywhere tonight."

"You can't keep us here, Rich. You can't."

He pushed his face close to mine and dropped his voice to a whisper. "There's that tendency of yours to go telling me what I can and can't do, Teresa. I thought we'd talked about that."

"We're going. There are so many others willing to follow you to the depths of the ocean. You don't need us here."

"You think you can just walk out of this life we've built, Teresa? You think you have that power? You were nothing when I found you. Nothing. If I hadn't saved you and Tom, you'd probably have gone crawling back to your father and Alice, precious Alice, would never have seen the light of day. I took you from the muck and mire and put you where you are now." He grabbed the back of my neck and pressed my ear right up against his mouth. His breath was hot and damp against my skin. "You're nothing without me." He let go of my neck and pushed his hair behind his ears. He straightened up and put on his placid smile. "You double check the weather before you head out, Teresa. No one likes to be caught unawares in a storm." He put his hands in his pockets and turned to go.

I grabbed the porch post to support myself but hadn't even caught my breath before Rich spoke again.

"Tell Alice she's got a good friend in Edwin. Always looking out for her."

I went inside and closed the door. Tom and Alice were still in the kitchen. They came back in the living room at the sound of the door clicking shut. I let my backpack fall to the ground, where it made a small dent in the carpet.

"Looks like the mission is postponed. We won't be heading out tonight after all."

"Why not? Are we going tomorrow?" Alice was a bundle of questions and energy. She almost looked like herself again.

"Bad weather," I said over my shoulder. I didn't look at Tom. I headed to the bedroom and tried to figure out where I went wrong.

-19-

ALICE

I'm almost back to my house when I collapse. The pain is rhythmic, clenching me hard in its grip, and then letting me go just long enough for a ragged breath before beginning anew. I wonder if this has something to do with Edwin, the lights, Brother Richmond. Not believing. Not following. Not obeying. That's always been my problem.

I curl up on my side on the Village path. The ground is so cool. The earth is already hardening for its winter nap, and I can almost see the steam rising from my body as the heat inside consumes me. Maybe this is how the world ends. Not in fire raining down from the sky, but in the spontaneous combustion of all those who dared not believe. I ache with another spasm of pain and think I may welcome the end. I roll over to my other side, desperate to find a way to make the pain stop. I see a wet patch on the ground around my knees and wonder if it's raining. No, that's not right. The ground's too cold for rain. I see feet coming toward me, hear yelling, but I'm too far gone to make out much else. I close my eyes.

Warm hands cup my cheeks, and I look up. Tabitha is perched above me. Concern creases the space between her eyebrows. One hand stays on my cheek and the other feels my stomach. "Alice, What's wrong?"

I try to describe the pain. A look of understanding dawns on her face.

"Alice, I think this baby is on its way. We need to get you inside."

I see another set of feet and hear Bekah's high voice screeching. "Alice! Alice? Is she ok?"

I moan with another spasm of pain and Tabitha's face shifts down into fear.

"Call Lorraine," I manage to say.

"What?" Tabitha says.

"Lorraine. Call Lor—" I squeeze my eyes tight as the pain chokes off my words.

"I don't know what you're talking about, Alice. Please, Bekah, help me get her to the house."

"Lorraine! Lorraine Cameron! She's married to the detective investigating the disappearance. She's a nurse." I push myself to sit up in the dirt.

"How do I get in touch with her? I don't know. Oh, god. We need to get her inside."

Tabitha is pulling at my jacket and there are tears in her eyes. I know I have Lorraine's number somewhere in my house, but the pain clawing at my body is uninterested in letting me sift through my thoughts long enough to find it. I breathe in a shuddering breath and lay back down on the cold earth.

"Bekah, go to the police station." It's Tabitha's voice again. It is sharp and determined now.

"I don't know if I can walk that fast. What if she needs someone sooner?"

"Don't walk. Take the farm stand truck." Tabitha pulls a key from her pocket and presses it into Bekah's hand.

"I've only driven once!"

"Good. That means you know where the gas pedal is. Go,"

Tabitha's voice leaves little room for dissent.

The pain is spasming against the inside of my stomach again. Bekah looks at me and gives her best attempt at a smile, but it's tight with worry and her face is streaked with sweat and tears.

"I'll be back as soon as I can," she says.

Tabitha heaves me up and I stumble forward. And then I'm on her porch. In her house. Laying on her living room floor. She bustles around me, fluttering in and out of the room like a butterfly. She tosses a pile of towels and sheets at my feet and then hurries into the kitchen. She comes back with a pot, steam rising from its surface, water sloshing over the slides. She sets it down next to me. I wonder what all these supplies are for and if Tabitha has ever delivered a baby before. I laugh out loud at the thought that it doesn't really matter at this point. My laughter draws more fear into her eyes.

"I think the baby is coming soon. I can feel it," I say.

"That's good, Alice. That's good. You just start pushing when you feel ready."

She props several pillows underneath me and then bends my knees and sets my feet on either side of a large sheet. She moves herself between my legs and removes my skirt and underwear, careful to drape a sheet over my legs as she does so. My bottom half is now tented under the fabric. I think, with growing horror, about what would have happened if Tabitha hadn't followed me out of the barn. I push the thought from my mind as another wave of pain squeezes me.

"I feel like I need to push," I grunt out between the spasms, which are coming hard and fast now. The sensation builds inside me, the baby asserting herself, making ready her plans to leave the safety and warmth of my body. Are you sure little one? The next contraction is an irrefutable yes.

"Ok, Alice, I want you to push as hard as you can," Tabitha says. She's on all fours, her head between my legs. Her face pops up above the great moon of my stomach. "I can see the head! You're doing great!"

I grit down, digging my fingers into the sheet that's been spread underneath me. Digging, digging, until I can feel my fingers pushing into the hardwood underneath the sheet. All the breath escapes my lungs and I push and dig my fingernails in deep again.

"Good! Good!" Tabitha encourages me from between my legs. "A few more big pushes and this baby will be here."

I repeat the process, breathe, grip, dig my fingers in, push until I feel faint and lightheaded from lack of breath, and still Tabitha tells me to keep pushing. It goes on for ages. Pushing, breathing, almost fainting, and all the time I feel the pain will soon consume me and all that will be left of me will be the series of crescent moons my fingernails have carved into Tabitha's floor.

Finally, there's a push that feels like it will be the end of me. I scream with a force I didn't know was in me. But at the tail end of my scream is another scream. Tinny and mewling, but unmistakable. It's the scream of new lungs filled with the first glorious gulps of oxygen. Tabitha holds a wrinkled, writhing thing up for me to see. It's covered in white goop and flailing in her arms. It's my baby, I think with a start.

"It's a girl! Alice, you did it. It's a girl."

She places the bundle on my chest with great care, but the surprise of it still takes my breath away. Everything else fades for one moment, and I can't believe she's here and she's mine and she's perfect. I cry and laugh at the same time. I touch her toes, her fingers, her nose. The whole while she screams, determined to make her displeasure known. I know, I know. The world's a scary place.

Tabitha tucks a blanket around us both and rushes off for

more towels. I hear the door bang open and feel the rush of cold air from the outside as Bekah charges into the room. She stops in the doorway, her face fixed in horror at the scene of the blood and the sheets and me on the floor. Then her eye finds the baby tucked in my arm and she's on the floor crying and mouthing something I can't understand. Lorraine is just behind her and Detective Cameron a little further back. Lorraine's carrying a black bag and sits on the floor beside me.

"Would you look at that. She's beautiful. Just beautiful. Told you she wouldn't need my help," she says to Detective Cameron, who is still lingering in the doorway. She looks adoringly at the baby for one moment more and then switches into nurse mode.

"Now, let's make sure everything is ok here." She moves everyone out of the way. "Someone turn on some lights for goodness sake."

She disappears into the kitchen for a few minutes. When she returns she smells strongly of soap. She moves around my legs and pulls away the blood soaked towels. She puts on blue latex gloves from her bag and rummages around below my waist. I don't really care what she's doing. I just want to hold my baby and sleep. She's calmed down now, and I tuck her up under my breast, amazed at the way she wiggles her face over and sucks hungrily. I am happy and in so much pain, and exhausted and joyous, and I just want to sleep and hold this baby forever. I close my eyes, knowing I'm safe and surrounded by people who love me.

*****

I wake encircled by blue curtains with fluorescent light overhead. There's some kind of beeping happening to my left, and weak sunlight is filtering in through a large window that takes up the whole of the right wall. A plexiglass bassinet sits next to me. I reach over, only to feel myself tethered to the beeping machine on my left by a thin tube and a needle that's been taped inside my wrist. I sit upright, and a dull ache spreads down my body. It dawns on me that the bassinet is empty. My baby. Where is she? Fear floods my veins, and I throw my legs over the edge of the bed and pull myself forward. I feel caught again by the cords attached to my arm, and I pull hard against them, determined to get to my baby. The soft beeping turns into a moaning alarm. The curtains in front of me whoosh open with a *clickit-clickit-clicit,* and a woman I don't recognize moves toward me. She's wearing scrubs covered in paw prints. Her mouth is a thin, set line.

"Whoa, everything alright, Mrs. Greene? Looks like your IV came loose. Let's get you back in bed and fix that."

She reaches for my arm, but I jerk it away, banging it on the little metal tray next to my bed.

"Where's my baby?" Tears fall hot and fierce down my face. "Where's my baby?"

The nurse reaches out and grabs the cords and tubes flying around and presses a button that makes the alarm stop. "Mrs. Greene, I understand you're confused. Your baby is perfectly safe. She's healthy and happy. We took her to the nursery while you slept. Just give me one moment—" she presses another button on the wall, "and I'll have her brought down, alright?"

"She's here? She's ok? Where's Tabitha? Where's Lorraine?"

"Yes, Mrs. Greene. She's perfect. Looks like you." The nurse smiles, and I think maybe she's ok. "Let me check in with the doctor, and if she's ok with it, then I'll send in your visitors. They're in the waiting room."

"What happened? Why am I here? Is the baby ok?" I know she's already told me the baby is fine, but I can't let go of the fear that something's happened. Not until I have her in my arms again.

"You lost a lot of blood, Mrs. Greene. It's a wonder your friends were able to deliver the baby and get you here without any further complications. Now you sit tight, and I'll go get your baby and check in with the doctor, but only if you promise to get back into bed and not rip out your IV again."

I climb back into bed. Everything hurts, everything is swollen, and laying against the pile of cushions in the bed does feel better than stalking around the room. The nurse assures me again that she'll be right back with the baby. She pulls the curtain back and leaves me alone.

Now that I'm no longer panicking, I look around the room. There's a balloon bobbing in the corner with a smiling sunflower; pink rays shoot out from behind it reading "It's a girl!" There are some drooping daisies in a vase by the window. It's clear they were once hot pink and neon yellow, but the color has drained from their petals, seeping back into the water in the clear vase. How long have I been here? The jacket I was wearing is hung up on a hook to my right, and something is sticking out of the pocket. I reach over, careful to avoid pulling on the cord attached to the monitor, and grab at it. I feel the soft leather of the journal I took from my mother's bathroom before everything went upside down. I draw it to my chest, freshly aware of my mom's absence as I sit alone in this hospital room, waiting for a baby. My baby.

I hear the door to the room open, and then there's another bassinet, just like the empty one beside me, but this one is filled with a baby. My baby girl. I set the journal on the table beside me and reach out. The nurse lifts her into my arms, and it feels like being home. I loosen my hospital gown and let her nuzzle her way to my breast. It hurts, the pain is sharp and pointed and brings tears to my eyes, but I adjust her and try again, determined to give her whatever she needs.

The doctor comes in and says a lot of words I don't understand.

They boil down to the same thing the nurse told me. I lost a lot of blood. Things were touch and go, but she's confident I'll make a full recovery. I can probably go home tomorrow. Then she's gone and the nurse is back and showing me how to change a teeny tiny diaper. Then she leaves as well and it's just me and my baby. The pain hasn't gone away. It's there in every part of my body, but I feel like maybe it won't be there forever. I doze in and out of sleep with her in my arms.

I'm not sure how much time passes, but the light through the window has faded when I feed the baby again. Long shadows fill the empty space on the tiled floor. There's a gentle knock at the door, and I see Tabitha's head peak around the curtain.

"Hey, kiddo. How ya doing? How's the little one?"

She pushes the curtain back and comes into the room. Bekah bounces up behind her followed by Lorraine. I can see Detective Cameron hanging sheepishly in the hall.

"She's pretty great, isn't she?" I hold her up for them to see.

"What's her name?" Bekah perches lightly on the end of my bed.

I look down into the baby's little eyes, so dark, so uncluttered by life.

"I think I'll call her Caroline. Hello, Caroline," I say, to test it out. It feels right.

"That's a sweet name, dear." Lorraine edges her way past Tabitha to look over Bekah's head at Caroline. "Family name?"

"I dunno, but I think my mom liked it. Whenever we played dolls when I was little, she always chose that name."

"It's a nice name," Detective Cameron calls from the doorway. "Glad to see you're both doing well."

"They said I can probably go home tomorrow. But what happened? How did I end up here?"

Bekah speaks up. "Lorraine called the ambulance pretty quick after she got there. A few people stood around and gawked when it came for you. Edwin shooed everyone away. Said there had been enough excitement for one day and that everyone needed to go home."

I cast a wary eye over at Tabitha, and she tells Bekah to get off my bed. Then she turns back to me. "We'll be back in the morning to pick you up and take you home. We'll get everything sorted after that."

Everyone visits a little longer and then takes one last look at baby Caroline. She gives them a tiny coo for their trouble, and then we two are alone again in the room. The nurse comes in to check on us and suggests that I let Caroline sleep in the bassinet next to me and try to get some sleep myself. I decide it's a good idea and reach up to turn out the light next to the bed. As I do, my hand brushes against the journal I grabbed from my parents' house.

I pull it into my lap and open the front cover again. My mom's handwriting fills page after page. It goes back to before I was born, but judging by the dates it looks like it was all written down in the last year. Someone must want me to read this journal because Caroline sleeps for four hours while I pour over every entry, every note, every little scribble in the diary. When I am done, I am sobbing. A sloppy strand of tears falls under my chin and drenches the neckline of my hospital gown. Then it's over and there's nothing left but blank pages. There was so much she didn't tell me. So much I didn't know. I flip past the rest of the unfilled pages. Desperate for one more note. One more scrap of information. One more connection to her. On the back inside cover, there's an address.

Michael Andersen
65 Jessup Way
Carpinteria, CA 93013

-20-

TERESA

I knew the day Jason Greene joined the Collective that he and Alice would be together. We had all gathered to welcome new members that afternoon. It was hot, so we used the shade of the pavilion instead of the meadow. Alice appraised the newcomers. Her eyes lingered on Jason, and he returned the look, a glint of curiosity in his eyes.

It had been a year since the debacle of our botched escape. Alice was working with me at the farm stand, and seemed to be growing out of the churlish teenage years. We never told her what we had really been planning that night. She never asked any more questions about why our mission was canceled. I prayed she never did. I didn't want to lie to my daughter again. Rich hadn't met with her anymore as far as I could tell. Things had settled down for the time being. I wondered sometimes if I'd overreacted to whatever I saw when she came out of his office that day. I figured the answer was no, but Rich had scared me. Tom and I still talked about leaving, but we'd never worked up the courage to make another plan. I guess we stayed out of fear, if I'm honest. Fear of what Rich had done. Fear of what Rich could do.

And he hadn't been wrong that night on our porch. Damn him for that. We'd have nothing on the outside. So, we stayed.

We made a pact, Tom and me. As long as our daughter was safe, we'd remain a part of the Collective. It wasn't the same anymore though. I never missed a devotion and baked the bread every week for Evening Table. I sang the songs and said the prayers, but I no longer had any desire to follow the God that Richmond Preston worshiped.

People had always married young in the Collective, and after Alice offered to show Jason around the Farm on that first day, I knew it would only be a matter of time before they'd be standing at the altar. Tom teased me when I said I thought Jason would be knocking at our door soon.

"What are you now? Some kind of a love prophet?"

"I don't think prophecy has much to do with it. I see the way Alice looks at that boy and it's the same way I looked at you. And we both know how that turned out," I said.

"It turned out very well, I think," Tom said as he pulled me into a hug.

It was autumn by the time Alice and Jason figured out what I already knew and dashes of flaming red and orange peeked through the still mostly green leaves. The breeze carried the scent of burnt wood from the bonfire the night before and that crisp smell of air that's about to turn cold. There was such hope and promise in Alice's face as we walked to Rich's office to get his official permission for the marriage. I wanted the world to be all she thought it was at that moment. I was so relieved that whatever atrocities Rich had wrought in her life, she seemed to be coming through it. Jason was quiet next to her, but no less joyful. His mouth turned up at the corners like he had no control over his smile. He hovered next to Alice, like he couldn't stray more than two steps from her, like they were tethered to each other with some unseen string.

We said hello to Marie and Sam, Jason's parents, and settled ourselves into the chairs we'd pulled into a crooked circle inside the meeting house. Frank was there too. No doubt he was recording everything on some hidden device to scan for any untoward conversation or behavior later. That Frank had become Rich's right hand man still baffled me. He hadn't been there in the beginning. He didn't know what we knew. Tom said that's just why Rich took him on. He could mold him how he wanted without any of the pesky knowledge of the man he'd been before he became 'Brother Richmond.' I missed Anthony and his quiet voice. I wondered where he and Jennifer were. I wondered if they ever thought about coming back for Edwin.

We waited a half hour and then another. Alice wilted a little as she perched on the edge of the metal chair. Finally, Rich swooped in, dressed head to toe in pale blue, like the sky on a cloudless day. His shirt sleeves were rolled up to the elbow and his hair, forever long but now streaked with gray, was pulled into a tidy ponytail. His beard was still dark brown, and I wondered if he colored it. He smiled at everyone, but it was tight-lipped, and I felt my stomach tense as he looked at me.

"Welcome, friends. Let's start with a prayer, shall we?" I bowed my head with the others, but I didn't close my eyes. I didn't think I could pray to the same God as Rich anymore, so I just stared at the whirling patterns in the planks of wood at my feet.

"Dear God, thank you for the prophetic vision you've lent me about this couple. Thank you for the foresight to see what's ahead for them and how I may best shepherd their path. I am, as always, humbly grateful for the opportunity to lead them and all our Collective family on the path to truth and love. Amen."

Alice looked at me as we all sat up. She'd brightened back up a bit now that Rich was in the room. I had to admit, the prayer seemed positive. I smiled at her and gave her a little wink.

"So, Brother Richmond? Do we have your permission to pursue a life together?" Jason seemed tenser than Alice and less sure of himself after the prayer.

"Jason, you've been a great addition to our family here on the Farm. Always loyal, always hardworking, devoted to God and the Collective."

Alice beamed. Jason turned slightly pink and sat up a little straighter.

"That's why it pains me to say that I can't lend my hand of blessing to this union. I'm sorry, son. But the Lord has given the final word. Alice is intended for someone else."

I felt the air go out of the room. Alice still had the beaming smile of pride in Jason on her face, as if it was frozen there. It lingered only a moment more as she jumped to her feet.

"Promised to someone else?"

"Alice, please sit down. The vision came to me a few nights ago. I wrestled with it, believe me, I did. But God was clear. And who am I but the messenger?"

"But that doesn't— It's not—" Alice sputtered, and Jason reached up and pulled her back down into the seat next to him.

"Brother Richmond?" His voice was cool water to Alice's fire. "Might there be some way you could intercede on our behalf with the Lord? Plead our case? I know that's been done before."

"I'm sorry Jason. God was clear. Alice is intended to marry Edwin Belfry."

At this statement, several things happened all at once. Marie and Sam stood and pulled Jason into the corner with them. They gestured toward the door. Tom started listing off on his fingers all the ways that Alice and Edwin were an unsuitable match. Alice started laughing. A loud harsh laugh that blotted out all the other sounds in the room. I closed my eyes against the noise and tried to find a quiet space in my head to process what had just happened. Edwin and Alice weren't in love. They had always been friends but nothing more. I'd wondered a few times myself about the possibility, but I couldn't see it. In either of them. They were more like brother and sister than betrothed. But it didn't matter. Rich had given his decree. Nothing was going to change his mind now.

Back at home, Tom and I walked tracks into the faded carpet of our living room. After the meeting, Alice had said she was going to walk Jason home, and we paced back and forth waiting for her return.

"How could he do this? After everything he's put us through? After all we've done? Why couldn't he just give us this one thing?" My voice shook as I spoke.

"Who knows the ways of the father?" Tom said with a grim smile. "She's never going to marry Edwin."

"No, she won't," I agreed. And then a thought dawned on me.

"Tom, we've got to try again. To leave. What if Rich tries to force her to marry Edwin? You know what he's capable of." I shuddered, still remembering his hot breath in my ear on the night we'd tried to leave.

Tom stopped pacing and scratched his head and then nodded in a slow and certain way. I felt a small sense of relief. Maybe everything had been leading to this time, this escape. I was sure Alice would understand now. She may even welcome the departure. And I wouldn't make the mistake of not sharing the plan with her this time.

But we never got the chance to share our plan with Alice because she didn't come home that night. We went to Rich. Where else could we go? He sent out the search parties. They combed the fields, they sent folks into town, and they put out announcements over the loudspeakers that ran through the Village. Someone in the post office said they saw Jason and Alice walking together down Main Street, but they weren't sure where they were headed. I wanted to scream, to run, to shout. I worried they were in trouble, and then I wondered if they'd left. My heart flip-flopped a little at the idea of my daughter being far away from this place, but it sank again wondering how I would get to her and if she would know that we too were searching for a way out.

Around 4am, Alice and Jason walked into our living room. Rich was there with us, with Frank on standby via walkie talkie. When the screen door banged shut and we saw them in the door-way, I shrieked and launched into one hundred questions about where they had been. Tom went to call Jason's parents, and Rich radioed Frank that we'd found them. In all that commotion I didn't notice the matching silver bands they wore. But Rich noticed. Rich noticed everything.

"You've gone against my wishes. You've gone against the wishes of the Lord." He spoke in his most dangerous voice, a low and omi-nous tone that barreled through our small living room.

I clung to Alice. I was ready to protect her, to shield her from whatever Rich would do next. I hadn't been there last time but let him try and get to her this time. I was ready. But he didn't do any-thing or say anything else. He simply left the room and walked out the door. This was our chance. I hadn't foreseen Jason and Alice getting married, but all the better. They could both leave with us tonight. I started to share the plan Tom and I had hatched in their absence, but I couldn't get the words out before Jason launched into his own plans about currying favor with Rich and begging his forgiveness and the life he'd planned for the two of them on the Farm. I frowned. Alice had never begged forgiveness in her life.

"Mom, this is a happy occasion. Don't look so down. God

works all things together for good, right?"

I shared a glance with Tom across the room. We were stuck yet again.

A week went by before Rich called the two families to his office. I readied myself for a reckoning, but Alice, basking in the newlywed glow, seemed unbothered. "He'll come around," Alice said with all the hope and stupidity of youth. I knew better.

Rich started the meeting by asking both Jason and Alice to give an account of why they had disobeyed. Alice spoke first.

"We love each other. We want to be together, to have a life together, to serve God together. Edwin and I, we don't have that. We love each other, sure, but not like that. We'd have made each other miserable."

Rich nodded and turned to Jason. "And you?"

"All I can do is ask for your forgiveness, Brother Richmond. I knew I was going against your wishes, I knew it was wrong, but my flesh overwhelmed me." He stole a furtive glance at Alice and added, "And my love for Alice."

Rich nodded again and drummed his fingers on top of the desk. "And what of your part in all this?" He looked past us, and Edwin stepped forward. I hadn't noticed him in the corner of the room, quiet and unseen as a ghost.

"I'm sorry, Brother Richmond. I wanted to help. I love Alice like my own sister, and I wanted to see her happy. I know now that it was wrong."

Richmond nodded a final time and then raised his hands to indicate that we should be silent as he issued his pronouncement. "You have all sinned in the sight of the Lord. You have disobeyed the orders of God's messenger, and that cannot be ignored. But," he held up a finger as if he thought we would interrupt though the room was silent, "the rite of matrimony is also a holy thing which cannot be undone by any man, even me. Therefore, Alice and Jason shall live in Separation for three months. Afterward, they may come together as husband and wife. For his part in aiding their scheme, Edwin shall live in Separation for one year. This is my final word on the matter."

Relief swept over Jason's face along with an odd mixture of gratitude and shame. Alice looked torn between crying with relief and mourning over Edwin's outsized punishment. She let go of Jason's hand and, with a small nod toward Tom and me, left the room. Edwin followed her, as ever. Jason walked out a few paces behind his parents, who still seemed dazed from their first real brush with the authority they'd sworn themselves into when they joined the Collective. Tom stood in front of me, his hand outstretched for mine.

I told him I'd be along soon, but I needed one more minute to sit and collect my thoughts. Edwin's terrible sentence didn't make sense, unless it was an extra punishment because Edwin was Rich's son. Still, a year's Separation was longer than anyone had been given before. I didn't understand. I could never get ahead of Rich, could never figure out his next move. So many plans had been dashed by his penchant for making things up as he went along. I stood and moved toward the door, but Rich called after me as I left.

"Teresa. I have bigger plans for Alice. Plans you can't even comprehend. God works all things together for good. Remember that."

-21-

ALICE

When I'm released from the hospital, the Camerons offer to bring me and Caroline to their house. They say I never have to go back to the Farm again. It's a generous offer, but having Caroline makes me more aware than ever before that I can't leave Bekah to fend for herself. I've got to get her away from the Farm before whatever is going to happen at the second Homegoing. My mom would have wanted that, I think.

Lorraine tried to convince Bekah to leave the Farm when they were waiting for me in the hospital, but she refused. I know she'll never trust a worldly person, no matter how sweet they are. It's gotta be me. I promise the Camerons I'll leave before the second Homegoing, so they drive me home, their reluctance evident in the way they drive the car down the path toward the Village at just under five miles an hour.

Bekah is waiting on the porch with a sign that says "Welcome Home, Caroline!" and a plate of chocolate chip cookies. After I've put Caroline down in the cradle the Camerons brought over, I invite Bekah to have some cookies with me.

"Thank you for going to get Lorraine for me, Bekah. I know that must have been scary."

"Considering I'd only ever driven on the Farm? I'd say yes," she says, before looking bashful and backtracking. "Not as scary as having a baby though."

"You know, the Camerons have offered to let me stay with him while I figure out what's next for me and Caroline. I'd like you to come with me."

"But what about Brother Richmond? And the second Homegoing?"

I remember our last exchange about Brother Richmond and try to soften my words. "I don't want to be here for a second Homegoing, Bekah. And I don't want you to be here either. I want to have a different kind of life. One that's not controlled by Brother Richmond. I'd like that life for you, too."

"Edwin was right about you."

I'm thrown by this accusation.

"He says you've gotten too comfortable with the world, just like Brother Richmond warned us."

"Bekah, no. That's not what this is about. I want you to—"

"I don't care what you want, Alice. You're not going to make me leave my home. No one is."

"Please, Bekah. Just think about it. Please."

"I don't have anything to think about. You go if you want. My place is here."

She tosses her half-eaten cookie on the table and lets the door slam as she leaves the house. Caroline wakes with a cry.

*****

I'm half-way on and half-way off the couch, trying to get comfortable and sleep a few minutes before Caroline wakes to eat again when I hear the front door creak open. I groan. I've just gotten Caroline down to sleep after my fight with Bekah. I still haven't yet figured out how to smooth things over and get her to leave with me in the next few days. I force my eyes open, and Edwin is standing over Caroline's crib. I bolt upright and wince as my sore body protests the sudden movement.

"I thought you were Bekah." The things I learned in my mom's journal burn bright in my mind.

"I thought I'd come to see the new baby. And apologize. I'm glad you're ok, Alice. I was really worried. I'm sorry I didn't come to the hospital. I hope our disagreement in the barn didn't have any adverse effects." He looks exhausted. His hair sticks up in odd angles and his clothes are rumpled.

"It wasn't anything that happened in the barn. She was going to be born regardless of the stunt you pulled in there."

"It wasn't a stunt, Alice. The dream, the message, the sign. That was all real."

I look away from his forced sincerity.

"I want you to know, I know I'm not Brother Richmond, but I would be honored to perform the naming ceremony, even though I've heard you already selected one."

"There's not going to be a naming ceremony. Haven't you listened to anything I've been saying?"

He looks hurt. "You saw the sign. You heard the letter. You were there. You know Brother Richmond will not accept your new daughter into the second Homegoing if she hasn't been through the proper naming ceremony." His eyes glitter and he's talking in a rapid, stuttering voice that doesn't sound like the Edwin I've known all my life.

"Edwin, listen to me. I am not going to participate in a second Homegoing. I'm not going anywhere. And neither is my baby. The Collective is over." He takes a step back and sits on the chair across from me. "Edwin," I begin, but I'm not sure how to tell him what I've learned. Part of me is angry with him for his part in keeping us from leaving all those years ago. Part of me is grateful to him. Part of me doesn't want to look at him. I'm afraid all I now know will spill out across that invisible tether between us.

"The Collective lives and breathes. The Collective is a body alive as long as there is someone to lead it." He quotes the old mantras at me as if I don't know them. As if I didn't learn them alongside him.

"Please, Edwin. You'll wake the baby. I'm not doing a naming ceremony. There's no more naming ceremony. There's no more Collective." I want him to leave me and Caroline in peace. I want him out of my house.

"No more Collective? Watch yourself, Alice. Pride goes before a fall, and everyone's watching you dance on the edge. These people, the ones left, are more committed, more in tune with things than we ever were. And they will do what I say we should do." He's near shouting now, and I think we've maybe crossed a line we can't come back from. I grab the edge of the couch and pull myself upright.

"Get out of my house, Edwin."

He turns toward the door but looks back over his shoulder at me. "God is always watching, Alice. You'd do well to remember that. You think I don't know you sent those people out here to look for Brother Richmond's tape?" His face twists into a sneer when he sees the surprise in my face. I decide not to give him the satisfaction of reacting and instead switch topics.

"Was God watching when you betrayed my family? That night we were supposed to leave? Was he watching then?"

He wheels around to face me again and his face crumples with anguish. It's such a startling transformation from the angry snarl of a moment ago that I take a step backward.

"How do you know about that?"

"It doesn't matter. I just want to know why."

"I didn't know, Alice. I swear it. I met Brother Richmond walking home from your house. I knew the mission couldn't be a secret from him. I didn't tell him on purpose. It was only later, after Brother Richmond had commended me for my service that I realized. I swear I didn't mean to betray you." His voice is sick with grief, and he looks so boyish that I hesitate. My anger abates some, but then he keeps talking. "In the end it was good you didn't leave. God works all things for good."

My anger whips itself back into a fire. "You know, Edwin. Don't pretend you don't."

"I told you. I swear I didn't know your parents were planning to leave."

"I don't mean about the plan to leave. I mean the reason my mom wanted us to leave."

"Everyone has doubts, moments of weakness, of course I know that."

"You knew what Brother Richmond was doing to me, to all the girls. You knew. Everyone knew. You knew what it was doing to me. You held my hand by the lake all those times I cried, cried so much my throat hurt, cried without being able to say out loud what was going on. You knew it. And you think I could stay here? Think I could somehow be a leader?"

"It's different now, Alice. I'm different."

"What's so different, Edwin? You think you're so unlike your father?" The words tumble out in my fury, and I press my hand to my mouth, as if I can put them all back. "I didn't want to tell you I knew about you and Brother Richmond that way. I only just found out. My mom left a journal and I..." Words always seem to fail me when I need them the most.

Edwin wilts under my blather. "It doesn't matter. You might as well know. Besides, Brother Richmond was more of a parent to me than Jennifer and Anthony ever were."

"They loved— They love you, Edwin. You know they do. They could be on their way here right now. It wasn't easy for them to leave. Other families have come for people. Maybe they—"

"Do you see them anywhere? No. They made their choice, and I made mine." He looks at the floor as he speaks, and I can feel something's not right in his words. There was a time when I would know exactly what the problem was, but I'm too out of practice and we've been out of synch too long for me to find my way back.

"All I ever wanted," he continues, "from the time I found out about my father, was to please him. I know we played around at rebellion as kids, but once I knew, really knew, who Brother Richmond was, I did everything I could to make myself worthy of being his son. Until I screwed up."

I know he means helping me and Jason, and the guilt nibbles away a little more of my resolve.

"I know that cost you a lot."

"No, you don't know. You and Jason, you went off and had your little Separation and then you built a life together. You can't know what it was like to have to see you, your parents, to have to see everyone, to live here and be ignored, shamed, discarded for that long. You can't know what it's like to live like a ghost among the people you love the most. A year, Alice. Brother Richmond was the only one who really cared for me during that time. Even though I'd betrayed him, he still fathered me. He still loved me and taught me. He helped me get back on the path. That's why I've got to make it right now." Edwin is on the verge of tears and all the words I think I'll say to him dissolve on my tongue.

"You're right. I don't know. That must have been a lot to carry around," I say, finally.

"Yeah."

Years ago, we would have sat around my bedroom and eaten contraband candy from town while we talked through all these revelations. We would have worked it all. It would have made sense somewhere between the Mr. Goodbars and the Twizzlers. We would have made it make sense. But now, in my living room, after everything, all the words feel stuck like glue.

"Why didn't you ever tell me any of this?" I ask, knowing it's a stupid question.

"Like you told me all your secrets?"

"Fair point. So," I say, clearing my throat of the lump that's lodged itself there, "let's start new. No more secrets. It's all out in the open now. We can put it all behind us and make new memories. We can get away from this place and do anything we want."

His head snaps up, and I see that too bright light in his eyes again. "No. Don't you see, Alice? My father entrusted me with this second Homegoing. It's my last chance to get things right."

"Edwin," I start to mount another defense, but I am so tired of having this argument. It feels like we've been doing this for years instead of weeks. And, in a way we have. I've been pulling away from the Collective for as long as I can remember. And Edwin's always been there, trying to coax me back in. I wonder how we can keep it up. The pull to just give in is strong. I can feel it beneath my skin, thrumming like a song I've always known. But there's a new lyric there now. I'm surprised to find the words are in Tabitha's voice. Something she told me her mom said about her sister. *If you don't want her in your room, don't leave the door open.* Caroline stirs in her crib, and I go to her.

"Edwin, I think you should leave." I pick up Caroline and press my face to the top of her head, so I don't have to look at him. I hear him get up and leave the house without a word. I pray this is some kind of ending.

*****

Days go by in a blur. Caroline sleeps, wakes, eats, cries, and needs to be attached to me at all times. Lorraine comes by with unidentifiable casseroles. I do the laundry. It's like I'm a hamster and everyday I convince myself that my wheel is finally going to take me somewhere. But all I do is go round and round in circles.

Bekah flits in and out of this cycle, and I try to find a way to convince her to leave with me. She seems far away even when she is here. She's left a part of herself somewhere else. I know this, but Caroline is all consuming and I can't find the energy to pin Bekah down. I tell her I'll give her until the day before the second Homegoing is supposed to happen and then I'm leaving with or without her. She doesn't seem to register my words. The day before the second Homegoing Tabitha offers to drive me to the Camerons' house. I tell her I want to wait until the last moment so I can try to convince Bekah to come with us one last time. She tells me to call her when I'm ready. I'm rocking Caroline in the living room when Bekah comes in. Her face is streaked with tears, and she falls down in a heap in front of me.

"I'll go with you."

I stand and put Caroline in her cradle. "You'll come? Just like that? You haven't seemed to hear a word I've said the last few days."

Bekah looks at the floor. "I've heard every word you said, Alice. And you said you'd be there for me, and you have been. You're the only family I have left. I'm sorry for the things I shouted at you. I'd like to go with you, if it's still ok. I can even watch Alice for you while you finish packing. Maybe take her on a little walk? It's not too cold out today."

"Nothing like leaving things till the last minute," I tease her. "Let me give Tabitha a quick call to let her know we're ready to go. You go gather whatever you want to take with you." Bekah nods and heads into the bedroom. I call Tabitha. Bekah comes back into the living room with a small canvas tote bag while I'm still listening to Tabitha's phone ring without answer. I hang up.

"Tabitha's not answering, so I'm just going to get Caroline and run over to her place. You finish grabbing whatever you need."

"Don't worry about taking Caroline. She's sleeping. I don't mind sitting with her. Tabitha is just down the path, and there's not anything else I need to gather."

"If she wakes up, just sit with her in the rocking chair. She calms right down when she's in that."

Bekah settles herself in the rocking chair, and I rush out of the house and down the path. I'm still a few paces from Tabitha's porch when I hear shouting. The door is ajar, and I push it open to find Tabitha shouting and throwing couch cushions against the wall.

"Where is it? Where is it?" She's yelling to no one.

"What's wrong, Tabitha?"

"My gun. My gun is gone." I wonder for a minute when Tabitha got a gun, but then I remember the bulge in her shirt that day with the reporters. I feel that tingling at the back of my neck that I felt in the barn.

"Ok, I'll help you look. Where was the last place you saw it?" She looks at me like I'm an idiot. "Wait, where's the baby?"

"Oh," I say, realizing I've left out the reason I'm here. "Bekah finally decided to leave with me. I tried calling you, but you didn't answer, so she offered to sit with Caroline while I came to get you."

"Is Edwin with her? He didn't have anything to say about her going?"

"Why would Edwin be with her?"

"He's always with her," Tabitha says.

"No." I think over the last few days. "She bakes the bread—"

"With Edwin," Tabitha interrupts.

"He's been baking the bread with her all this time? Not just that first Evening Table after everything?"

Tabitha nods.

"Ok, fine, that's a couple times a week. Otherwise she's at the library—"

"With Edwin."

"Or taking a walk or at your house," I finish before Tabitha can interrupt again.

"She hasn't been to my house in weeks."

My head starts to spin, and I feel like I need to sit down.

"I told you. She's always with Edwin," Tabitha says.

"So why would she agree to leave with me all of the sudden?"

Tabitha doesn't answer. She's already putting on her jacket and heading out the door.

I run as fast as my legs will carry me to my house. My lungs, no longer squished by another human, take in long gulps of air. I crash into the door. Caroline's cradle in the living room is empty. The tote bag is in the chair where I left Bekah, but she's gone. I pull it open like I'll find my baby inside. It's empty. Tabitha rushes down the hall to check the bedrooms. My vision doubles as I call for Caroline. This isn't how this is supposed to go. I was supposed to get out. Caroline was supposed to get out. I imagine Brother Richmond laughing down at me from wherever he is. *See, Alice? This is what happens when you stray outside the lines. Obedience is the path to happiness.* I dig my palms into my eyes to soak up the tears and try to breathe.

"She's not here. They're not here," Tabitha says, breathless from rushing through the house.

For a fraction of a moment, I think maybe things would have been simpler if I'd walked into that light with my parents and Brother Richmond. But then I think about Caroline's tiny nose, and eating meatloaf with the Camerons, and waking up each day to decide what I want to do without fear of punishment or eternal damnation or worse. I breathe and breathe and breathe. Tears won't find Caroline. Worrying about the right choice won't find Caroline.

"We'll have to split up to look," I say to Tabitha. "This isn't Bekah's doing. She loves Caroline. This is some kind of ploy from Edwin. I'll check the other houses in the Village and the barn in the north field. Can you check the meeting house, the pavilion and the library?"

Tabitha nods her head yes. I'm already sprinting out of the house when she calls after me, "I'm going to call that detective just in case."

I rush through the Village, not really believing they will be there. I bang on doors. Peer into windows. House after house. I beg anyone I see to tell me if they've seen Bekah or Edwin. They all shake their head no, and I wonder if they're in on it too. Edwin's lived in Brother Richmond's house since his parents left, so I head there next.

The house is dark from afar, but I see a faint light in the front window. Inside, it's still a mess from the search. There are books tossed everywhere and ashes from newly burned incense scatter the floor. One curtain on the far window is torn and all the furniture is pushed up against the walls. I go over to the front window to let in some light. I think I see another light in the reflection of the glass, back toward the kitchen. I whirl around, expecting to be greeted by Edwin, but there's nothing there. I hear rustling coming from that direction, so I walk into the kitchen. The rustling grows louder and morphs into a banging. I follow it to the basement door. I press my ear against the wood. Not a baby, but something, someone, is crying. I unlatch the chain lock pulled across the door and swing it open. Bekah falls smack into me and both of us collapse backward into the kitchen. I scramble away from her and onto my feet. It's hard to make eye contact with her, but I force myself to do it for my daughter.

"Where's Caroline?"

She looks up at me. Her eyes are swollen red, her long brown hair is tangled and there's snot streaked across her face like a spider web. Her clothes are smeared with dirt and cobwebs from the unfinished basement. She must have been in the dark down there.

"Alice. He told me—I thought—"

"I don't care, Bekah. I just need you to tell me where I can find my baby."

I try to keep a calm tone, but it is a monumental task when I want to scream and shake and curse her. It doesn't matter. She stares straight ahead as if I haven't spoken at all. She pulls at her hair and looks down at the floor. She speaks not to me, but to the doorway opened down into the basement.

"Edwin said I was special. When everyone else left me, he was there for me. When Sarah said Brother Richmond was bad, Edwin showed me he was good. When you were too busy, he was there for me. He said I was the only one who was truly faithful. He said God gave me a special light. He said he just wanted to see the baby. He said he wanted to bless her. But it wasn't true. Not any of it. I tried to stop him taking Caroline. I really did. But he was too strong. I couldn't do it. He put me down there like I was a dog and—"

She breaks down sobbing again. She is ripping out bits of her hair now. A new tuft comes away with each sob. I sink next to her on the floor. I reach out my hands and place them over hers. One by one, I pull them away from her hair. They go limp as soon as they're free, and I set them in her lap. She doesn't raise them again.

"Bekah. Look at me. Look me in the eyes." I remember what

Lorraine told me, the stern way she spoke to me. I try on that tone like I'm trying on my mom's clothes. "There's not a lot of time, but I need you to look at me right now." I want to shake her, but I wait for her to raise her eyes. Each second feels like a year. Like we're running out the clock on how long I have to find my daughter. Finally, she looks at me.

"What Edwin did to you is wrong. There's no other way about it. It's wrong. And it's not your fault. I have been where you are." Here I pause, unsure if I can say the next part, but I think if I say it then maybe it will be true.

"I forgive you for taking Caroline. I know it wasn't really you. I understand that. And I will do everything in my power to make sure Edwin atones for his sins against you, Bekah, but we can't do anything until we get Caroline back. So, please, please, Bekah. Where did he take my baby?"

She looks at me, bewildered, snot still running down her face, and her mouth gaping open. I'm on the verge of screaming when she says, "The barn in the north field. Where he made the lights change. That's where he went with Caroline."

Bekah gets up, unsteady on her feet, but I don't stay to see her out. I'm already flying north toward my daughter.

-22-

TERESA

I stroked Alice's hair and let her cry into my lap after Rich told her and Jason there would be no baby for them.

"It's punishment for getting married against his wishes. I know it is," she said between whimpers.

I could do little to contradict her. Rich had doled out harsher punishments for lesser sins. Maybe it was punishment for getting married, maybe it was punishment for rejecting Rich's plans so publicly, maybe it was just a whim of Rich's carried by the wind, or maybe God really had shown him something about Alice. That was the thing with Rich. For all his violence and lust for control, he did seem to have real flashes of the divine about him. I'd seen and felt it in the early days. And though I'd put away my belief, that didn't mean he wasn't still capable of it. It was also part of what made leaving so hard. Perhaps he did have the divine power to ensure our utter destruction once we'd left this place. We never spoke to anyone who'd left, so we had no way of knowing what became of them.

I'd thought about trying to convince Alice to go after she and Jason were married, but then there was Jason. He was too committed. I knew he wouldn't leave, and Alice wouldn't go without him. I couldn't go without Alice. So, we stayed. Some days I even saw sparks of that man who gave out quarters in the laundromat. The man who helped Tom and I find a place in the world again. On those days, I wanted to put away all the other things. All the fear, the shame, the guilt. I wanted to lock it in a box and pretend it never happened. Pretend Jennifer and Anthony never left. Pretend I never saw Alice coming out of his office crying. Pretend he hadn't left a fleck of spit on my ear when he grabbed the back of my neck. Pretend I didn't ignore the letter telling me my father had died. Pretend my brother hadn't stopped speaking to me when I didn't show up for the funeral. But all those moments made up as much of my life as the quarters for our laundry and the view outside my kitchen window and the pies I made to sell on Saturday mornings. We were bound to it all, to this land, to Rich. To leave would be to sever part of ourselves forever. So, we stayed and stayed and stayed until I couldn't look out at that view of the hills without tasting bitterness in the back of my throat.

"It's not fair, Mom," Alice was saying. "It's just not fair. I told Jason that maybe we should..."

It was dangerous to have these kinds of conversations out loud and she knew it. My hand paused above her hair. "You don't have to say anything else, Alice. I know. We've all had those thoughts before."

"You have?" She sat up and pushed her long black hair out of her face. "Did you ever do anything about them?" I looked at her. Really looked at her. My little girl was all grown up. She wasn't the kid reading books under her pillow anymore, or the scared teenager I'd failed to protect. She was an adult. Jennifer had been right, then. Children have to grow up to make their own choices.

"You know it's never been easy to leave this place. Even if you want to."

"Yeah." She looked down at the pillow in her lap. "I tried to talk to Jason, but he just spouts off 'God works all things together for good' and talks about all the good we can do in the world without children to hamper us. But can I tell you something?"

"Always."

"I don't really care about doing good anymore. I know that's awful, but it's the truth."

"You'll care about doing good again one day. I promise. You know, your father and I always thought we would have more children, but it didn't happen."

"Because you couldn't have kids or because Brother Richmond didn't let you?"

"A little of both, maybe." I didn't want to admit that I wasn't quite sure which side of that answer was truer.

"Did I ever have any cousins? Does your brother have kids? Geeze, I've never even thought to ask. You never talk about him much."

"Yes, a little girl. I'm sure he's a great dad. He used to come visit us at the apartment when you were first born. He loved you so much."

"What happened? Why did he stop coming around?"

"He went to California for college and stayed. And then we kind of drifted apart. He didn't really understand what we were doing here. He always thought we were a bit..."

"Crazy?"

I smiled. "Yes, I suppose he did think we were a little crazy."

"Well, he kind of had a point there. What did you tell him?"

"I told him that I was doing things for a higher purpose. That your father and I felt called to this life."

"And that was true, right?"

"Yes, partially. But the part I couldn't tell him was that we'd found a family here. I felt like my own family had turned its back on me. All except my brother. And I didn't want him to feel like I was cutting him off by coming here."

"Do you miss him?"

"Every day. We're only eighteen months apart. We were close growing up. We used to exchange letters. Christmas cards. He came to the Farm once, when we first moved out here. I don't know if you remember. You were really young. He didn't like it. Where I saw unity and harmony, he saw conformity and too much authority. Maybe he could see something I wasn't yet ready to see." I said the last part almost to myself.

"You could get in touch with him again."

"I don't think we'd have much to talk about anymore. But I'm telling you all this to say that I really wish you'd had someone like that growing up and I'm sorry you didn't."

"I had Edwin."

"Yes, but you know what I mean. I feel like we may have lost some things by choosing this life."

She stood up. She was so tall looking down at me. I marveled at the way the sunlight glinted off her black hair and the way she narrowed her eyes just like Tom.

"What are you saying exactly, Mom?"

"I'm not saying anything, Alice. I'm just musing about the past."

*****

I found out Alice and Jason were planning to leave in the middle of the night. Edwin tapped on our bedroom window well past midnight. Scared me half to death. Only when we'd all settled down at the kitchen table did he reveal what he knew.

"Alice and Jason were planning to leave." He looked toward the ceiling as if he were worried someone was watching over us, hovering unseen among the light fixtures. "Alice is pregnant."

Alice pregnant. I would be a grandma. I let the thought wash over me.

"Jason agreed to leave with her so they could keep the baby. They planned to leave during the Homegoing, while everyone else was distracted with preparations. But Jason got cold feet. He was in Brother Richmond's office tonight telling him everything. Brother Richmond said to leave it with him, that he would take care of everything and for Jason to show up at the Homegoing as usual."

Tom's arm was tense as it pressed against mine. Rich wouldn't let this go. Something terrible was going to happen if we didn't intervene.

"How do you know all this?" Tom asked.

"Brother Richmond left the door between the house and the office open. I was in the kitchen getting a snack when Jason came in."

Tom appeared to consider the veracity of this statement. "Thank you, Edwin. I appreciate your sharing this. We'll figure out what to do next."

As soon as I closed the door on Edwin, Tom and I started talking at the same time. I didn't know what he was saying. I'm sure he didn't know what I was saying. We were both formulating plans and contingencies for every letter of the alphabet.

"We have to get her out of here before Richmond does something," Tom said.

"He always seems to cut us off though. We need to do something he won't expect. And we can't tell Alice that Jason betrayed her. She won't believe us, or worse, she'll confront him. That's probably what Rich wants her to do." We both sat and thought for a while.

"What if," I said at last. "What if we make Rich think Alice isn't leaving? What if we go to the Homegoing and tell Richmond we know what Alice was planning? We tell him Edwin came to us."

"And we intervened, and convinced her to come after all?" Tom asks, picking up my train of thought.

"Yes, exactly. That will give Alice enough time to get away and we can stall Rich for a bit. Remember the last Homegoing? We were out there for six hours. We can probably stall him for at least a couple."

"I don't know. Two hours seems generous."

"Ok, but we can stall for some amount of time, and we'll have to pray that's enough for Alice."

"But we need someone else," Tom said. "Someone who can help Alice if things go wrong."

We went to bed uncertain who we could trust with Alice's safety. Edwin had come to me, but he wouldn't cross his father outright. I was sure of that. Besides, it would look too suspicious if Edwin wasn't front and center on the day. And we hadn't gotten close to anyone since Jennifer and Anthony left. It seemed like too much of a risk with everything else that had happened. I barely slept as I wracked my brain for someone who could help our girl without making things worse. I couldn't think of a single person who wouldn't report us to Rich. Tom tossed and turned next to me. I knew enough to know that nothing ever went according to plan. We needed to find someone to be there for Alice.

When morning finally arrived, we decided to go about our normal routines. Tom went off to the garage and I met Alice at the farm stand for the weekly farmer's market. Alice kept looking at me with her head tilted to one side and asking me if I was ok. I told her I had a headache. Halfway through the market, Tabitha Morales pulled up in a pickup truck to drop off more vegetables from the Farm. If I remembered correctly, she'd only been at the

Farm a few years, and she didn't seem too plugged in anywhere yet. She was always bouncing from task to task, and I didn't notice any particular closeness between her and Rich. Maybe, just maybe. I hurried over to help her unload the boxes.

"Thanks, Tabitha. The corn is selling like crazy today," I said.

"Sure. Brother Richmond wants to get rid of as much as we can with the Homegoing coming up." I looked over my shoulder to make sure Alice was out of earshot and then I lowered my voice anyway, just in case.

"And what do you make of all this Homegoing stuff, Tabitha?" Her face betrayed nothing, but I thought I saw a glimmer of curiosity in her eyes.

"I mean, you've only been here a few years, so you weren't here the last time. The time we thought was the Homegoing. So, it all must feel rather different to you." Tabitha blinked at me a few times before speaking.

"You know, Teresa, when I was little, my aunt came to stay with us for a whole summer once. She brought all her house plants with her and taught us to take care of them. She showed me how to French braid hair. She taught my sister how to do a cartwheel. She took us to the grocery store one day when my mom was working. She said we could pick out one thing each, whatever we wanted. I knew what I wanted. I raced over to the cereal aisle. All year I'd been begging my mom to get me Sparkle Puffs. They were dusted with some kind of edible glitter and each box came with 'a prize fit for royalty.' Those commercials really got me. I just had to have them, but my mom said they were overpriced and probably tasted like sawdust."

I looked back toward Alice and prayed she wouldn't come over while Tabitha was talking. I wondered where this story was going.

"Anyway, my aunt bought the cereal, and I was so excited to try it that I asked if I could have some for dinner instead of waiting for breakfast. She agreed because she was cool Aunt Abby. And you know what?"

I shook my head, hoping this story had a point.

"They were terrible. The sparkle dust got stuck in your teeth and the prize was just a cardboard crown. It was a total disappointment." She stopped talking and I was about to just carry the box of corn back to the farm stand and come up with a better plan when she added, "Ever since then, I don't get too excited when I'm offered something shiny. Just between you and me, I figure it's always going to disappoint, whatever it is." She looked into my eyes then, and I had a feeling, like a sudden jolt of electricity, that I could trust this woman with my daughter. It was a risk. Tabitha was an absolute risk. But I was running out of time and options.

"Tabitha," I said, "would you like to come over for tea this afternoon?"

*****

We made the plan tonight. Tom and I will distract Rich, and Tabitha will linger in the Village as long as she can. She's kept a key from the motor pool in case Alice needs to make a quicker getaway. I'm not sure what Jason is planning to tell Alice, but whenever he leaves for the Homegoing, Tabitha will go to their house. She'll tell her the truth. Convince Alice she has to go on without Jason. For the baby. I'm not sure if Alice will go without Jason, but we have to try. Tabitha won't tell Alice that Tom and I know. I want her to be far away from here before she worries about us.

I think time is on our side. The last Homegoing was only a test. I hope and pray it will be the same this time. Just a show of bravado from Rich. Maybe it's even some kind of test for Alice specifically. This time, I'll make sure she passes, or at least buy her enough time to get herself far away from the Farm. And once she is away from this place, we can leave too. She'll need help with the baby. She has no idea how it will turn her world upside down, but she won't be alone. I'll be there to help her.

-23-

ALICE

When I get to the barn, lights shine out from the uneven beams that line the outer walls. I throw open the heavy door. Caroline is tucked into an old feed trough. She's asleep with a blanket tucked around her. Even so, her nose is pink with cold. I rush over and scoop her up in my arms. She's breathing. She's alive. Relief floods my body, dampening the adrenaline I've been running on for the last hour. My legs weaken underneath me. I sit on the dusty floor. From this vantage point, I realize that the string lights that flickered and danced when Edwin called everyone here are gone. In fact, I don't see any lights at all. But there's still a brightness here. An eerie bluish white light hovering in the barn. I don't know where it's coming from, but I don't care anymore. I gather my strength and push myself back up to my feet, careful to support Caroline's head in the crook of my other arm. I'm almost to the barn door when Edwin steps out of the shadows, blocking my path. Tabitha's gun dangles from his left hand.

"Glad you could join us, Alice. I hope you won't be upset at me borrowing Caroline too much." He must see the murder in my eyes because he hesitates for a moment before he speaks. "I didn't harm her, Alice. Don't worry about that. I just didn't see another way to get you here, to make you listen to me."

"So, you thought kidnapping my daughter was the best way to get me on board?"

"I needed to get you here, so you could see the light and know that it was true, so you could finally accept what you've been called to do. What we've been called to do."

"And what about Bekah? You've traumatized her, Edwin. More than I can say. You've made her do things she'll regret for the rest of her life. What about her? Where does she fit into all this?"

He looks ashamed for a moment. Color flairs in his pale cheeks, and the wildness in his eyes dims, but he shakes his head, and it's blazing again. "That was unfortunate. I didn't want to hurt her. I didn't want to hurt anybody, but she was part of the plan. We're all part of the—"

"You didn't want to hurt anyone, but you did it anyway, Edwin. You've hurt Bekah, and me, and now you're hurting Caroline by keeping her out here in this cold. And you're hurting yourself by clinging to this madness, Edwin. There's nothing left for us here. Can't you see that?"

"There's a presence here, Alice. The time for the second Homegoing is drawing near. It will all make sense in the end. Please, Alice. Please believe me. Think of all we've been through together. Think of how many times I've been there for you. Now I need you to be there for me."

He's manic. His eyes are wild, streaked red, and stretched wide as if he's trying to see more than is actually in front of him. It's clear he hasn't slept in some time, and a small piece of me, the child still inside, wants to hug him and let him know it's ok. That he's ok. That it's all going to be ok. But I'm not that child anymore, and neither is he. I keep an eye on the gun and try to sidestep my way toward the door.

"This doesn't have anything to do with me, Edwin. This is

about some unfinished business between you and your father. I wish I could change things, but I can't. Look around. We've all got unfinished business. Sometimes you don't get to make things right. Sometimes things just move on."

"No, Alice. Brother Richmond was right about the prophecy. If he was right about that one, he's right about this one. He's sending signs. I know he is. If I don't follow, what will he think? What will he do?"

"The bigger question is what will happen if you do follow? The world hasn't ended. We're all still here. The seasons keep changing, the sun keeps rising. He was wrong about that. And you know what else he was wrong about? Me. I'll never lead a Homegoing. I'll never follow Brother Richmond again. That part of my life is done. Just because Brother Richmond was right about one thing does not mean he was right about everything. He was wrong about so, so many things, Edwin. So wrong. And he hurt so many people. You and I included. It's time to let him go. Let them all go. There's nothing here but ghosts."

"No! You don't know what you're talking about, Alice. You're always trying to convince me you're right. But you're not right about this. This is my last chance. It's our last chance."

He paces the floor in front of me, mumbling. He moves further into the barn, his body half in shadow. There's a clear path to the door now, and I sprint toward it with Caroline in my arms. I'm a foot from the handle when Edwin grabs my shoulder and jerks me back. I wrench forward, trying to get free of his grasp, but he holds firm. Caroline wobbles in my arms, and I lose my balance in my effort to steady her. The wood beams rise up fast to meet me, but I catch myself before I crash to the floor. Fury overtakes my senses, and I hoist Caroline onto my shoulder with one arm and shove Edwin with the other. I hope he'll fall or at least drop the gun. He does neither.

"You say you don't want to hurt me, Edwin? You say you care about me? You don't care about anything." Dust from our tussle swirls and catches the blue light shining from somewhere in the rafters. It stings my eyes.

"Alice, don't. I love you. That's why I need you here. That's why I have to keep you here. You're my family. We've got to be together now. It's important we're together now. That's the only way it will work." He starts talking to himself again, though he's careful to keep his body between me and the door. His mumbling takes on a rhythm, like a song or a prayer. "Maybe two months wasn't enough. Maybe it should have been longer. How does it work? How do I know when I've got it right? How did he know?"

"Edwin, what are you talking—" Realization dawns on me mid-sentence. "You wrote the letter." I'm stunned I didn't see it before. "You wrote the letter," I repeat. "There was never any message from Brother Richmond. It was you. And there was never anything on that tape, was there? Did you rig the VCR to shred it before you called the meeting or was that a happy accident?" My heart is racing again, and I can't square this new information with Edwin's attempts to help me leave. "But you went to my parents, Edwin. You were trying to help me get away before any of this happened. Why create this whole charade once everyone was gone?"

He looks up, a spark of confusion in his eyes, but it's not the time to explain anymore. Then he looks down again and speaks at the floor, like he can't bear to look at me. "I...," he starts, but the words seem frozen in his throat.

"You didn't believe it would happen either," I finish for him, understanding washing over me again. The tether that's always bound Edwin and me is once again taut between us. I can feel the feverish struggle for the truth emanating off Edwin the same way it must have once radiated from me. I wish it hadn't taken me so long to realize he was just as scared as I was. I wish it hadn't taken us to this point, to this ending, to find him again.

"I couldn't let you lose your baby. Not if the Homegoing wasn't going to happen. But it did happen, so I went to Brother Richmond's office. I knew there would be some instructions, some explanation, but there was nothing. How could he have gone without leaving anything to guide us forward? That's when I knew I was still being punished. I didn't go to paradise because I wasn't yet finished atoning for my sins."

"What sins, Edwin?"

"We were supposed to be married. Not you and Jason. I knew how important that was to Brother Richmond, and still I disobeyed. And then I went to your mother, knowing Jason had already told Brother Richmond about the baby. I wanted to help you, but it all adds up. Every mark we make against the father has to be answered for."

"So why make up a story about a second Homegoing? Isn't that a lie? Another mark against you?"

"Don't you see? If it was true once, it can be true again. How else to show Brother Richmond I am finally worthy of him than by bringing about another Homegoing, just as he did? I studied the *Collective Code* and all his other books, and I made the best prediction I could. The final Homegoing will happen tomorrow. And with you here, we can set things right. We can do what he always wanted for us. Don't you see? You've got to understand, Alice. That's why I brought you here. It's the only way. We don't have a choice."

He's shouting and waving his arms now. My eyes never leave the gun as it jerks toward the ceiling, behind his back, and then, chillingly, just past my head. I press Caroline to my chest.

I can't seem to breathe and think and hold Caroline at the same time, but somehow I am doing all three. How can we have gotten to this place? How can Edwin be so close and so far gone from me now? And why isn't Brother Richmond here to answer for any of the destruction he's created? Caroline stirs in my arms, and I understand the time for finding answers or justice or even peace in all this has passed. I tuck the blanket a little tighter around my daughter and speak to Edwin in a calm and easy tone, like we're kids sitting out by the pond again.

"Edwin. Caroline is cold. She needs to get inside. It's not safe for her out here. She didn't ask for any of this. She didn't ask for it any more than we asked for it. That choice was made for us. But now we get to choose. You and me, Edwin. We get to choose now. And you already chose, Edwin." He winces but doesn't say anything. "You chose when you went to my mom and told her about Caroline. You saved her by not going to Brother Richmond. You made that choice. Just you. No one else. You saved me too that day, Edwin. You saved us. And I can never say thank you enough for being there for me that day. For always being there for me. I know. I'm always asking you. I know it's a lot. But I'm asking you to be there for me one more time, Edwin. Please put that gun down and let me take Caroline home?"

I don't think it's enough. Edwin sways where he stands, his eyes are unfocused, and the gun is still pointed too near us. I clutch Caroline and pray to whoever may be listening. *Please keep my baby safe. Just keep her safe.* I don't know if it's the cold, the wild beating of my heart against her little face, or an answer to prayer, but at that moment she cries. The tiny, soul-pricking wail of a newborn. Edwin's eyes snap back into focus. His shoulders unclench and drop. The gun dangles toward the floor, his fingers barely gripping the trigger. He backs away from the door.

"Alice, I..." But nothing else comes out. He collapses and puts his head in his hands. The gun clatters as it falls onto the wooden floor. Dust motes swim in the hazy light. I move slowly, my gaze flitting between Edwin and the gun. The wooden door is coarse under my fingertips. I pull it open with one hand and hold Caroline tight with the other.

"Goodbye, Edwin," I say, but I don't know if he hears me. He doesn't move from this spot on the floor. I let the door fall shut behind me, and I run until the barn is a large smudge on the horizon.

I don't hear the gunshot, and Edwin's already gone by the time blaring sirens blaze blue and red against the barn. But I don't hear of any of that. I hear only Caroline's tiny cries as the wind carries them up and over the Farm, where I imagine they fall back down to the earth like rain.

EPILOGUE

Bekah, Caroline, and I stay with the Camerons till spring. Some people question me bringing Bekah along after everything that happened. But I know what it is to feel powerless and alone, and forgiveness has a funny way of creeping up on you when you least expect it. Lorraine introduces us to a therapist. It helps.

All winter long, we watch Caroline wrinkle up her little nose every time a snowflake lands on her cheek, and we smile, in spite of ourselves. When spring finally peaks its head over the hills, I am amazed to find that it makes the world feel brand new again. I wasn't so sure the earth could perform that same magic trick this year. I thought maybe eternal cold would be our penance. But still it comes. Every new bud and leaf is a sign the world lives on.

The FBI ramps up their investigation after Edwin's death. Not that it does any good. I tell them Edwin wrote the letter, but the next day they still stake out the meadow where the remaining faithful few gather for the second Homegoing. Not so much as a leaf trembles. I imagine the weariness that haunts those left behind again, and my heart breaks. The FBI searches the Farm again. This time they find a remote-controlled tape player loaded with orchestral arrangements of old hymns, a smoke machine, and a blue lantern in the rafters of the barn where Edwin died. But no video tape.

You can't find something that doesn't exist.

Detective Cameron says the FBI isn't likely to take spontaneous rapture into serious consideration, so they'll just keep spinning their wheels. I hear reporters talking about it on the TV in the Camerons' living room late at night when I'm up making a bottle for Caroline. I know Lorraine follows every development, even though she never says anything to me about it. From the kitchen I hear them say it's the largest missing persons case in U.S. history. They bring on panel after panel of experts to guess at what happened. They all have a different theory: mass kidnapping, spontaneous combustion, elaborate hoax with a secret tunnel to Canada. Lorraine switches off the TV when I come into the room, but one night I catch a clip of a stone-faced Angelica refusing to answer questions before the screen goes black. Another morning, on the way to the grocery store, I hear a snippet of Justine doing an interview on NPR. She's writing a tell-all memoir. *Collective Chaos.* I don't think I have the stomach for much more than the title, so I switch to the oldies station before Lorraine can hit the button. Somehow Bekah and I are never mentioned in these reports. Detective Cameron's doing, I'm sure. I still can't help calling him that, even after all this time.

I stay out of the news, but people find me anyway. The phone calls are unending. We ignore most of them: reporters, Brother Richmond groupies, personal injury lawyers. A few break through the clutter. Like the call from Jennifer and Anthony. They'd been trying to reach Edwin since the disappearance, they say, but he'd refused all attempts at contact.

We spend an awkward dinner together. They ask question after question about who Edwin became in their absence and what led to his death. I think about the day Edwin told me they'd made their final choice when they left. I wonder if they'd already tried reaching out to him by then. They tell me about their life in Kentucky and the good work they do at a school for underprivileged kids. How they hoped to bring Edwin there one day. I can tell they are searching for something, anything, to cling to in their grief. Absolution. Condemnation. Forgiveness. But I don't know what to say or what to give them. How do I bridge the chasm that's grown between us since they left? How do I put Edwin's life into words? I just say "I'm sorry" over and over again till the words lose all meaning. Jennifer pats my shoulder and tells me she'll call again. We both know she won't. It's too much.

There's also a call from a man who tried to stock my mom's pies at his restaurant in Dover Springs. He never got Brother Richmond's approval, but Lorraine tells him I can recreate mom's rhubarb crumble to perfection, and he offers me a job making the desserts at his diner. Bekah can help in the afternoons after school. I can bring Caroline with me until I get some kind of childcare sorted out. It's not much, but it's a start. Going back to my parents' hometown without them is bittersweet, but I like to think they'd be happy for us.

Tabitha comes by the Camerons' house the day before we leave for Dover Springs. She waves away my thank yous and makes googoo faces at Caroline. We sit on the back porch and watch Gracie and the breeze tangle in the grass.

"I would say don't be a stranger, but I don't think that's such a good idea in this case." She leans her shoulder into mine as she smiles.

"What's next, Tabitha? Have you been in touch with any of your family?"

"I think my little sister's going to come out in the fall."

"Here?"

"Yeah, I don't think I can leave this place now."

"Why not?"

"Someone's gotta be here to tell people what happened. To give 'em the real story. There's already so much garbage out there about the Farm."

"What are you going to do? Give tours?" An image of Tabitha leading a group around the Farm, waving a little flag, and pointing out the gift shop makes me smile.

"Maybe something like that," she says.

I still don't know what happened to everyone. I know what I saw, but knowing a thing isn't always enough. Maybe it was all exactly like Brother Richmond said it was. Or it was something else. It doesn't really matter much anymore. My therapist tells me she's impressed by how well I've adjusted. And I guess I've made an uneasy peace with the uncertainty. I'm hopeful that somewhere past the end of all this I'll find rest. But for now, I lay awake at night wondering what I'll tell Caroline when she asks about her father, and the ache of missing my parents gnaws at the pit of my stomach. Edwin's always there too, asking me why I didn't take him with me. None of it goes away, it just grows a little dimmer in the light of day.

By the time we leave Cyrene, Tabitha's the only one left at the Farm. The others are all scattered. Justine's on a press tour for her upcoming book. Angelica's gone to live with her sister in New Hampshire. They haven't spoken in thirty years. There are a couple postcards from Sarah down in New York City. She's taking college classes. She's learned to play piano with her aunt. It seems we all had family out there waiting for us to come to our senses. It makes me wonder why they never reached out before. Maybe they did. It wouldn't have mattered. I know that.

I get a few missed calls from a California number before I leave the Camerons' house. I write the number down in the back of my mom's journal. Sometimes I flip to that last page and read my uncle's address out loud like a prayer. I imagine we both have my grandmother's nose and that his daughter loves babysitting Caroline. I picture us swapping stories about my mom and soaking up the California sun. A family again.

ACKNOWLEDGEMENTS

You always hear about how many people it takes to get a book from idea to print, but you never know how true that is until you set out to write one yourself. So many people contributed to this story in ways big and small, and I'll do my best to remember them all here.

Many thanks to Kevin, Rylee, Molly, Olivia, and the entire Apprentice House team for making this dream of mine a reality.

I'm much obliged to Ona, Sara, Shay, and Brittany for reading this story and offering their kind and gracious thoughts.

To Dana, I'm so glad you wrote to me on Twitter to ask if I wanted to be critique partners. Your encouragement and notes were invaluable when I wasn't sure what the future held for this book.

I would be remiss if I didn't mention my friends in #MomsWritersClub. Your friendship, encouragement, and accountability have meant the world to me even if we've never met IRL.

I'm also incredibly thankful to the Tioughnioga River Writers, my wonderful writing group. Thanks to Laurie and Mary Anne for reading an early version of this story and giving specific and needed feedback on making it a better book. Thanks also to Lynn, Meghan, and Kris, who not only read and offered feedback but listened to me complain about the process, continually asked me how things were going, and were fabulous friends throughout this whole adventure.

Thank you to the bookstores and libaries who have carried my book and made it possible for this story to find new readers. And thank you, reader. There are so, so many books out there, and I'm honored you picked up mine.

Even though she isn't here to see this book, I owe a huge thank you to my grandmother, who first showed me the joy of reading and always encouraged my writing. I'm certain I can't buy us a log cabin with the proceeds from this book, but I'll be dreaming one up anyway.

Many thanks to my in-laws, Terry and Phyllis, for their love and support and for always being willing to play another game or two with my kids so I could get in a bit of extra writing on summer trips.

To my parents, Tony and Loretta, you've both supported me in all the various things I've wanted to do over the years and have never for a second believed I wouldn't achieve what I set out to. Thank you for the love and encouragement I needed to do absurd things like try to write a novel. Special shoutout to Laken, Shelby, Sydney, and Crystal for always being in my fan club.

To Clara and Miles, I couldn't have written this story without the experience of being your mom. Thank you for being such amazing kids!

Finally, to Evan. You knew this book would make it into the world when it was only an idea and a few roughly sketched notes. Thank you. You're my favorite forever.

ABOUT THE AUTHOR

Alexandria Faulkenbury's work has been featured in *The Maine Review* and *Mom Egg Review*, among others. She lives in South Carolina with her husband, two rambunctious kids, and one ornery dog. Read more of her work and stay updated on her writing journey at alexandriafaulkenbury.com

Apprentice
House Press
Loyola University Maryland

Apprentice House is the country's only campus-based, student-staffed book publishing company. Directed by professors and industry professionals, it is a nonprofit activity of the Communication Department at Loyola University Maryland.

Using state-of-the-art technology and an experiential learning model of education, Apprentice House publishes books in untraditional ways. This dual responsibility as publishers and educators creates an unprecedented collaborative environment among faculty and students, while teaching tomorrow's editors, designers, and marketers.

Eclectic and provocative, Apprentice House titles intend to entertain as well as spark dialogue on a variety of topics. Financial contributions to sustain the press's work are welcomed. Contributions are tax deductible to the fullest extent allowed by the IRS.

To learn more about Apprentice House books or to obtain submission guidelines, please visit www.apprenticehouse.com.

Apprentice House Press
Communication Department
Loyola University Maryland
4501 N. Charles Street
Baltimore, MD 21210
Ph: 410-617-5265
info@apprenticehouse.com • www.apprenticehouse.com